The Light Thrower

When Violet Took Flight

by allison keli

The Light Thrower|Book 2|When Violet Took Flight

First Edition

Copyright © 2024 by *Meditating Squirrel.*

TRIGGER WARNING: Some scenes may cause some discomfort for certain readers—in particular, the birthing scene. You've been warned!

www.MeditatingSquirrel.com

ISBN: 979-8-218-53974-0
Book & Cover Design by allison keli.

Author's Note & Dedication

Dear Reader,

Firstly, *thank you* for your support! This may be my fifth book published, but finding the elusive reader is a daunting task. So I thank you, thank you, THANK YOU for having this in your hands! I hope you find yourself entertained.

Secondly, here comes the inevitable Allison-babble. My mom and I don't call me 'creamily verbose' without reason! So here's my spiel—The ever-present "they" say writing can heal, and as one who writes, I'm inclined to believe them. Through Violet's full story, I was able to deal with some of my own demons and trials. By the time I was finished writing her tale, I realized that I had completed not only one book, but three! There is a truth to certain stories writing themselves. This was one of them.

These books are echos of my own existence here on Earth. I have known I was a writer since I was a very young girl. It is only recent, though, that I started to understand what exactly that means. Sharing my writing never seemed possible, nor was I sure I was meant to do it. Then it dawned on me that I was *already* sharing my writing across various internet platforms, and then *it* happened—I chose to be an author. *Phenix & Fox* and the first *Violet* darkened some bookshelves in 2022. Two years later, it is all still unfolding.

The online writing community is supportive and encouraging. The in-person community—still a WIP. I'm not giving up. I'm just getting started.

In spite of the inevitable pain and tragedies of life, I try to be as painfully optimistic as possible. And so, I end this part of the story, not with a more negative *what could go wrong?*, but rather, *what could go right?*

I'd like to think *many* things can go right.

Shipping some peace your way,

allison keli

November 23, 2024ce

Oh, this book? It's for you, Pat.
It was your destiny to be next. 😆

The Before Times

My official job title, as named by the United States' deep and dark underground, never-mentioned, hardly legitimate, entirely woo-woo operations division was *Consultant*. That's it. That was the amazing title that earned me more money than I needed, and more trouble than I desired.

I was part of the hokiest branch of the government, possibly under the Department of Defense, but who really knew? It was the teeniest, tiniest, most insignificant branch that was only whispered about in the presence of fine whiskey and the sound of clinking ice. Those who knew about us, ignored us. Those who didn't know about us, made fun.

To the people who were in charge, though, the job was taken very seriously, often without smiles, and generally while wearing incredibly starchy suits. While it seemed unbelievable and silly in the regular lexicon of speech, my essential job as this particular brand of consultant was to fight *Darkness*. This Darkness that I aimed to extinguish was created by people referred to as *Scouts*, as well as whomever was in charge of organizing them. It changed depending on where the Scouts were located, and trust me—they manifested all across The Great Divides of the Earth. They came in many shapes, sizes and power with various intentions and abilities to create real chaos in the world.

I fought these enemies with some sort of innate ability I was born with, but also developing, with the aid of various guides and gurus. I fought them with my own *light*. This light energy was something I was able to channel through magical intonations evolved from these ancient, hidden Germanic rune-staves. Although not everybody in my field of work used the runes and chants, I personally was trained in them because I was somehow genetically tied to the magical blood from Vikings of Yore.

Did this make me more effective and efficient at my job than others in the field? That was for the Suits to figure out. It did not matter to me.

Imagine a real life Wanda + Hermione + Ladybug mix. We're talking full-on woo-woo—prophecies, clairvoyance, clairaudience, clairsentience. All the damn clairs, except the best tasting kind—the *eclair*. It was all rather hard to believe. I was in the thick of it and still couldn't believe half of the shit that happened.

My personal problem was that I had always prided myself on being a realist. Nothing about my current life seemed particularly real. My greatest ally was something deep inside of me that would well up and boil over at every critical part of my existence.

Humor.

You betcha, I was awesome at laughing off whatever I couldn't quite figure out.

My paychecks were signed by nobody but a bank account number, and prior to direct deposit, the envelope had merely been marked 'US Government'. My healthcare—including mental health, dental health, maintenance care like chiropractic and even massage—was completely covered by the Feds. I possibly had better care than the President. I also got hazard pay instead of worker's comp—and while I did have to file claims when I was injured (which that point was almost moot when magic could often heal my boo-boos), the regular pay was so ridiculously insane, it made you wonder why people were starving in all corners of the world.

Clearly money wasn't the issue.

Due to the nature of the work, I also was assigned a psychotherapist. I had to see her once a month to help deal with any of the multiple insane things I'd undergone in a previous month's work. Her name was Dr. Angevin. She was in her mid-50s with thick, greying hair piled onto her head in a loose bun. She described herself as someone adept at dealing with the supernatural through scientific means. I'm pretty sure she only tolerated me because she *had to* tolerate me.

My area liaison was Nicole Barton, a mid-40s walking-library of information. She rented out a dojo once a month for weekend meetings for her *Party of Five* to make sure we were keeping up with our personal training while in our individual, metro Atlanta area cities. She would quiz us, whip our butts into shape, force us to fill out paperwork if we needed, answer questions if anything had come up in the past month, lead us into meditations and then after we'd cleaned up for the day, make nice with delicious meals in the city, typically somewhere on Peachtree Street. I mean, come on—it was Atlanta. How could it not be on a street with peach in the name?

I digress. Nicole was not the only liaison in the area, nor had I met them all. I never even thought to ask how many of "us" there were… I didn't really care, my personal life was hard enough to keep track.

Nicole's *Party of Five* consisted of Duane and Victor—the jokesters of the group—and Tollie and Janine, the two I relied on the most for companionship in our careers of weird. The head honchos of the Southeastern Branch of Atlanta were

Misters Michael Perez and Robert Cox, two of the aforementioned suits without personalities. I mean, they must be good with whatever it was they did, and I'd met with them on occasion, but I mostly interacted with Tollie and Janine. I was able to meet with Nicole outside of our monthly weekend meet-ups, but I typically did not.

I lived south of Atlanta is a sleepy little community which gloried itself on golf cars and being safe, so theoretically I shouldn't have had too many Scouts to fend off, right? Unfortunately, this wasn't the case, and I had been in some pretty gnarly situations in the past. However, at the current moment, things were relatively calm.

My roommate and I had contemplated moving into the city, but I would have lost my clientele for my part-time job. Speaking of my clientele, I somehow had enough time to keep the business I had been doing prior to the consulting work. I was a licensed massage therapist who dabbled in other healing modalities. It was steady work which was rewarding. I enjoyed helping people, not just by being a detective when it came to muscular dysfunction, but also helping them reset their Soul when they needed it.

Now, it could be argued that I dabbled in real world magic preceding my work with the government. After all, I was a Reiki Master, someone who worked with energy. I also did reflexology and cranial sacral therapy in addition to the regular massage therapy. While there's plenty of science to back up a lot of these esoteric modalities I practiced, nothing compared to the leveling up that happened once I accepted my role in the new career. A lot of my regular job was deemed woo woo in its own right, but my bodywork career was actually quite the relief, considering my magical consulting career was so messy.

My personal life was *also* a mess, and even with my monthly visits with Dr. Angevin, sometimes I had a really hard time staying tethered to the planet. My local friend group had been rapidly dwindling since I'd started my new career. My closest friends and I had met during yoga training several years in the past. We were all a part of this larger, slightly incestuous group of locals who jumped from yoga studio to yoga studio, bodyworker to bodyworker, soothsayer to soothsayer. These same people would sample whatever hot new modality someone had picked up without showing any allegiance to any one place or person. This group always seemed to be seeking and striving for more, more, more, rather than just be, be, being!

My beautiful blonde best bestie, Liz, had moved closer to the city with her new wife. Layla, with her black hair and spunky eyes was still around, but we didn't see much of one another. One of our other friends, Sam, had entirely moved out of the area to help take care of her mother.

Other than some local law enforcement involving a super-hunky ex of mine, the only people who knew what my other job was were Liz, Layla and dear Sam. They had been cleared by the government to be included in as much of the insanity as I felt comfortable sharing with them. It had been a stretch to get them in on it, but eventually they had come to realize that all of the chaos that had followed me since my trainer and recruiter, Nathan, had entered my life, was real.

Was it destiny or fate that had made Nathan choose me as his next apprentice? Was it the blood that ran through my veins that destined me to be able to develop this type of work in the world? Or was it Nathan's fault as he exhibited *his* free will, choosing *me* to be the next apprentice that sealed the deal? There was also some shabby parchment that had been involved in my choosing—seriously, don't get me started.

The higher-ups didn't explain anything to me, so I had to take most things at face value. Usually it was easy to go with the flow, do what I was supposed to do, and move on to the next big thing. But there were times this unknowing, this feeling that shit was being kept from me for some reason, *really* pissed me off.

At any rate, Nathan became my trainer, and during the time I was under his tutelage, I had been a part of the biggest "takedown" of Scouts in my career to-date. Sadly, my pal Sam had been in a really terrible personal space when I'd been recruited and was used to lure me to a gaggle of lost souls who wanted to destroy me before I was even fully trained. Liz had been with me when it happened, and… I almost died.

Or maybe I *did* die. That part is unclear. I'm doing my best to forget this event.

Luckily, that unearthly teacher of mine had tapped into his otherworldly skills to bring me back to existence. Not only did I survive death, heal remarkably well, but then I lived long enough to meet Nathan's brother, Grayson.

One wonders why this matters. *I'm* still wondering why Grayson matters.

I mean, Grayson really shouldn't matter at all.

See, Nathan wasn't *just* Nathan, and Grayson wasn't *just* Grayson. When Nate and I met, there had been an instant connection, instant attraction. When he was in my house, though, teaching me the ways of the wise, that connection and attraction turned into something else; something deeper. It was hard to describe, but imagine meeting your best friend for the first time, only with that same level of comfort from having been best friends for eons. Millenia. Whichever one was longer in duration. I thought Nathan and I had this forbidden love thing going on since he was my boss, but as it turned out, he had secrets from both of our pasts that he thought would change how I felt about him.

It didn't.

Unfortunately for me, the connection I had with Grayson was almost as strong as it was with Nathan. Truth be told, our pairing was more realistic in terms of age, things in common and a history of self-bashing. One wasn't better looking than the other; Nathan with his dark hair, toned muscles, crazy upper arm tattoos and dreamy green eyes with golden flecks was only slightly shorter than his taller, leaner brother. Grayson had dark auburn hair with eyes that were the opposite his brother's: hazel with green flecks.

Beautiful-looking men aside, Grayson was not-always-so-good, but more importantly, missing-in-action after a gigantic debacle across the pond on a small German island near Denmark. This precious little town was where Nathan and Grayson's mom, Alexandra, lived in a picturesque cottage. We'd all flown in together on Lübeck Air on a wing and a prayer...

This was also the trip that Grayson had confronted his mother *as* his mother. Before that, she'd merely been Auntie. These boys came with more drama than a telenovela, and somehow the tendrils of my own destiny had become intertwined with theirs. While their mom took off on a short-trip to retrieve sacred information that shadows *and* governments alike wanted, more terrible moments in time happened that I'm additionally trying to forget. I'll sum it up with a few words: dark magic, singeing flesh, Nathan almost dying; Grayson, naked.

After Alexandra returned, the nefarious parties were dealt with and the boys and I sought asylum back at the cottage to recover. Well, until Grayson decided he didn't love me enough to get over his own bullshit. He hopped on a plane and disappeared with the information, purportedly to share it with his *own* nefarious parties. Remember when I said he was not-always-so-good?

Grayson's isolation from his family had led him down dark paths. This loser firefighter, Jason, had taken him in, and then tried to repeatedly exploit Gray's weaknesses. Jason was a part of a group called *Vendetta Veritas*, or the stupid *Veritites* that they called themselves. They were essentially home-grown terrorists who walked the fine line between career criminals and utilizing their first amendment. Somehow they always walked away clean, though. I feared the lines were becoming less blurred and their mission to destroy hope, joy and freedom were becoming more solidified by the minute.

The information Gray had was something called a prophecy. Not the hokey ones we've all read about in fairytales, science fiction and Potter—no, legitimate ones. More legit than anything that furry-bearded Nostradamus had ever shared. This prophecy had been about an unnamed entity who was essentially supposed to give birth to the *second coming of Christ*. Alright, I'm being a little glib here, but it's hard *not* to be glib when you're living a life of unbelievable, fantastical proportions.

Even so, with the prophecy tucked away with Grayson and us having no idea where he was, life had been somewhat normal since the return from Germany. My roommate? Yeah, that's Nathan, and no, we had not become an item even though the players would so have it be. Apparently he and I were destined to be together, but I didn't believe in any of that.

I saw humans playing dangerous games with real people, trying to give meaning to words that didn't have to have any special significance. Unfortunately, I was a part of that meaning, as everyone thought I was the person being referenced in that darn prophecy as *The Weapon. I* was the one who was supposed to give birth to this amazing child who was going to save us all... save us from our darkest thoughts, desires, and manifestations.

That's all Darkness really was. It was when humans, or any animal for that matter, let out all the light. When all hope was lost.

I tried not to dwell on Darkness—certainly I had some within myself—but after seeing how one of my very best friends had been taken advantage of during the darkest times of her own mind, I knew I'd never let it overcome me. I couldn't.

And so, my particular careers—part-time day job or part-time secret wizard job—were really two aims at the same goal. To help people be the best version of themselves.

But since these prophecies were thrown into the mix, and the bloodlines of the brothers and I were somehow intermingled in time and space, the three of us were on the radar of all sorts of people—good *and* bad. People wanted to stop *The Weapon* from birthing *The Bullet.* People wanted to know what exactly this prophecy said so they could control *The Weapon*, or, shudder, control *who the father was* of *The Bullet.*

See where I'm going with this? One of the *brothers* was supposed to be the *father.* Here's the actual translation of the prophecy, per Alexandra:

The Brothers in youth must be separated to keep The Order or one will perish; The Weapon will bestow upon a brother The Bullet. All will be in peril during these times. Pairing brings forth Peace, or War. Sacrifice leads to Safety. The Bullet must dislodge correctly, or else—

So why did their mother even *have* this prophecy? Oh, that's another shit-show of when one of her former lovers—I think—who had been connected to all this mystical madness —broke out into a scary voice by speaking and writing runes by way of trance. Well-versed in magic and runes, she instantly knew what it meant, and so mortified, locked it up into a box and buried it, hoping to never reveal its contents.

It became pretty evident that she was going to have to share it, and so Alexandra translated the prophecy into English. Nathan certainly didn't need help with the translation, but I was a mere novice in understanding runes when my psyche was alert. When I myself was in a trancelike state, though, my mind knew *without* knowing.

These runes predated the more common Elder Futhark runes which Odin supposedly gave to the people. The markings were like a rare alphabet that few could garner true meaning from, written in a magical ink that gave an additional boost of power to each utterance written, read, or said. These far more rare runestaves supposedly came from bloodlines directly connected to Odin himself.

And yes, the same Odin from all those Thor movies and mythologies. I mean, I go for jogs and eat at restaurants and watch movies at the theatre. Listen to music. Yet somehow I have a direct line to Odin? The same guy who wanders around the MCU with an eye patch?

Makes you giggle.

The prophecy had made the boys' mother do the unthinkable. Alexandra had felt so strongly about the stupid thing that she separated her sons as children, choosing one to stay with her, and one to be raised away from her. That action would haunt all of us for eternity, I suppose. Grayson was the son who was raised in the states by his father and others. Nathan, while sent to boarding schools across Europe, but also stateside with his father, had spent a lot of time with his loving, doting mother.

My relationships with the brothers, my crazy ass job at hand, well, none of that compared to the prophecy and the power people were giving it.

Anyway, all that stuff was behind me now. I wasn't worried about it anymore. At least six months had passed since Germany, and life was pretty sweet. Let the psychos who wanted to believe all that nonsense keep chasing fairytales and ghosts. I was going to keep helping people the ways I knew how to help, and that was that.

I was happily single, and ready to mingle. My hair had recently been cut and dyed to its natural color. I had fresh clothes, new eye cream for my blue eyes, a new lotion for my face. Fresh sheets were on my bed. I was taking care of myself and it showed.

But even so… maybe not ready to mingle so much. Let me reiterate… *Nathan* was my roommate. Once he and I had decided to get an apartment together is when I had made these changes to my outward appearance.

But, I mean, we were just friends…

Part I: Prophecy Schmophecy

The Brothers in youth must be separated to keep The Order or one will perish; The Weapon will bestow upon a brother The Bullet. All will be in peril during these times. Pairing brings forth Peace, or War. Sacrifice leads to Safety. The Bullet must dislodge correctly, or else—

1

On this particular day in my life, the rain was coming down in large plopping droplets, each splash on the ground soaking another inch of yoga leggings. I was closing up shop for the day, having just had my last bodywork session thirty minutes prior. It had been a long day and I was covered in oil stains and now cold, wet pants. I wasn't thinking about the Brothers Hotness at all; nope, I just wanted to get home into some sweats and hang out with my fur babies.

Dammit. My car was within eyesight, but underneath the same awning I was standing under, a body hidden by black hoodie was walking towards me with purposeful steps. I had a very bad feeling this person was looking for me. Call it sixth sense, call it bad luck. I couldn't quite make out if this quickly moving shadow was male or female; it didn't seem particularly threatening, but if I could just hurry up and make it to my car...

I turned my back to the person, hastily sliding the key into the lock. My red hood slid off my head, and my tangled brown hair started sticking out and around a thousand directions at once. I was holding a dirty crock pot on my left hip, while balancing on one foot. *Crap.* The person had passed the juice bar and was definitely making a beeline for me.

I surrendered and turned to address the hooded entity, ready to let him or her know that I was closed for the day, but then I saw her face. She was younger than me, by maybe about ten years or so. She had telltale green eyes that a certain family I was close to had, and dark red, wavy hair was draping her face like Merida. *A cousin?* It dawned on me that maybe it was time to sit with Nathan for a history lesson about family trees.

The gorgeous female spoke and tentatively asked in a childish tone, "Are you Violet? Violet Moore?"

"Yes... How can I help you?"

She dropped the hood, her long hair pulled back in a high, messy ponytail. It was the end of summer, and her freckled nose was hidden under a slight sunburn. I inadvertently thought to myself that gingers weren't supposed to tan. Looking at her more closely, I realized she was quite a bit younger than me.

"I believe you know my aunt Alex and cousins Nathan and Grayson?"

My innards did a crazy tumult upon hearing Grayson's name. I nodded, and stepped closer to the door of my business as if seeking shelter of the heart. Nathan and I rarely mentioned him, and almost never by name. It was always 'he', or 'him'.

The rain from a small crack in the awning began to steady stream onto me as I blankly looked up at it. The girl hesitantly, yet wisely asked, "Should we step inside?"

"Yes, of course," I murmured.

Once inside, after I turned the light back on and dumped my bag and crockpot back down, she instantly apologized. "I'm so sorry to interrupt you—it looks like you're going home—I just didn't know who else to contact—"

I furrowed my brows again, wanting her to get to the damn point. Her cousin, Nathan, was literally about seven minutes up the road, so why she was approaching me and not summoning him was beyond me. She had a northeastern accent, maybe New York. A little Jersey? I wasn't terribly good with accents and so I couldn't place it.

"It's about Grayson. He's not doing well. He's sick."

Whoa. What? Air got sucked out of me, and lightning streaked across the sky. I felt punched in the gut. She was in contact with *him*. Thunder boomed, shaking the walls of my office. The girl looked nervous. "Who are you again?" I warily asked.

"I'm Gray's cousin, my mom is aunt Alex's sister. They call me Blaze, but my actual name is Gertie, or rather, Gertrude."

I closed my eyes and shook my head quickly, as if trying to hit a rewind button. "Okay… First things first. Should I call you Blaze or Gertie or…?"

She sat down behind a desk and started wailing. "I'm so sorry! I'm so scared! Gray is so sick! And I didn't want to call Nate because, well, Gray would *kill* me!" She paused for half a beat, throwing her hands dramatically up into the air, voice deepening, "And my dad would be *furious* if he knew I was even here! He can't stand my mom's side of the family." Her voice rose several scales on the octave chart. "He thinks they're all nutters but, I mean"—she stopped crying and gulped, swallowing air—"Magic is real, right? What's cooler than that?"

My eyes positively popped out of my head. I wondered if this girl was actually in high school due to her theatrics. Maybe I had completely misjudged how old she was. I had never seen such a creature in my *life*—her energy was positively amplifying the outside electrical storm.

BOOM went the thunder. "Gertie… Where are you

supposed to be?" My eye began to twitch.

"I'm attending college in Syracuse, but I caught a flight down here to find you. I have an exam I should be studying for!" She choked on a sob.

"Okay. So where is…" I paused, trying to figure out how to get the foreign word out of my mouth. "Grayson?" I licked my lips and tasted the word on my tongue. *Grayson.* I sat down in my relaxing recliner meant for post-session, extremely de-stressed clients. I, however, was electrocuting the poor chair with my anxiety, creating high levels of static.

"He's in Brooklyn, staying with one of his friends. Just a few weeks ago, I visited him right before I went back to school. His roommate called me the second he got sick, because, well, there's nobody else in the family who is close to him!" She was essentially shrieking at this point, and my temples were bursting.

She stood up and started to pace. "What's wrong with him?" I closed my eyes and tried to remain calm as my heart loudly thudded on the outside of my ribcage. The crease in my brow deepened, and my breathing grew shallow.

"Tim didn't know." She swallowed. "Gray sounded awful on the phone. Tim said he'd been really lethargic this past week and then all of a sudden had hallucinations—no fever or anything—and kept mentioning the name *Violet.* Of course, *I* know who you are, Gray told me all about you when he moved back to New York. But anyway, some guy from here had been up to see him, and—"

"Wait, what? Someone from Georgia visited him in New York?" This Blaze-train was almost impossible to follow.

Crap. My mind started to calculate the probabilities. "Yes. I can't remember his name, though, he was—"

"Jason?"

She shook her head. "No, not Jason, but a Guh, Juh—"

"Jared! Jared Tenebris?!"

"Yes. That's what Tim said. Jared Tenebris. What an interesting name!" She erratically spoke. "Grayson apparently hadn't been very happy he was there. They went out one night and Gray didn't return until the following morning, exhausted. From there he just kept getting worse."

Tenebris. Tenebris was a name I hadn't heard in months. After Nate and I returned stateside and Tenebris had found what happened in Germany—months afterwards—he'd been livid and let the Feds know it. Seeing as Jared was no longer employed *by* the government, nobody had felt compelled to tell him. However, he was often utilized *by* them, so I kind of understood his point.

But—I didn't trust the guy at all. I also didn't know too much about him. Nathan, forever an information hoarder, hadn't quite elaborated about his part in our collective stories. All I knew was Jared had once infiltrated my friends to try and get closer to me. This was even before I'd officially become sucked into this mystical world. Once Nathan officially deemed me the next apprentice, though, Jared had stepped back. Or at least I had thought. I never figured out what exactly he wanted with me.

In summation—Jared was oily and gross and operated outside of the governmental red-tape. This of course is why he was useful *to* the government. At the time, Nathan's blatant dismissal of Tenebris hadn't seemed like such a big deal, but I wondered if it was the reason why he'd sought out Grayson.

Unsure how long I had been silent and inside my head, my eyes refocused on the frozen and terrified cousin. "Gertie, we've got to tell Nathan—sorry if Grayson gets mad, but—he can just suck it up. I won't let him get mad at you." She looked unsure. "Nathan will know what to do." I stated with conviction. She still looked unsure. "We'll get you back to Syracuse before your dad finds out. Does your mom know?"

"If she didn't before, she probably does now. Gift of sight and all."

I rolled my eyes. I was over all of these stupid 'gifts'.

"C'mon, I'll drive you home."

"Home?"

"Yeah, Nathan and I are roommates."

"Oh, right. Gray said you guys were an item or something."

We went back into the rain, and charged to get to my car. Blaze shook out her beautiful red hair like a dog just out of a bath; I eyeballed the wetness on my car door and dashboard. This car was fairly new—I didn't own much, but my car was my baby. "An item? Now why the hell would he say that?" I growled. She looked at me and narrowed her eyes.

"Well, he told me you guys were in love and destined to be together or whatever, that it was written in the runes. Honestly, after how he talked about you this summer, I think *he's* in love with you." She looked out the window. "And of course, all of those hallucinations. Tim said he was blabbering about energy and swirling and you and…" She blushed. "And stuff I don't want to repeat."

Both eyes twitched. "Have you eaten?"

"What?" she seemed taken aback, and looked at me. "No, I haven't… I'm actually pretty hungry."

"Here," I said, pulling into a parking lot across from my apartment complex. "Let's run in here and get takeout. Let me text Nathan I'm on the way." I glanced over at her with a sideways glance. "And tell him I have a surprise." No sooner had I hit 'send', did Nathan write back.

Blaze! You're kidding me.

I quickly wrote back. *Home soon. Grabbing dinner.*

From the driver's seat, I ordered a ton of food for dinner. I knew it would take several minutes to get ready, and so Blaze and I were going to be enclosed in a tiny vehicle, with no escape, for much longer than I was comfortable. "I'll get a text when it's ready. Technology, eh?"

She looked unaffected. "Right... I usually do it that way, too." She looked at her fingernails, seemingly bored.

"How old are you?"

"Twenty-one. I know. I look and act super young, but I graduate college next year." She grabbed my hand and endearingly asked, "Are you sure you guys can help Gray? He's been such a good cousin to me. He really helped me out in high school when my life went haywire because of all this psychic stuff."

I moved my hand from hers, and tapped at the pane of my window, tracing a water droplet. "I promise, I'll do whatever I can for him. I have a feeling Jared poisoned him — either energetically, or with an actual herb." I looked over at her before continuing, "We may have to go up there..." I trailed off, looking back at the droplet. My heart flip-flopped again, and this time not out of anxiety. One of my last memories of Grayson was of him... *naked*. And damn if that memory wasn't a fond one.

He looked pretty good naked.

I inadvertently laughed out loud. I was thinking of how great he looked, but chances are, the last memories he had of me were not so good. I had had massive bruises, scabs, a twisted knee, and remnants of a stab wound that had just been stitched up when we'd done the tango between the sheets.

Embarrassingly so, this was the true reason why I was trying to forget the whole Germany trip. Not just from having been attacked by a bunch of crazy people who wanted to use me as *The Weapon*. No, really just because Grayson and I had slept together.

"Violet?" Gertie asked, breaking my reverie.

"Nothing." *Buzzzzz*. Dinner was ready for pick-up.

2

"Cousin!" Nathan happily exclaimed to Gertie as he greeted her at the door. "What brings you here? Shouldn't you be up at school by now?" He asked and grabbed her in a giant bear hug.

He closed the door behind her with one arm, and I started to pull out the food, placing it onto the countertops in the kitchen. I had ordered dinner from our favorite restaurant—the little Mediterranean place across the street that he and I frequented. We went so much, the owners knew us by name.

I had gotten more than enough food to feed us all. I peered through the kitchen pass-through window, listening to the two of them talk at the dining table. I started to vigorously saw away at some pita bread as soon as Grayson's name came up. You know. To share with the cousins.

Nothing was *ever* lost on Nathan, though; it was so damn annoying. "Ahh... Yes... Grayson's in Brooklyn? I should have figured that out." *Clang, click, bang!* "And you say he's sick?" He entered the kitchen and came up behind me. He grabbed the knife out of my hand and pushed me aside with his hip. He began to slice the pita bread himself.

Gertie trailed behind him, framing the doorway and looking unsure. "Did I say something wrong?" She nervously asked, glancing at my fuming figure by the stove.

"Umm… no. She's just —" He paused, not having an answer. He glanced back at me a warning look to calm down.

I exploded instead.

"You know," I said, voice thundering as I reclaimed the knife, pushing Nathan out of the way to ferociously cut into the food, "If he had just *listened* to me and not left, I guarantee you, he wouldn't be sick!" I turned to Nathan. "You and your brother *always* run away, two peas in a pod, really, I just —"

A slice of bread flew across the room with hummus following along like a stream of contrails behind a plane. We all watched it drop onto the floor in silence.

Nathan smiled at Gertie, put a hand over my mouth, walked me out of the kitchen and to the table, then returned to the kitchen, pulling out a beer from the fridge. He popped the top, stepped around the hummus for a second time, placed the beer in front of me, and slid back into the kitchen.

It was still quiet, save for the hum of the fridge. I could see Nathan's hand wiping the hummus off of the floor, and tossing the bread into the trashcan. Gertie stood between the kitchen and table positively beaming. She blurted, "I just *knew* he had a thing for her!" As my eyes crossed, I imagined her as a seal clapping its paws. Its fins. *What the hell do you call a seal's hands?* She continued, "And it looks she's got some unresolved feelings for him, too. And he said *you* two were an item! Well!" Her eyes were wide and astonished, staring at me in wonder until a flush began to creep into her cheeks.

Unable to control his true feelings, Nathan's mouth was about as gaping as mine as he looked from her, to me, back to her. "Sorry. Daddy says I don't know when to keep my mouth shut. Can we just start over?" She grabbed an olive and stuffed it into her mouth, her face completely red as she sat down at the table with me.

"They call you Blaze, do they?" I asked, regaining composure, warily eyeing her as I popped a pita slice with hummus into my own mouth. I figured chewing was as good as any activity to keep from turning into a tornado of rage.

Just then my pug, Phang, chose to bound into the room, snorting happily at the fact we had a new visitor. Barnaby, my cat, trailed behind her, but when he saw Gertie, stopped, crouched low and let out a warning mew. I felt like Barnaby. "Ooooh, how cute, a pug!" she exclaimed, standing up and scooping up my traitorous dog into her arms.

Phang farted on her. "Ewww, stinky," she said, putting Phang back down.

From Nathan's room came another pug, Mina, at full charge. Mina was my recently deceased father's dog—sister to Phang—and when dad had died, guess who got Mina? "Oh my gosh! Two pugs! Wow!" Mina didn't fart on her, but rather left behind a dampness from her hello snorts. "This one's wet." She looked grossed out for a moment before her overtly perky behavior consumed her. "I can't wait till I'm officially grown up and can have my own place! Two dogs and a cat! How great!" She dropped back down into the chair, happily adhering hummus to her bread slice.

I continued to cram food into my mouth so I wouldn't say anything else. My right eye resumed a steady twitch. Nathan glanced at me, saw my coping was going extremely well, and sat down at the table next to Gertie. I accidentally stepped on his toe as he sat down.

Okay, I deliberately stepped on his toe. Hard.

***

Dinner had been a terrible mess in execution as expected, but, short of my continued silent infuriation, the apartment was finally quiet and peaceful. Gertie was comfortably tucked beneath heavy covers in Nathan's bed. I'm not going to lie—

suffocation from my downy pillow that she had stolen had crossed my mind.

Nathan and I were in my room, quietly talking to one another. My nightlight was on, creating a dim, warm glow in the room. I flopped onto the bed, not knowing Barnaby was hiding under my now single pillow. He angrily meowed, and took his time stomping off of my bed with his tail slashing the air like a sword. He gave me the stink eye before disappearing. "Sorry!" I exclaimed, hurling myself onto my stomach.

Yes, I was having a tantrum. Nathan sat next to me, and patted me on my back.

"I'll get Blaze back to Syracuse tomorrow or the next day. In the interim..."

I rolled back over, waving a fist into the ether. "I'm not in love with him anymore."

"Of course not."

"I don't care that he's... *hurting*... and *alone*... and *hallucinating* about when we—"

"Violet," he weakly interrupted. "Sometimes you forget who I really am."

I looked over at him, and saw him with one leg on my bed, the other not, his hands in his lap, nervously turning them over and over again. "But we... but we.. We have our thing... And our thing is *good*." I sat up and forced him to look at me. "It's good, right?"

Fuck. That face! That face! I hadn't seen *that* expression on him since I'd been his apprentice. With my eyes actually *seeing* for quite sometime, I took him in; the tousled, dark hair with streaks of grey at the temples—Nathan was pushing mid-40s—; the grim way his lips pressed together on his sharp jawline; the beautiful green eyes, flecked with gold... and *pain*. And *longing*. And *defeat*. He looked away and cleared his throat. "Sometimes it's hard. That's all I mean."

"Nathan." He looked back at me, like a wounded puppy. "I... I didn't know. I really thought... Should we not have moved in together?" I hesitantly asked. *Jesus*, I could be naive. I didn't want to hear his answer. I was such a jerk.

I saw his crude, remarkably deep blue tattooed runes on his upper arm. *So in life, is death.* It had been everything to him. The runes, the prophecies, his connection to me. It hadn't gone away like I pretended it had. I felt the old, familiar rhythm of our connection begin to throb between us.

"It's okay. It's really okay. Most of the time. But when it comes to Grayson... Ahh." He looked away again and kicked at the ground. "Look, I don't want to talk about us. Or you two as a couple. Can we just talk about how we're going to get him back here?"

I didn't like that he was avoiding the conversation—or did I? But when he said get Grayson back *here*, I positively froze, my brain stuck on the current issue at hand. "Uhhhh, what do you mean, *here*?"

"Exhale, Vi."

Breathe out. I cleared my throat, and again asked, "Uhhh, what do you mean, *here*?"

"If we can't get him to... feel better in New York..." Nathan trailed off, looking ready to defend himself. "He's going to have no choice but to come down here. Most of our resources to help are here, and while I've got a few people that may be able to help in DC, Atlanta really is the best place."

"Oh, God." I lied back down and covered my head with a pillow. Nathan literally chuckled, enjoying my theatrics. "I'm glad my plight humors you," I said from underneath my cozy cavern.

He reached down, lifted up the side of the pillow and said, "Good night, Violet." He gently placed the pillow back over my head, clearly intending to head out into the living room for his sleep on the couch. I reached out and grabbed him before he could slide away. "Nate." I peeked out.

He leaned over, sliding his long, lean body on my bed next to me. "Yes?" He asked, as he still held the pillow. I could feel slight pressure from his knees touching mine.

"We're going to New York, aren't we?"

"Yup."

"With someone who goes by the name Blaze?"

"Yup."

"Any… Any visions about Grayson?"

Sigh. "No. Flying blindly, I'm afraid."

"Should we tell your mother?"

"Not yet."

I covered his head under my pillow, so we were now both under the oversized fluff. "Nathan," I whispered, barely having enough light to see him, but I could smell and feel his sweet, warm breath on me. He often smelled like cloves and pumpkin; no idea how he did it.

"What?" he conspiratorially whispered back.

"I haven't forgotten who you really are. To quote a popular song from my childhood, 'I'm just really boss at denial… best at forget."

I could sense that his face softened, but he also followed it with an audible groan at my reference. "I appreciate that. Now let's get some sleep. I have a feeling the next couple of days are going to be, what word would you use? Yes, A total clusterfuck." He said to himself. Nathan had much more eloquent speech than I did, but the more time he spent with me, the more I dragged him down to my level—no eloquence, sheer laziness.

I laughed, removing the pillow and tossing it away from both of us. "I'm sleepy," I said, closing my eyes, automatically reaching for his chest, simply to touch him as I fell asleep. It always felt so natural for me to do that when I wasn't stuck in my mind about what was right or wrong—when I was simply just being. As the darkness overtook my exhaustion almost instantaneously, I noted a slight shift in the rise and fall of Nathan's chest.

When I woke up a couple hours later, because I was cold, I blinked into the light; it was still on. Closing my eyes again, I leaned to the left to turn the light off and simultaneously grab the covers, only the covers wouldn't move. Nathan was asleep on top of my comforter with me! I had forgotten he had been in there when I'd fallen asleep.

With the light still on and my eyes now wide open, I looked at the scene before me. Phang was snuggled next to him, and Barnaby was at his feet. I wondered where Mina was—probably with Gertie. I watched him sleep for a moment, wondering what to do. I slid off the bed and walked around to turn off the light. Then I wiggled under the part of the covers that Nathan wasn't covering. Phang snorted happily in her sleep with the movement. Nathan made a small sighing noise, and I closed my eyes, warmer because I was under my comforter. I placed one hand on Phang, accidentally brushing hands with Nathan.

It was enough to wake him up. I kept my eyes closed while he figured out where he was. He sat up; I felt him shake his head, pet both Phang and Barnaby, then reach over to lightly kiss me on the head before getting up and leaving.

My bed got cold.

3

The following morning I awakened to glorious food-making sounds in the kitchen. I figured Nathan was cooking something for Gertie, and hopefully, for me. He was a pretty great cook when he was up to the task of doing it. "I'll take the little puppies out," I heard Gertie's voice from the hallway. The dogs began to excitedly yip as I imagined they had seen their harnesses being picked up. I heard the door close. I groaned into my pillow, and also into a cat's rear end that was unfortunately in my face.

"Dammit, Barnaby."

I got up and trudged my way to the bathroom. I quickly brushed my teeth, grabbed a robe, and leaned in the doorway of the kitchen. I had an image of Nathan wearing an apron with a chef's hat on, dark hair peeking out underneath the hat... But no such luck. He was just wearing a white t-shirt and dark blue, drawstring shorts. He smiled when he saw me.

"You saw the chef hat again, didn't you?" He slid a plate of what looked like tasty vegetable crepes towards me. I stifled a yawn, grabbed the plate, and walked to the kitchen table to release it.

"You will most definitely wear one, just as soon as I buy it for you."

I walked into the kitchen to grab a cup of coffee. "Excuse me," I said, trying to walk around him.

"Hey," he said, stopping me before I walked out. I took a sip of the coffee.

"Yeah?"

"Why didn't you wake me up last night? You must have gotten cold."

I took another sip, and then walked away without looking at him. "I was cold after you left."

"Oh." He said, and then began to scrape the pan clean. I had a good portion of the food shoveled into my mouth when Gertie came back in with the pugs.

"Good morning, Violet!" she exclaimed, a giant smile adorning her face. "Thank you so much for letting me crash here, I really don't know what I was thinking when I left school. Nathan told me what the plan is."

I counted to three. "Oh? I'm not sure *I* know what the plan is."

"These dogs are great, by the way. And your cat, too! He's got quite an attitude, but give him a treat…"

I closed my eyes and took two long cycles of breath. It was going to be a long day with Cousin Gertie—I had to get my shit together. I opened my eyes to Nathan placing a manila folder on the table. I opened it up, and saw three plane tickets. I looked up, confused. "Ever been to La Guardia?"

"Wow. What the hell time did you wake up?" I looked at the clock, and it read 10AM.

He grinned. "I woke up early to meditate, unlike some people I know."

"Dude. It's a Sunday."

"A well-disciplined mind is a well-functioning mind."

Gertie was watching the verbal volley with wide eyes. There had been a long time of when Nathan and I hadn't flirted with one another at all. Those times were becoming less frequent now that we lived together full time, and I was beginning to miss them. I felt like my world was starting to implode on itself, right when things had been going smoothly.

I changed the subject. "What about Jared? Are you going to reach out to him before we see Grayson?"

My mind drifted to a vision that Nathan had experienced regarding Jared. It had happened a mere moment before Nicole had called Nathan on the phone to let him know Jared was aware of what had happened in Germany. The vision was of Jared and Grayson at a bar, with Grayson apparently slamming an empty pint onto the counter, looking angry. Jared smiled his usual oily grin at Grayson's response. Nathan hadn't caught any words, but he was definitely unsettled that the two of them were together.

"No. In the off chance we're walking into a trap… I'd like him to be caught off guard."

"Would he really turn on you like this?"

"Grayson's an easy target, he's got too many demons."

"I meant Jared."

"Oh." Nathan looked uncomfortable

"Nathan Murphy. You're holding out on me again." I tried to be funny, but in reality, I could feel anger begin to well inside of me. After the takedown I did during my apprenticeship, Nathan had abandoned me. He had hidden things from me. I hadn't forgotten it—I had more or less forgiven him, though, when he had finally explained his own cowardice.

Nathan often said most when he said nothing at all. When we were in Sylt and the prophecy had been shared, Grayson and I had become very close. So close in fact, I could still remember some freckles on his backside. Nathan was mum when I told him I wasn't going shack up with either of them, nor would I fall prey to the stupid prophecy, to Vendetta Veritas or whatever other group erroneously believed they could use my imaginary child for their own whims.

Gertie cleared her throat. I had kind of forgotten she was there.

"Oh hey, guys, I was just wondering if I could shower?" Nathan left the kitchen to grab towels and get her situated while I went to clear my plate off in the sink. By the time I had put the dishes in the dishwasher, Nathan was back and the shower was on.

"Welllll?"

He stood in front of me, deliberately towering over me to faux-intimidate me. "Not gonna work, Nate. You've got food stuck in your whiskers." He hadn't shaved in a few days, and there was a teeny crumb caught in his chin hair. He groaned as I brushed it out of his hair. I pushed him back until he ran into the counter, poking his chest. "When did you meet Jared?"

"He and I finished apprenticeship at the same time with the same regional group. Obviously this is before he went rogue. He didn't like being under direction of the government; he wanted to do his own thing. He didn't last long. We may or may not have majorly butt heads before he left."

"Where was this at?"

"I was in Washington at the time."

"How long ago?"

"Over twenty years."

"How long were you a light bearer?"

Remember when I said my title was consultant for the government? While this was true, the unofficial title to those in the know was *light bearer*. In the beginning, though, since I hadn't been given a title at all, I had jokingly called myself a light thrower. I mean, that was sort of what I was doing to the Darkness, right, throwing light?

"Not long, just a few years. My strengths didn't lie in that type of field work. I sort of went rogue, too—but by following the rules."

"Thus why you and Jared didn't, and don't, get along. I mean, other than he's potentially evil." I was deep in thought, chewing on my hair, still standing practically on top of him, keeping him trapped against the counter.

"Yeah, there's that."

"I have such inexplicable bad feelings about the guy, Nathan. It's almost nauseating."

He propped himself up *on* the counter, thoughtfully looking at me before rubbing his hands through his hair. "Yeah, I'm starting to feel very ill about him, too." He set his jaw, looking off into the distance. I knew he wouldn't tell me if he sensed something. Nathan was too good at keeping secrets.

And so, I resorted to *my* typical behavior. I threw my head into his lap, whining, pounding the counter with my fists. "Last tantrum, I promise," I said into his lap after I was done with my fists. He awkwardly pet me on the head.

"Sure thing, Vi."

I looked up at him, and scowled, placing my hands on either side of him. "Support me, you jerk!"

He turned me around, trapped me in between his legs and said into my ear, "I am." I felt the warmth from his breath, and then he released me.

His touch lingered as I went to my room to pack for the trip.

***

It was very early the following morning, and we were already on the plane. I had my eyes closed, pretending to be asleep, but really I was wide awake with overflowing anxiety. I was sweating from every orifice in my body.

Over the past few months, I had played a million and one scenarios in my mind upon seeing *him* again. There was one very bright image of me strangling him. I liked that one a lot. There was another one of him waking up from true love's kiss, followed by us running off together and disappearing into dusk, never to be found again.

Then there was Nathan's warm body pressing up against mine on the plane. *Sigh.* Steady. Strong.

We'd been twenty thousand feet in the air for some time when the silence was broken by Gertie "Nathan," she whispered. I was falling in and out of sleep at this point.

"Yeah?" I felt him look up from his book about the nature of reality. Choice read for a short flight. Only Nathan would pick such an impenetrable tome during travel in an encased tube hurtling in the air at 900 km an hour.

Gertie was seated by the window and Nathan had the aisle. As I was in the middle, I felt her body lean up close to mine as she leaned towards him.

"What's the deal with you and," her voice considerably lowered, "Violet?"

Nathan's body stiffened and I felt him glance my way. He somehow knew I was awake. "There's nothing to tell."

"That's not true. I know about the prophecy."

Nathan's body managed to stiffen even more as he leaned in, turning his back towards the aisle as if to block anyone else from listening. "How do you know about that? Grayson swore he wouldn't tell anyone!"

"Not Gray, my mom. Auntie Alex told her about it ages ago."

"That can't be right. She said she hadn't shared it with anyone, even the man who had spoken it."

"Hmm... Maybe she told Mom about a vision then? Either

way, we still all know about the prophecy and Violet. One of you is going to be the dad to someone incredibly powerful!" Her voice was hushed now. "So cool."

"You know the prophecy and our visions are two entirely different things, right?"

"Yeah, I know, but—"

"Nothing is set in stone unless it *actually* happens."

"Well, right, but the prophecy was transcribed in the runes, though—I thought that solidified everything once Odin's magic got involved."

Well, hell. I didn't know *that* theory. Odin's magic, that one-eyed Tony Hopkins fellow from the MCU had to do with this madness? This crud was getting too esoteric again. I emitted a fake snore to keep them talking.

"It's complicated." *Complicated?* All I could think was that the prophecy she was speaking about didn't specifically name me *as* The Weapon, nor Nathan and Grayson *as* The Brothers. Nathan had unwittingly named *me* as The Weapon when I had become his apprentice.

"I can see. But beyond that—you're in love with her, aren't you?" Nathan must have answered by a look on his face. "I'm so sorry, Nate… I know Grayson sorta loves her, too. This is so awful." She let out a huge sigh, and I felt her turn to look out the window.

Nathan moved to rest his back against his seat again.

"Does she know?" Gertie turned back to Nathan.

"She knows… enough."

"Does she understand that she can't get out of it?"

He shifted again, this time because he was extremely uncomfortable. My breathing changed and became incredibly shallow. No, in fact, I did *not* know that. This was treading into the territory of *What Pissed Me Off Most*—my free will being taken away from me. It wasn't about being in denial, or being stubborn. The fact that I was supposed to believe my free will didn't matter—That. Pissed. Me. Off.

Like you wouldn't believe.

"Does she get that she and her daughter may have to go into hiding? I mean, what of you, or Gray? Ugh. It's like some sick and twisted fairytale. Fairytales always end badly, don't they?" Gertie sounded forlorn.

I must have been gripping the seat at that point, because I felt Nathan try to pry my fingers off of the armrests.

"She and I are going to have to have a long talk, yes." He squeezed my hand, my guess out of sight from Gertie's eyes. "But not for awhile." His hand remained on mine, trying to send calming vibes into my system.

"Oh—cause you've had another vision or something?"

"Something like that."

Nathan's effect was taking its toll on me—I was drifting off to sleep, finding comfort in the nothing. Yet, there was this tiny part of my brain that was angry at Nathan for calming me down.

The last thing I caught wind of was a flight attendant asking the cousins what they wanted to drink. Nathan ordered me a ginger ale for when I awakened.

4

I woke up with a start, forgetting where I was. I opened my eyes and saw Nathan latching the tables onto the backs of the seats in front of us. My dry mouth frowned as my full glass of ginger ale walked away in the trash with a flight attendant. I sighed, stretching my legs and rubbing my neck.

Gertie hogged the window, staring out of it like she'd never been on a plane before. Nathan pushed back into his chair, closing his eyes, mumbling something under his breath. I reached across him to catch a glimpse of Lady Liberty from a window on the opposite side of the plane. I saw her proud, green crown reaching to the heavens, her torch aflame with hope. I glanced up and saw that Nathan was watching me. He softly said, "Hi." I kept eye contact for a beat, trying to read him, but to no avail.

We landed without a hitch, left the airport, caught a bus to the subway, and took off to Brooklyn. Gertie had time to see Grayson before we put her on a bus for Syracuse, so as we got off of our train stop in Brooklyn, the three of us were still together. Nate and Gertie were arm in arm ahead of me, leading the way to Grayson's friend's place. Nathan had apparently never been there, but clearly Gertie knew the way by heart. We walked by a little corner store on our right. From there, it turned into sidewalks that led to multiple, oddly scattered dwellings. I heard a basketball dribbling on a court somewhere in the distance. With my sunglasses on in the afternoon light and my backpack slung on my back, I followed them, my thoughts jumping all around.

It dawned on me that I had no idea where Nathan and I were supposed to stay that night. I assumed we weren't going to be very welcome at Grayson's place. We approached a small house that had a tiny, brickyard in front. Gertie stepped up to the door, and buzzed to be let in. Presumably, the voice on the other end of the intercom was roommate Tim, telling us to come on upstairs. We stepped inside the door, and Gertie took us upstairs to the first door on our left. She knocked, and a man, probably around Nathan's age, opened up the door.

"Blaze! So glad to see you again so soon—but obviously under these circumstances it's terrible." He gave her a big, strong hug. This Tim guy was only about 5'8" or 5'9"—not particularly tall— but a solid guy, stocky. His blond hair was grey at the temples, and button down shirt was half-untucked.

"I take it you must be the brother?" Blaze stepped beyond Tim, and disappeared into the apartment.

Nathan shook his hand, and said, "Yes, I'm Nathan. This is —"

"Yeah, Violet I take it. Grayson sure has been mumbling about you since he got sick." He suspiciously eyed me, noticeably not extending his hand to shake mine. Turning to Nathan, he continued, "I don't know what happened, man. One second Gray was fine, but that guy showed up, kept him out all night, and he just hasn't been right since then. I called

Blaze 'cause I don't have any other contact info for his family, you know? I know his dad's a schlep, and he *just* told me that his mom was alive and all, but I don't even know her name."

He stepped aside so we could come in, keeping a sharp eye on me like I was about to spew forth spider webbing to ensnare him. "He's right down that hallway where Blaze went." He nodded down a hallway. "He's been crashing in my spare room for awhile."

Nathan and I stepped inside. Tim grabbed a blazer hanging on the back of a chair, slipping some loafers on. "Look—I've got to get to work. There's a spare key in the cabinet right next to the fridge inside an old coffee tin. If you could lock up before you leave—maybe just slide the key under the mat." He paused. "Actually, do you know how long you'll be here?" He slid a daypack over his shoulder, placing keys on an inside pocket while holding his cell phone. "I have a pull-out couch if you need it."

"Violet!" shouted Gertie, and I excused myself, not sure what Nathan was going to say.

The hallway was dark; it smelled a little musty, or at least like men lived there and no women. I followed the voices, and almost immediately picked up on Grayson's energy. It had reached around the doorway to me, tendrils of desperation grasping at my general essence. It broke me out into a cold sweat as I stepped inside the doorway, seeing the back of Gertie's curls kneeling at a bedside. Just beyond her was Grayson who was slightly slumped in the bed. His skin looked pallid, his cheeks hollow. He looked awful, almost like he was dying. He had an unruly 5 o'clock shadow and heavy eyes. His beautiful auburn hair was predominantly slicked back against his head, sticking out in odd places as if his fingers had been repeatedly running through it.

He weakly looked up at me from his slightly propped up position, and then closed his eyes, wheezing out my name. I hesitatingly walked into the room, placing my sack by the door along with Gertie's. "You say it's only been a week that he's been like this?"

Gertie's wide eyes met mine. "Yes. A week. I can't believe it. A few weeks ago he looked so good, so healthy."

I kneeled next to the bed, Gertie sliding closer to his feet to give me space. I took one hand and cupped it underneath the base of his head; I took my other hand and placed it on his chest at his heart. I muttered a healing chant under my breath, one that wasn't terribly familiar. Even so, it seemed to naturally flow out of me, as if from a memory.

"What's wrong with him?" Gertie whispered next to me.

"Grayson," I murmured softly. "Is this poison?"

He opened his eyes, and I could see the focus happening, almost like when a wild animal makes eye contact with you. "You look like someone I once knew… I was no good for her, though." He closed his eyes again and started rasping.

"Grayson, focus! Look at me!" I softly commanded. "It's Violet. I'm here. In New York."

I did an energetic scan of his body, trying to figure out where the imbalances were. I called on intuition to show me the *hibiki*—any of these imbalances "shown" to me by feel as I hovered above each chakra. I looked at Gertie. "Can you see if Tim has any tea here? He needs some ashgawandha, kava kava, or any anti-stress type tea—maybe some lemon and lavender for clarity and focus? Maybe a combo?"

I needed to be alone with him, and I figured if I assigned Gertie a fool's errand, she'd be content. She stood up, red hair tucked behind her ears. "Yes, I'll look." She walked out of the room, clearly on a mission, and I glanced up to see that Nathan was quietly standing in the doorway.

"Can you do something?" I asked, suddenly very afraid. "He isn't coherent."

"I'm good at helping heal physical ailments… Not so much

emotional."

"This is emotional? Or did he get poisoned?"

"Maybe both?"

"But it's been a week—that's a really long time—shouldn't a high be over by now?"

Nathan shrugged. "If magic's involved, who knows?"

I did a quick rub on Grayson's sternum, seeing if that would awaken him. His face looked irritated, and he said, "Stop that. That hurts."

"Grayson—it's me—it's Violet."

"Violet's not here. She's in Atlanta with Nathan," he mumbled.

"Grayson—open your damn eyes—Nate and I are *both* here, in Brooklyn. Gertie got us!"

Grayson opened his eyes again, trying hard to focus on my face, and then on Nathan. "Blaze?"

"Yes, she's getting you some tea," said Nathan.

I stood up and crossed my arms looking at Nathan. "Do you know a shaman? Priestess? Witch doctor? Medical doctor?" I started to get a little hysterical, and Nathan put his arms on me.

"We'll figure this out, Violet. I promise."

"Brother?" questioned a weak voice behind me.

"The one and only," Nathan replied over my head. I turned away from Nathan and slowly walked back over to Grayson.

"Violet?" asked Gertie who had taken the space I had just emptied. I turned to her. "I found chamomile. Do you think that's good? It says it's medicinal grade."

"Perfect." She walked back out.

"Violet?" This time my name was uttered by the man in the bed. Stubborn man at that, as he was trying to sit up even more to get a better look at me. I dropped to the floor next to the top part of his body, putting on a brave face.

"Heeey," I said. "You look terrible." I smiled, brushing his hair out of his face taking on the role of caregiver. "And in major need of a shower." I wrinkled my nose, my heart rapidly beating, fluttering my shirt just enough to betray my calm appearance.

"Water?" Grayson asked.

"Gertie's getting you some tea. What... What happened? What can we do for you?" I looked back at Nathan who was standing just behind me.

"Jared," Grayson managed to croak out.

"Yeah, Blaze told us—but—" Nathan said.

"Violet," Grayson reached out to me, hands roughly gripping my hands. He had finally fully propped himself up, awakening more with each word, blurting the words out with a sudden alertness that was shocking. "I had to tell him about the prophecy... His threats... I had visions... He knows you're *The Weapon*. You aren't safe."

I pulled away from Grayson, suddenly scared for myself. I was a *fool!* I hadn't given enough thought to my own safety with all of this nonsense! How naive I had been to think that this irrational prophecy would have any bearing on my little, boring life—but others were going to *give* it weight. "Nathan! I'm *not* this weapon!"

Nathan gave a small shake of his head, trying to let me know that now was not the time to tackle this refusing-to-die issue. "Nathan... She still doesn't get it?" Grayson groaned. "God dammit."

I stood up, feeling a small shake inside my body start to form. "Nathan." I turned to him, begging his eyes to make sense of this nonsense for me.

Gertie interrupted, rushing into the room exclaiming, "Tea! I've got tea!" The smile on her face when she saw Grayson sitting up was out of place with the tension I had created. Gertie sloshed the tea onto a desk as she hurriedly placed the mug down, rushing to Grayson's side. "Oh my Gooooood,

Grayson, you're awake! I've been so scared! I'm so sorry about getting Nathan, but I didn't know what else to do!"

"It's okay, Blaze." He looked at the tea. "Can I have some?"

"Oh, yeah, sure!" She handed it to him and he sipped some, clearing his throat. While I was trying not to hyperventilate from fear, or die from the pure adrenaline pumping through my veins because of seeing Grayson for the first time since the *last* time, those damn reunited cousins carrying on a normal conversation as if none of this chaotic crap was happening was about to render me furious.

5

"Are you freaking kidding me?" I blurted out, interrupting the chattering cousins who were discussing their favorite teas. "You three aren't really just sitting here talking about tea, are you? Grayson literally just underwent some sort of psychic attack and you guys are discussing the benefits of chamomile?" I was incredulous.

For a moment, the three of them looked like beautiful, wild animals realizing an outsider was in their midst. The creature in the bed narrowed his eyes, assessing how I might taste for dinner. The female animal's eyes opened in abject terror, wondering where she could hide from the intruder. And the third entity, well, his eyes softened, and while they didn't offer an invitation into the conversation, they tried to offer understanding.

However, I was pretty livid.

"Look," Grayson said, point blank. "This attack took me by surprise. I wasn't prepared for it and lost myself for awhile. I'll be okay, now, though... I started getting better a couple of days ago. Now it just comes and goes, this incoherency left lingering."

I took a step back. "You're getting *better*?" I asked, and I could feel the air still around me. Gertie's terror continued as she took a safe space behind Nathan. Nathan looked to Grayson, looked to me, and began to slowly back himself into the doorway.

Nathan took Gertie by the shoulders and said to me, "We'll just be out here when you need us." He closed the door behind him, leaving it slightly cracked.

I barely looked at them as they left. "Look, Violet, I'm still recuperating here so if we could avoid any theatrics..." He trailed off, placing his tea on the side of the bed, normal cockiness failing just shy of pulling it off.

Good. He damn well deserved to be apprehensive in regards to my presence.

"*Theatrics*? Do you mean, the drama of how you ditched us? How you ditched *me*? Of how you disappeared into thin air like you'd never even existed?" I began counting each drama on each fingertip, exaggerating each one as I counted it. "No utterance at all from you!" I dejectedly looked on at him. "No whisper of you on the wind." I paused. "I pretty much told you I *loved* you and *poof*! You were merely of my imagination."

"You never told me you loved me," he said quietly, interrupting me. "But I told *you* you loved Nathan more than me." I paid no mind to what he was saying—I was on a a roll and he wasn't about to stop me.

"And then when *you* need *us*, somehow here *we* are here for you? Only, I'm so sorry—you're actually getting *better*, and so you *don't* need us." I was irate and pacing as he looked on, no doubt calculating how to get me to stop. "You're just like your damn brother. Both of you—running away when things get tough—"

"You're one to talk," he spat out.

It was unbelievable. If it weren't for his thinned body and

sallow skin tone, I wouldn't have ever thought anything had been wrong with him only moments before. His voice was strong, his bitterness stronger.

I still had the upper hand, though, as he remained in bed. I glowered down, using my full height as a weapon. "I'm one to talk? What the hell does that even mean? I haven't run away."

"Ha, Violet, that's pure crap." He sat up straighter. "You run away every day from your feelings for Nathan. You run away from your *gut* which tells you there's merit to this prophecy. Your greatest betrayal will be your running away —"

"Oh yeah? *Will* be? Is this some bogus vision you're talking about?" I clapped my hands together like a crazy person, tears of frustration beginning to pour down my face. "If you guys have this great gift of 'sight', then, why don't you just tell me what you effing see? I'm beyond tired of your psychic bullshit." The tears were freely streaming now.

"Clearly, Nathan doesn't think it's a good idea." Grayson's face hardened as he turned to sit on the side of his bed with the intention of standing up to challenge me.

"Nathan? What the hell does he have to do with any of *your* visions?" I took a step back.

"You'll have to ask him." Grayson drily responded, finally reaching full height.

I pressed my lips hard against one another, and turned to look back at the door. Nathan was back in the room, Gertie nowhere to be seen.

"You weren't gone long." I stiffly said to him.

"I didn't get far," came his soft response.

Silence.

I was half-turned to the door with Nathan's eyes affixed on mine. The left part of my body was mere inches from the now standing tall Grayson. The electricity between him and me was palpable, and I was doing my best to ignore it. I finally broke my stare on Nathan to gave Grayson what he wanted; my blue eyes on his hazel ones. His eyes were narrowed, taking in my wet face with no ounce of regret buried anywhere in those eyes. He was deliberately trying to intimidate me by his mere stature.

We stood there outside of time, frozen in confrontation, confusion. I felt Nathan's eyes travel from my backside to Grayson's face, who was still inches from mine. "Stand down, Grayson," Nathan murmured, crossing across the room and reaching towards me. Before he could grab me, I dropped onto a desk chair by the bed, leaving the two of them standing, eyes on one another.

"Are you going to explain any of this shit, or per the usual, keep me in the dark?" I sourly asked, addressing Nathan. He looked down to me, breaking whatever silent communication was going on with his brother, and his expression cleared.

I had misjudged him.

"I honestly assumed you didn't want to know." I raised an eyebrow, Grayson let out a small groan. "The things I see in my visions... These dreams I have... I just assumed you didn't want to know about them because of their lack of *significance*. You know fully well visions and dreams don't necessitate reality." He kneeled down before me as I sniffled a little bit more.

Grayson had moved to his closet and started gathering what appeared to be clothing. I wasn't thrilled that I was crying in front of him. "Violet," Nathan murmured, taking his sleeve and gently wiping the wetness off my face. My eyes welled up again, and I looked away from him, using my own sleeve to dry my face. Nathan kept his hands on my knees, then turned part-way to Grayson. "But I feel like this particular discussion should be tackled later, if that's alright."

"That's fine," I muttered, as Nathan stood up, turning back

to Grayson.

"We first need to take care of you, brother. You look terrible."

"Why, thank you," he said curtly. "You look great yourself."

Nathan ignored his response, and continued, "So why don't you tell us what happened, from the beginning?"

"Yes, well, I think I'd like to take a shower before we talk. *If* you don't mind." Grayson showed us the clothing in his arms, clearly irritated Nathan was about to interrogate him. "While I really am feeling a lot better, my preference is to continue this dreadful conversation *after* I've washed off this insidious week."

Nathan nodded, "Sure."

"Violet," Grayson abruptly turned to address me as he was about to exit the room. "Whatever you just did, well, it really did help me. Just so you know." His eyes looked earnest and his voice without its usual edge, but I merely glared in response. He stepped out of the room and in the distance, I heard water turn on.

"Violet, are you okay?" Nathan asked, showing real concern.

My tears were dried up, though. My frustration had been replaced with resolve. "I'm fine," I said, standing up, brushing off my legs and stomping past Nathan to exit. "I will be in the kitchen, waiting to hear the story." I walked out, leaving Nathan behind.

Behind me, I heard Nathan emit a long sigh and, "That went well."

6

Nathan, Gertie and I were in the kitchen, waiting for Grayson's reappearance after his shower. Gertie had poured tea for the rest of us, and I was grateful for it to serve as a distraction. Nathan had tried to console me after I'd stormed out of the bedroom, but I brushed him off. Gertie was confused about what was going on, but also clearly excited that Grayson was feeling so much better.

A loud noise came from down the hallway, and then some cussing.

"Ummm," said Gertie. "Should someone check on him?"

"I will. He's my brother."

"Yes," I said, standing up, pushing the table away from me with fervor. "But *I've* seen him naked." I started to forcefully stride to the bathroom, but Nathan blocked me.

"Don't remind me. *My* brother, *my* responsibility." He wasn't budging, so I growled and then went into the attached living room and plopped down onto the dingy, plaid couch.

Gertie ran over to the fridge, pretending to be studying its contents. "Awkward!" Her big eyes peeked out from behind the top of the door.

Nathan disappeared down the hallway, and I closed my eyes, muttering things to myself. "My poor cousins," Gertie sadly said into the refrigerator. She pulled out a carton of milk. "Want some for your tea?"

I opened my eyes and looked at her still standing by the fridge. "No. Why are you saying 'poor cousins'?"

Her face turned as red as her hair. "Sorry. I didn't know I had said that out loud."

I narrowed my eyes and stared off down the hallway as she splashed some milk into her tea. My right eye began to violently twitch again.

Nathan came back into the kitchen. "He's getting out of the shower now. He caught himself while falling, but bumped his elbow. I guess the side effects of whatever happened haven't completely worn off yet." He trailed off, daring to glance at me. Nathan audibly sighed, yet again, then sat back down at the kitchen table. He took in the red faced Gertie. "What did I miss?"

"Nothing," she squeaked, returning to the refrigerator.

I chose to ignore the current conversation by changing the topic to what it needed to be. I stood up and marched over to the round table. "Perfect time to tell me whatever it is you've seen and haven't told me about yet."

Nathan grimaced, glancing down the hallway. "Look—I've told you before—these visions change, they aren't necessarily set in stone. We make them what they are."

"What did you see?" I slammed my hand on the table, beyond angry. This was my *life* he was messing with by continuing to keep secrets from me. If he didn't think I could handle it, then why was he wasting time with me at all?

A throat cleared from just outside of the kitchen; Grayson stood framed in the doorway. His hair was still wet, shirt off, towel wrapped loosely around his hips. All at once, my mind started traveling in sixty-five million directions. Good *God*, that man needed to put some clothes on. Practically naked in front of his own cousin! It was hard not to appreciate how good he looked, especially since his skin coloring had come back. While he was definitely thinner than when I'd last seen him, he still had enough muscular definition to make someone's head turn.

Nathan followed my eyes as they flickered towards Grayson, and then he barked at him to get dressed. "Of course, brother, do excuse me," Grayson said, smile widening at our discomfort.

"Well," I said drily, "At least we know he really *is* feeling better." Even so, my cheeks felt a little warm.

Gertie's eyes were about to pop out of her head. Noisily slurping her tea, she said, "I really should be leaving soon, Nathan."

He looked at his phone. "Crap, Blaze, I totally forgot you had to leave. Look—when Gray comes back out, tell him bye real quick. I'll get you to the bus stop and head back here afterwards."

He stood up, placing his phone in his back pocket. "Will you be okay alone with him?"

"Yeah." I said, holding eyes with him.

"Don't let him get to you."

"I won't. I'm going to get some answers. Unlike from *you*."

"Violet, I have reasons for my—"

Gertie ran up to Grayson as he reentered the room and Nathan stopped speaking. Gertie and Grayson exchanged goodbyes. He assured her he wasn't mad at her. She told me she was super happy to finally meet the famous Violet. The door closed, and then there was nothing left but awkward silence.

At least Grayson allowed for that now that he and I were completely alone. After a few moments, we spoke at once, sharing a short, uncomfortable laugh.

Across the table from me, he began. "Jared visited me about a week ago. I hadn't seen him in, say, over five years? I didn't even recognize him at first—he approached me in a convenient store up the road. After he reminded me of who he was, we agreed to meet for dinner later on. He's still pissed at Nathan for not letting him know what happened in Germany."

"Why does he think Nathan owes him an explanation?"

"No idea," he shrugged before continuing. "Anyway, he starts to rant about how much Nathan really goads him, and I get the feeling he's trying to bait me. Of course, I don't fall for it, but then he starts to talk about *The Weapon*, and the prophecy... I just listened, didn't offer anything."

He slammed his fist on the table, and I jumped. "Then he mentioned how several groups of people are looking for *who* this weapon is, and that *he* was the only one able to protect *her*, because he knows all of the invested parties looking for her." He spread out his hands on the table like a fan. "You know, when I met Jared all those years ago, I didn't like him. I already knew Jason and all about Vendetta Veritas. I wasn't involved with them, but I wasn't *not* involved with them if you know what I mean. Jared started hanging around, and I could never figure out whose side he was on."

"What... What did you tell him?"

"He kept going on and on about protecting this woman... and then he mentioned Alexandra, and then *you* by name. I don't know what I did to show a reaction, but by whatever I did, it confirmed that you were *The Weapon*."

I could barely move.

"Violet," his hazel eyes turned sincere—this being something they didn't look like often. Grayson was one of the most guarded, wounded individuals I knew. "Tenebris rattled off where you worked, where you live, where you run, who your friends are… The guy is no good."

"And?"

"And then he wanted to know what the rest of the prophecy said."

I felt like I'd been punched.

"You've got to understand, Violet—Nate and I had visions with you in them before we even knew the prophecy existed. Nathan also had his thoughts that your connection with him was," he tossed his hands up in the air, as if reaching for the right word. *"Unique.* But once chatter started around someone referenced as *The Weapon,* well, our visions crossed and the prophecy was no longer a secret. Apparently it had been rumored amongst certain parties for a long time. How? I don't know. Nathan and I didn't know anything about that."

"Why does everyone think it's me?" I quietly asked.

He harshly laughed. "Your gifts precede you, Violet. That first takedown you did with the Scouts… You shouldn't have been able to do that. Your bloodline is noted by the Feds, *our* bloodline is noted by the Feds. Our families are so intertwined, even without us having sought out one another. This prophecy was told *to* Alexandra, written for *her.* She promptly hid it, but not without telling her sister, and God knows who else. People talk." He looked off in the distance.

"But… Even so. I mean, the prophecy didn't mention my likeness at all."

"I had a vision first… Of this woman I had never met, carrying a small child on her hip," he rushed, holding his hand up not letting me interject. "I didn't recognize her, but she had this tangible power about her. She then looked back and smiled at someone—possibly me. She was holding a man's hand as she walked, and there was no telling who the man was. It was vivid as hell, the most vivid and real vision I've ever had. Nathan already knew you when he had his vision. He saw you pregnant, but walking with *me.*"

I blew out and swore. "If your mom didn't know about the rest of the prophecy beyond giving away one of her sons—"

"No," he corrected, "She didn't *have* to give one of us away. She *chose* that."

"I'm not here to argue the actions of a desperate woman. I'm just saying, so *what* if you guys saw me pregnant, or with a child? Why does that mean I'm some weapon, or that *either* of you are the father? Or why was it even out that there *was* a weapon before hearing the rest of the prophecy?"

"Obviously Alexandra lied. Or maybe she just meant—"

"About the missing part of the prophecy. In which case, we need to talk to her. Where is the rest of it?"

We sat in silence for a few minutes, questions with no answers swirling around us. Well, other than one. "I'm not choosing either of you. All I have to do is keep my wits about me and then I can be left out of this! Maybe I *will* become a mother one day, but it seems fairly easy to keep either of *you* from being the damn father."

I sat back, proud, smug, clueless.

Grayson leaned forward, mood changed, very seductive, clearly accepting my unwitting challenge. "Oh, is it?"

"Stop that," I muttered. "Don't put images in my head of the past."

He scooted his chair next to mine. "You think you can stop me—either one of us for that matter— when your connection to us is beyond rational thought? Beyond logical explanation?" He angrily whispered in my ear, taking a finger to brush my hair from behind my ear to the top of my shoulder.

"Stop it, Grayson. Yes. I can."

"You weren't able to before." He sat back, arms crossed and eyes narrowed.

"That was different. I was caught up in everything."

"Aren't you now? Aren't you caught in the middle of

everything? Because you're *The Weapon*?" He cruelly laughed.

"Fine," I growled, leaning into *him* this time, taking his bait and raising the ante. "Then why the hell aren't *you* the father? Why is it Nathan? If it can't be stopped, then it's *my* decision, as I've said before. *Not* yours. I can choose who I want to be with."

He didn't say anything, just pressed his lips against one another. Then a softness violently came across his face, across his entire body, and he leaned into me. His hazel eyes were slightly closed with burning green embers in them; his lips hovering above my lips for a hesitant second before pressing down hard against my own. His hands reached the sides of my face, along my back, pulling my body even closer to his, and I found that he was right. This attraction was beyond rational thought. I couldn't think at all, I could only feel, and I could feel *everything*. The contours of his body as it curved into mine, the silkiness of his skin that wasn't covered by clothes; the stubble of his chin harshly brushing across my face.

He tasted like a deep red wine on a chilly, fall day. Spicy, and warm, and safe. *Jesus, why did this feel safe?* Nothing about this was safe. As I was trying to surf the waves of emotion, desperately seeking air and logic, it suddenly occurred to me that the man I held within my embrace wasn't behaving properly—he was convulsing. It happened so quickly that I was taken aback at first and didn't react, just dumbly stared at the body I was now holding upright.

"Grayson?" I breathlessly asked, holding him as I pulled away.

7

His eyes started to roll back into his head and he began to make guttural sounds. "Oh my God, what is happening? Grayson!" I shouted, attempting to drag him over to the worn couch before he hurt himself on the wood of the table. I didn't make it very far, and ended up straddling him on the floor, trying to keep him down. I pushed the coffee table out of the way, then moved back to him, wrapping him as best as I could in a blanket I'd yanked off the back of the couch.

"Grayson! Can you hear me? Do I need to call 911? Is this another psychic attack?! Grayson!" I grabbed at his face, trying to get him to see with his eyes again. His head was lolling side to side, strange noises still coming out of him. My veins were pulsing with the fire of adrenaline, and my tunnel vision was overcoming me. *I had to focus. I needed Nathan.*

I fumbled in my pocket for my phone, and frantically called him, interrupting his hello. "Where are you? Grayson's seizing or something, I'm trying to pin his arms down and hold his head and—" I tossed the phone, keeping the line live and gave my attention back Grayson.

As tears of fear streaked my face, I began to notice that my muscles were relaxing. Grayson had stilled. A herd of elephants raced up the stairs to the apartment and the smack of metal came from outside as Nathan's key fidgeted in the lock. Once inside and out of breath, he asked, "How long?"

"Just a few minutes—he's calmed down but still isn't coherent—what do we do? Call 911? I mean, is this psychic or is he having a stroke or are they one and the same or—?"

Nathan held a hand up to me and closely listened to Grayson's breathing while taking his pulse. "His breathing and heart rate are elevated but... But he seems okay?" He questioned, looking unsure. Nathan and I sat in loud silence, not knowing what to do.

Fortunately, the silence was almost immediately interrupted by violent coughing. "Gray!" I exclaimed through a mouthful of anxious spit. I squatted next to him, helping him prop up against the couch. Sliding next to him on the floor, I was painfully aware of every bit of his body touching mine. I carefully cradled his head against me as best I could. His eyes were open, but they were heavy.

Nathan crouched before us. "We've got to break your connection with whomever is attacking you, cut the cord. Is it Jared, or someone else?"

Grayson managed to get out, "Not Jared." Nathan looked at me with huge question marks replacing his pupils.

"What do we need to help you? A chant? Forcefield? Crystals?" I rattled things off, recognizing the uselessness of it all.

He looked a little strung out when he replied, shakily drawing in a deep breath, "I don't know."

Nathan sat down on the couch behind us, and as I continued to cradle Grayson's head, I looked up at him. "Grayson told Jared about the prophecy when he visited him."

Grayson cleared his throat and sat up away from me,

slightly turning into me to speak with Nathan. "I just confirmed there was a weapon. I did not mention the child."

I chimed in, "And as long as I'm *considered* this stupid weapon, I'm in danger. And if they find out about the child… *she's* in danger."

We all looked and felt helpless. "I'm so sorry." Grayson really did look sorry, his now-dried hair askew. "He was already threatening you." He looked into my eyes, asking for forgiveness, hazel on blue. He coughed again, hanging his head low after the fit ended. I was still turned into him, but rather than wrapping my arms around him, I sat back a bit and wrapped my arms around myself.

"It looks like I don't have a choice. Everyone's decided it for me." With my knees pulled into my chest, I hung my head down feeling scared, and more than a little angry. I squeezed my eyes shut, trying to figure out a plan to get us all out of this mess.

Nathan stood up and grabbed Grayson some water, and Grayson sipped on the water for a few beats before speaking again. "Yes… and this is a huge problem, your safety. As well as trying to figure out who is invested in this information, and why they're all so desperate to get to you."

"And the rest of the prophecy," I dully said, looking up.

"I completely agree, Violet, and we have to figure this out. But right now we have a much more pressing issue. My brother cannot keep having attacks like this. We have to help him."

"But how? We don't even know if it's Jared or someone else. Who else have you come in contact with? Did Jason ever find you?"

"Jason's looking for me?" Grayson groaned, almost completely having returned to normal again, except for looking tired in the eyes. In fact, he was so normal, so nonchalant, I wondered if he had completely forgotten about the kissing assault on my face about twenty minutes prior. He stood up and leaned on the kitchen counter next to Nathan.

"Did you really think you could just abandon everything, Grayson?" Nathan asked. "You, more than anyone, should know how things cannot be left alone, no matter how much we try. Suffering comes from denial of the truth. Destiny always finds a way to grab you—"

"You speak of fulfilling destiny! Rubbish! Why the hell haven't you claimed our dear Violet for yourself then? Why is she still wandering about by herself, thinking there's a way to escape her *own* role?" He hissed with as much fervor as he could muster after the attack. "She still thinks I could be the father. You and I both know this will never be the case. Just end it."

I was silently standing now, watching them have this encounter. I was mere feet from them, but they were so engrossed in their verbal battle they didn't see me.

"She has to find her way on her own. It has to be her decision. *Neither* of us can make that for her." Nathan was looming close to Grayson, and in spite of his brother just having recovered from the attack, seemed hostile.

"A ring was not made for me. One was made for you, her and the child." Grayson angrily leaned into his brother.

My mind drifted to the rings Grayson was referencing. Of the many gifts Nathan and his family had, one was craftsmanship. They were able to create beautiful pieces of artwork with magic embedded into them. Grayson was talking about rings their mother had hand-fashioned—there had only been three of them, not four.

"I saw *you* in the vision."

"Yeah, because I *know* her, not because I'm the damn father." Exasperated, Grayson took a step back from Nathan, and the tension snapped a bit.

"Guys?" I asked, stumbling then reaching onto the table to

steady myself. Tunnel vision was taking over my senses again, but this time it wasn't from fear. It was uncontrollable, and with it I felt woozy and totally detached from reality.

Four eyes turned to look at me; two a brilliant green with gold flecks, and two a shocking, deep hazel with green flecks. All I could see were their eyes. The image began to weave in and out, as if underwater, to clear, back to underwater.

"I don't feel very good." All of a sudden I felt very faint and a great darkness overcame a large portion of my senses, this great disconnect. My hand slipped off the table, and if Nathan had been any slower, I would have fallen to the floor and potentially hit my head. It was terrifying. I could see Nathan and Grayson staring at me, but I felt unplugged and incredibly empty, like my body didn't matter anymore. A part of my brain registered Nathan was holding me upright, but most of my brain registered the nothingness.

And then there was a connection. A horrible, incredibly intense connection reached out to me. I could feel tendrils of Darkness embrace my being, grasping at me, trying not to just hold me, but to entirely envelop me. "Grayson?" I asked, trying to be present as it gripped. "What is this?" I whispered.

He reached for me, taking me from Nathan, roles reversed. Grayson held me close, looking into my eyes with what I thought was sorrow. "It's... It's taking over." I trailed off, oddly having the sensation of being in two places at one time. Darkness continued to tease at my senses to entirely overcome me. I couldn't focus.

"Don't let it. You're stronger than me, Violet. You're so good. Your force field... Just push it out... Don't—don't let it win." He seemed so sad, and so surrendering. Underneath the fear I could sense a stronger emotion trying to break through, but I just knew it couldn't. Wouldn't.

This part of me that was still trying to keep a hold on

reality, was still assessing Grayson and his inability to love. Nathan took one of my hands, and it was just terribly quiet as the lights started to fully turn off. By Nathan's expression, I knew he was pumping me full of his light to fight off whatever was happening. It was so still, and dark, and quiet. An orange glow surrounded Nathan, and then greens and purples wove in together with shades of blues, odd shapes of color moving in and around him.

With my last gasp of consciousness, I took both men in. One was full of soft power, and the other, the other one was totally defeated. My body went limp; my vision dark.

8

"She's fine, Grayson, her vitals are all good."

"But she's still out cold!"

"No she's not. Look, she's stirring."

I could hear them talking, but they seemed far away. I felt something soft touching the backs of my arms and legs. I had a feeling they had placed me on the couch after I had passed out. I was too spent to open my eyes, but I felt the urge to try to communicate with them, so I said in a low voice, "I'm fine. I know who is doing this, how and why."

"What did she say?" asked Grayson, leaning forward. I felt his concerned breath bathe my face.

"I don't know," said Nathan in a hollow.

I faded out again.

Sometime later, I heard scraping sounds, for sure felt a blanket on me, and heard the sound of finger tips tapping, quite impatiently, on what sounded like a table. I smelled delicious curry scents wafting from what I was assuming was the kitchen. It was mixed with the scent of orange and bergamot. I heard and felt my stomach growl. It must be dinner time.

I tried to sit up, and when I was able to, the images started to come in. Living room. I was in the living room of the man named Tim, a man who was letting Grayson crash at his apartment. That's why the place didn't look familiar. I looked to my right and saw the brothers in the kitchen. Nathan was the one tapping; Grayson was the one cooking.

"Tim will be home soon and then we won't be able to talk. I wonder how much longer she's going to be out."

I saw that a giant fluorite crystal was sitting on the table in front of me. I wondered where they had gotten that from, and hell, I wondered how long I had been out. The light coming from outside the window looked like it had somewhat faded; nighttime was nearing.

I stood up, and had to steady myself I felt so wobbly. *Why weren't they looking at me?* I hovered near Nathan at the table, and he still hadn't looked my way, although he stiffened a bit. "Do you feel that?" He turned and looked through me. *What the hell?* He was looking *through* me.

I started to panic. I looked in the direction he was looking, and sure enough—my body was still asleep on the couch. *Ummmm.*

I reached, *reached* into Nathan's mind, willing him to communicate with me. I had no idea how to get back into my body. Was I still asleep? Was this astral projection? *How do I wake up?*

Grayson looked right at me, but not meeting my eyes. Somehow, he must have seen something of *me* standing behind Nathan. He turned the stove on low and walked over to Nathan. "Look—just there. Can you make out that form? It almost looks like Violet—look—oh, it's moving—"

Nathan stood up to join him. "I don't see it, but I can feel it trying to approach my mind. It's benevolent, whatever it is."

"I'm going to try to wake her up, Nate."

The second Grayson touched my body, I flew, and I mean,

flew back into my body, jumping up with a tremendous jolt. Grayson had to hold me back as I about ran out the door in pure adrenaline. He met my eyes and smiled as I relaxed, creases deep in the outer edges of his eyes. "Cool."

I wanly smiled and shook my head. My throat was dry, and I croaked out, "Not for me. What the hell *was* that?"

"I suspect astral projection," Nathan rationalized. "You must have incurred a new skill." He gave me a goofy thumbs up, and I plopped back down into the couch, groaning.

Grayson had wandered back into the kitchen. "Dinner will be ready soon, but Violet—what the hell happened?"

Frustrated and completely back to normal, I described to them in great detail about what had happened while they filled in some of my own blanks. When I told them I knew who, what, and *how* the attacks were happening, they both stilled. The look of relief on Grayson's face was noticeable. "Thank God. I'm hoping this means you can stop it."

"I already did."

Grayson looked at Nathan. "Oh?"

"It was Jason." Jason, the guy who had been Grayson's firefighter mentor when Grayson lived in Georgia. Jason, the member of Vendetta Veritas, the small-town group who was steadily growing in number, size and power and wanted to 'correct' the world and make it better...by making it worse.

Grayson uttered a low groan.

"When I fainted, I landed in this sort of neutral space. Jason's image appeared, and while his lips didn't move, I understood everything he wanted me to understand. He believes Jared is working with him and is now a dutiful member of the Veritites. I don't believe for one second that Jared is a part of any group, though." I paused, looking to Nathan for confirmation. He subtly nodded.

"So whatever Jared is up to, it's not for Jason, but he gave him enough information to whet his appetite to reach out and attack you, Gray. He thinks he's saving you." I paused again, and Grayson's face turned several shades whiter than normal. "He wants *you* to be the father of *The Bullet*, Grayson," I quietly said. Both men were still, deeply engrossed in what I was saying. I could sense Grayson's dread, and Nathan's anger. "Obviously he wants this for his own selfish purposes," I spit out.

I knew that wouldn't sit well with Grayson—he still felt he owed Jason for being there for him when he felt nobody else was. "Anyway, when he reached for me, I was able to tell him to screw off, and I kicked him out."

"Does he know where we are?"

"Not exactly. He knows we're in New York, but other than that, no. He's still in Atlanta."

"So now what?"

"We find the rest of that damn prophecy before anyone else does. Nate—you need to get your mom to the states, and fast."

Grayson and Nathan looked at one another, long and hard, quietly communicating over my head as per the usual. This time, though, I wasn't irritated by it.

Nathan turned to me, looking at me from head to toe, silently assessing something I didn't understand. I simply stood there as he did it. A weak smile crossed his face, and my stomach did a flip flop in response. I turned to Grayson, and could tell that he was deep in his own private Hell as he scooped food into a bowl for each of us.

Nathan walked up to me and wrapped his arms tightly around me. His strength and calmness seeped into my bones as he murmured in a deep voice, "We will figure this out." I sighed a deep, full-body sigh, surrendering into him.

Over his shoulder, I caught Grayson's expression. He was absent from the present. I tucked back into Nathan for half a breath before shakily stepping away. I smiled and said,

"Tim's here."

The door opened.

***

Nathan and I were on the flight back. I had a window seat, and he was sitting next to me, leaning his seat back a bit. It was dark, and a few people were still awake with their ceiling lights on. Neither of us had on ours, and I had my body turned towards him as we spoke in low voices. We discussed what had happened in Brooklyn in depth. We wondered what to make of my new skill, what Alexandra was hiding, and how to help Grayson.

I was messing around with Nathan's hand in my lap as we spoke, half-aware that I was tracing the lines of his palm. "Ever had a palm reading?" I suddenly asked, with a slight smile in my voice.

He laughed. "No? Have you?"

I slowly traced the long line cutting across his palm, causing goosebumps to form in my own flesh. "This is your lifeline. Any major breaks in it would show major shifts in your life. You have a break right here, approximately in your midlife," I murmured, wondering what exactly that meant. He was more or less currently in his midlife.

"This is your head line. It indicates mental acuity." I smiled a large grin, and his dimples appeared in return. "You're a pretty smart guy." He laughed again, leaning back in his seat, closing his eyes. He seemed lighthearted.

I continued. I came to a small indentation on the side of his palm, and my stomach began to do somersaults. Nathan's last embrace while we were still at Grayson's had started a new epiphany. The embrace had elicited feelings of fullness—completeness. Nate had told me that we would figure it out, and in spite of the madness, those few words had consumed me with a knowing of peace.

Witnessing the line on his hand that demonstrated the

amount of children he was supposed to have may not have indicated my future life, but it *was* fully awakening me to my actual feelings. A child may or may not come into existence; that wasn't even the point. What really mattered at that moment was…what really had mattered ever since I had met him…

"This shows how many children you will have," I murmured. "It says you will have one."

"Oh," he said softly.

I turned his hand back over, and clasped my fingers into his. I felt the steady hum of his energy. This was a normal action, he and I held hands from time to time, in various situations and it meant nothing. We did it, maybe not all of the time, but often enough. I leaned my head back on the chair, and looked up at his closed eyes, thinking as our hands stayed held.

We lived together, and it meant nothing, too. We often worked together. I'd met his mother, and attended his father's funeral. It meant nothing. He'd attended my father's funeral, and it meant nothing. We had kissed in the past, and expressed love to one another, and it meant nothing. We were prophesied to have a child together. It… It all meant *something*.

"Hey, Nathan…" I paused, remembering the first time I had seen him. I had been in a yoga studio, having a meltdown about, of all things, being bored. Nathan had extended his hand to help me up. Of course, he had already known who I was on that first day, and I had no idea who he was, but… That was the thing. That was it. He *always* lifted me up, cheered me up. He was my rock. It may have taken me awhile to trust this fact, but I knew that the time he had abandoned what was between us was a one-time occurrence. He would never leave my side again. Even if we weren't together. Which…

His eyes had remained closed while I'd been lost in my revelation. My breath caught as it dawned on me. For the first time ever, I was clearly seeing things. *Yes.* I had strong feelings for Grayson, and some of it was inexplicable, and some of it was because I really cared about him, maybe even truly loved him. These feelings were unresolved with nowhere to go—there just simply wasn't a future there, and whatever needs it fulfilled, it was never to be a lasting relationship.

And this all primarily could be because, for the first time, I was *clearly seeing things.*

As it turned out, I was in a *relationship* with *Nathan.*

And had been in it for awhile. And it was, you know, serious.

I reached over to brush his chocolatey hair behind his ear, his temples speckled with grey belying his otherwise extremely youthful demeanor. His breathing deepened as I helped him relax, tracing his triple warmer backwards.

"Hmmm," he finally said, in response to my touch and inquiry.

I slid my hands off of his ears, to his face, on the angle of his cheekbone. My hand lingered, and he tilted his head a bit more into my hand.

I gasped, pulling my hand away.

His eyes opened and began to focus, taking me in. "Violet?" he sleepily asked.

I looked at him in open, adoring wonder. He let out a nervous laugh, not understanding what was happening. I re-clasped my hand with his, fingers intertwined. I held tightly and mystified, returned, "When were you going to let me know we were in a relationship?"

Initially the look that crossed his face was one of mirth, but seeing the expression on *my* face, it quickly was replaced by a pained, deep longing. Longing that he had been masking for,

God knows how long. Longing that I had missed because I had been so wrapped up in myself. I had been looking into these eyes for how long now? And they had been wearing a facade, and I had pretended to buy it, just as he had pretended to be okay with everything.

I removed my hand from his, and crossed my arms tightly across my chest, awaiting a response. He bit his lip, fighting whatever words he wanted to say. He heavily sighed, reclaiming my hand, bringing it up to his heart. "Are we?" he breathed, and re-closed his eyes, clearly trying to not push the issue. It was obvious he didn't trust it.

I took my hand from his heart, and slid my head onto his chest as best as I could since I was still wearing my seat belt. He was noticeably shaking as he wrapped his strong arms around me, neither of us saying anything. There was no more room for indecision. There was no more room for fighting the inevitable. I listened to his heart beat for a long while, until I drifted off to sleep.

When we finally returned home, it was around 3 AM. The dogs were super happy to see us, of course, and Barnaby barely greeted us, save one eye measuring our every movement. I washed my face, my hands, brushed my teeth, and changed while Nathan brushed his teeth. We hadn't spoken about anything important on the rest of the way home.

I waited for him at the doorway to the bedroom wearing a grey v-neck and sweat pants. He stepped out of the bathroom in a soft white t-shirt and his black harem pants that were so worn out now they had holes in them. My hair was brushed, tucked into a neat pony tail past my shoulders. His hair was messy across his forehead.

He shyly smiled at me when he saw I was waiting for him. He looked sleepy. I felt sleepy. I turned away from him and floated towards the bed, opposite side from the doorway. He did not hesitate, and followed me inside the room, clicking off the overhead light as I turned on a small nightlight. It felt routine, it felt normal. He belonged in my room; it was now his room as well. We were both exhausted. There was no desire, no lust, no need, no romance; just the simple sensation of belonging to one another, without question. I fell asleep in his arms, his snores lightly tickling my ears, his breathing easy and calm.

The dogs almost immediately jumped on our bed, resting at our feet. Even Barnaby wandered in at some point, because when I woke up late the following morning, his tail was underneath my nose. I woke up, yawning heavily, still exhausted, forgetting where I was at that point. But when I rolled over away from the cat, and saw sunlight gleaming off a part of Nathan's sleeping face, a warmth started at my toes and released out of my crown.

Nathan's eyes popped open at that moment, and once his eyes focused, he smiled.

Barnaby walked between us, and I heard one of the pugs fart at our feet.

His grin widened, and he purred over Barnaby's belly, "Reality."

"Reality." I returned his smile, pulling covers up to my mouth to save him from my morning breath. He let out a happy little laugh. I had never seen him this happy, or relaxed, even in spite of all that was going on.

"Tonight… tonight I want you to myself. They're all getting locked out." He promptly removed Barnaby from between us, reaching out to stroke my face. "At least for a little while." He winked.

It made me nervous, but in a good way.

"Tonight," I repeated.

9

The next few weeks rapidly crashed through time. When I wasn't *with* Nathan, I was replaying our time together over and over again in my mind. I couldn't wipe the silly grin off my face even if I wanted. I was consumed with happy jitters from the newness of everything. We had essentially been spending all of our time…unclothed. In the bedroom. On the couch. In the kitchen. Laughing, teasing, having a good time. We would venture out into the sunshine very raw, only grabbing necessities before locking ourselves back into the apartment.

The animals got fed up with seeing so much of us that they would wander out onto the balcony, together, just to get away. We were loud, we were messy, we were constantly touching one another. I couldn't cook a meal without him coming up behind me whispering words of love in my ear. He couldn't type up a report for work without me getting between him and the computer.

We were so happy, it was disgusting. If it had been anyone else I would have cracked obscene jokes and heavily judged the co-dependent nature that had been mustered. It was as if we were to suspending time inside those walls, pretending to be anyone other than who we actually were.

Oh, so lovely. So fleeting.

We didn't hear much from Grayson after we left Brooklyn. Somehow he had pieced together that his brother and I were *finally* together. I had know idea how he knew, and it seemed crazy to me that he seemed genuinely happy for us. However, all seemed well.

In spite of "losing" me to Nathan, he felt like his life was in an upswing. Those had been his words—not mine. His support was heartfelt, but he told me he would never forget our stolen moments together, and, I can't lie—it did make my heart race a bit. Whatever response I had made to his comment, with a laugh, he told me he hoped our time together would always have that effect on me. Not in a nasty way, though—just in a way that would have infuriated his brother. Luckily for me, while the steamy moments hadn't disappeared from my psyche, there was no desire to revisit them.

The boys had reached out to their mother, but had been playing phone tag. It was frustrating to say the least, but because things were so calm and enjoyable, it was also easy to ignore.

Except...there had been a lot of Scout-takedowns all around Atlanta. Not just from my partners, but rumors were flying about other government groups having issues with small, local terror groups, too. I tried to keep it out of my mind, and focus on enjoying Nathan's company, but the longer our honeymoon phase lasted, the stronger a nagging feeling poking at me became.

There was definitely tension filling the atmosphere.

Nate was headed up to Atlanta on this particular morning to meet with one of our suits, Mr. Perez. He wanted to speak to Perez about changing his position within the government. I hadn't even inquired because, honestly, I wasn't sure what his actual position was anymore, anyway. He was also going to finally bring up the dreaded topic—the prophecy.

Nathan was a polite man, earnest, an excellent worker bee. He aimed to please. He didn't push issues unless he felt like it was truly necessary. I was pretty sure Perez was going to see a side of Nathan that most people were not privy. He wasn't sure he'd get any answers, but was determined to try.

In spite of the building tension, in spite of Nathan driving up to Atlanta to speak with Perez, when I stepped out of my car that warm, sunny morning and began to unlock the door to my office, I was whistling a happy tune. I turned the knob to the door of my office, and stepped on the inside, inhaling the remnant oils from the last time I'd been in there. I flicked on the switch, watching the gentle light bathe the room. I walked inside and dropped my bags on the cushy couch for customers, and turned to lock the door behind me.

Only, the door was opening. "Sorry, we are by appointment only," I cheerily proposed to the man walking inside the door. My stomach dropped. I knew this man. It was *Jason*. Not my former boyfriend, hot-cop Jason, no, the *shithead* Jason who, a little over a month ago, had infiltrated not only *my* psyche, but Grayson's as well.

I groaned, "It's too early for this bullshit. What the hell do you want?"

"I have a message for Grayson."

I expectantly looked at him without fear, or frankly, care. He wasn't going to steal my good mood. "You tell him he and I have unfinished business."

"That's great, Jason. Really great," my mouth was dry and mind blank from cleverness. "Do you understand you don't have a hold on him anymore? That he is no longer prey to your attacks? You lost—okay? *The Prophecy* never mattered to begin with, and you seeking it out to control fate was a waste of time. Go find something else to obsess about." I turned my back on him and strode down the hallway indicating the conversation was over. I turned the light on in my treatment room.

"Oh, but it *does* matter, Violet," he followed. "Especially now that—*The Weapon*—has finally chosen a partner. It means we're that much closer to getting *The Bullet*, you see, and when *she* comes to fruition—well—the aim of *The Bullet* can be swayed, or haven't you heard the rest of the prophecy you seem to care so little about?"

I froze—but only for a brief moment. He had me on that. Had he really come across the rest of the prophecy, or was he just surmising what it was so I would take the bait and tell Grayson? And how on *earth* did he know that I had 'chosen' a partner? "Get. Out. Of. Here," I hissed, turning towards him with menace, gathering space and fury as I stalked him.

He looked amused as I altered the distance between us. I stood my ground, wringing my wrists around like I was getting ready to use my Dr. Strange powers to knock his ass out. A slow, dangerous smile crossed his face as I looked up.

He began to step back towards the door, never breaking eye contact with me. "Tell your fiancé I said hi. And tell his brother that I expect to see him soon." He stood at the door, pausing for one last moment before stepping out. "Oh, didn't Gray tell you? I have visions, too."

The door slammed shut behind him. I locked the door and watched him get into his car. My heart was racing and sweat was forming on my upper lip. I closed my eyes and tried to calm myself, employing all of the skills I had acquired since becoming a ninja, and all of the skills I had acquired being a bodyworker.

Nothing was helping. My heart still pounded, my breathing still rapid. Shakily, I reached down into my bag and grabbed my cell phone. Grayson answered on the first ring. "Viiiiolet." He drew out my name. "Something happened with Jason?"

"Yes." These psychic men were annoying.

"Dammit," he swore. "I should have known he wouldn't leave you alone."

"He said you have unfinished business, and that he expected to see you soon. He mentioned the damn prophecy and also said he had visions?" There was no breath between my sentences.

Grayson was quiet on the other end. "Grayson." I plopped down in my cushy chair, not being comforted at all by it. I hadn't even realized I'd started my portable kettle, but it began to shriek to let me know the water was heating up.

"Yeah—sorry—there're a million things swirling in my head right now. So yes, Jason has visions. You know he's a part of *Vendetta Veritas*. You know I loved Jason as my mentor, and you know I traveled with him, at times, to do things that never quite sat well with me."

"Yeah, like torturing me," I mumbled.

"Honestly, I turned a blind eye and tried to stay out of his crazy talk. I never really appreciated how dangerous any of them were until they crossed their paths with my family." He hesitated. "And you."

"I suppose you've come a long way from the man who tried to ruin my Christmas."

He bitterly laughed in response as he mused "That was almost a year ago." He was right. We were somehow in the following Autumn which meant the holidays were right around the corner again. He continued, "When I came back to the states after Germany, *yes*, I saw Jason, but I kept quiet about the prophecy. Obviously Jared gave him the information that I kept. And it sounds like they found the rest of it before we did."

"To be fair," I groaned, rubbing my forehead, "Since Nate and I got together, we haven't given it much attention. But he's literally in Atlanta right now demanding answers from Perez."

Grayson scoffed. "The Feds aren't going to share anything with him. He should know better."

"Have you ever seen Nathan angry?"

He was quiet. "Only in Germany."

"I hope Perez doesn't push him, because there's no guarantee he'd be able to keep this under wraps any better than *you*."

Grayson quietly laughed. "Brothers."

"Brothers."

I stood up, continuing to get ready for my client who would shortly be joining me in my now-discombobulated headspace. "So what do we do?"

"Well, we know they have the damn prophecy and they think this child of yours is going to help them achieve whatever crazy plan they have." He paused. "What they really want is to control the population at large and remove anyone in their way. They're gunning for a time period after something they call *The Almighty Cleanse*. It's disgusting what they want to do." His voice filled with woe. "And this guy is a sworn firefighter, meant to protect."

I interjected. "Look. There is *no child*. And also, there is *no child*. Nathan and I have been together for what, a month? We aren't talking about any future plans at all—we're just enjoy—"

"Violet, stop." He cut me off.

"At any rate," I muttered, "There is no kid."

I heard him plop down into what I assumed was a chair. I glanced at the clock; I had about thirty minutes to get ready for my client. I stood up and went into the massage room, making sure sheets were on the table and soft, soothing music was playing.

"Surely you don't think we're the only ones with these ridiculous gifts, right? It expands across the globe. Yes, there may be something slightly more powerful in our bloodlines since we're theoretically related to Odin—"

"What the hell are you *talking* about?!"

"But," he continued, ignoring me, "that doesn't matter. Everyone is essentially a 'psychic', Violet." I could hear him make air quotes through the phone. "They just have to tap into it. Some are more gifted than others. It's no different than someone being naturally skilled at playing basketball, or acting. The problem with these particular gifts, though, is that groups may use it for ill. Like Vendetta Veritas. *They're* really dangerous because they do it with such conviction." He sighed loudly to himself, and as I turned on the essential oil diffuser, I could tell my patience—and time—were waning.

"Gray, I've got to go. My client is going to show up soon."

10

Perez had not given Nathan answers that he wanted, but he had given him more questions. For starters, he wanted Nathan and I to go up to Atlanta and meet with him together, as the couple we were. "I'm sorry, this is bonkers!" I exclaimed for the fiftieth time, pacing in our apartment. "My personal relationship is none of their business! Technically you and I don't even work together anymore—"

Nathan was sitting on the couch, looking haggard. "I know Violet. I agree. But I don't think we should blow him off—"

"Argh! Why do you have to be such a rule follower?" I impishly smiled. "Why don't we just run away?" Here I was again, desperate to run away.

"Violet," he said in response, placing his head in his hands. "You know we can't run from this."

"We can tryyyy," I said in a sing-song voice, stopping before him and making him look up at me. For a half a second, his face drained white. Immediately color returned to his cheeks, leaving him a little flushed looking. "What?"

"Nothing."

"Nathan."

"I said nothing." He never took such a firm tone with me, but I figured he'd tell me when it was necessary, so I let it go. He stood up and walked into the kitchen, the air about him having changed. I was trying to not get angry at him for keeping something new from me—this was something he and I had been working on, together, in our relationship—but it was hard.

I knew the plan was for us to trust one another.

It still pissed me off.

"Ok, so nothing means I'm going to let that go. But can we still talk about ignoring Perez's request?"

This is how I found myself sitting *before* Perez one fine morning the following week. Nathan had spoken to his mother on the phone, and she and Grayson had agreed to come into town sometime after our meeting with Perez. Alexandra refused to share vital information over the phone —Nathan had not pushed.

We walked into a nondescript high-rise office building which housed insurance, health and other government agencies. I wondered if anyone else in the building recognized that Perez's office was for super-esoteric, super-Avengers' bullshit, sneakily hiding in the heart of Midtown Atlanta.

"Tollie!" I exclaimed in surprise, as she walked out of his office right as we got up on his floor. "What are you doing here?"

She grimly looked at us. "Hey, guys... Perez brought me up to speed. Well, as much as he wants me to know, I guess."

We just mutely stared at her. Her eyes darted back and forth, and then a huge smile painted across her face. "Even so, it is so good to see you two *finally* together!" She was looking down at my hand as it was wrapped up in Nathan's. He and I were standing so close to one another, a blade of grass could not have found its way between us.

I had had no idea. I melded into him without even knowing it. Our shadow probably looked like a two-headed monster. Don't cut one of the heads off, because..

"Yes," Nathan agreed, quietly, squeezing my hand.

I squeezed back, and smiled back to Tollie. "I concur."

"Mr. Murphy, Ms. Moore," Perez called from behind his door.

"Guess that's my cue," Tollie said, winking at us. She started down the long, empty corridor towards the elevator. I glanced back at her, and she mouthed, "You'll be okay." I furrowed my brows and let Nathan lead me into the room.

Perez was a tall, stoutly, no-nonsense fellow. We took our seats across from his desk, and I glanced around the room. I had never been in his office before. I'd seen him in conference rooms, but never in such an intimate setting.

"Good day," he muttered, placing his glasses on top of his head as he fiddled with his paperwork. I felt like I was in the principal's office. He cleared his throat, "Here is some paperwork to outline what we know—and while you may read it in here, you will leave it here and it will promptly be destroyed by me. I'll give you some time to look over it. It's basically a dossier on both of your families. Mr. Murphy, I assume you will know most of what is in here, but Ms. Moore, there's a lot in here you probably don't know about your own family."

My stomach instantly filled with a flood of snakes. Nathan had somehow taken my hand again after we sat down, and I felt him pumping his calming energy into me as per the norm. When was I not taking advantage of this guy's good graces?

Perez droned on, "The only reason why I'm giving you this information is so you understand all that the government understands. When your mother, Mr. Murphy, left the agency, we no longer technically had any rights, if you will, to information that she garnered, as she was no longer working for us."

Nathan snorted a laugh. "I bet you kept tabs on it all anyway." I was surprised Nathan was so blunt, but by Perez finally indicating he may be capable of smiling, I quickly realized Nathan's relationship with Perez perhaps ran a little deeper than I had given them credit.

"At any rate, when the prophecy was created by Klaus Dietrich for Alexandra, she quickly crafted the rings as a way to harness the information."

I couldn't help myself, I was feeling quite impulsive. "Whoa, what? Who the hell is Klaus Dietrich? How did you know about Alexandra's personal rings? What does 'harness information' mean?"

"Ms. Moore—this paperwork should clarify what I'm sharing with you, as I said when you first entered this room." His glasses had popped back onto his face as he peered down at me. I had somehow separated from Nathan's sheltering embrace; I was leaning forward, all-in. I glanced at Nathan again, and his face was not telling at all.

"It is well known that one of the gifts of Mr. Murphy's family is craftsmanship, mmm?" I sat back and nodded, feeling uncomfortable and hot. "So Alexandra created the rings and buried the prophecy, away from us all." He looked down at the paperwork, and then slid it towards Nathan and me, each of us having our own copy.

"Obviously it was not quite as hidden as she had hoped. And whatever energies were trapped within those rings may have additionally be sought by others. The fact that this prophecy is stirring up trouble again means that perhaps the prophecy is not merely a myth, but something of real concern."

Perez looked squarely at me, this time all joking aside. My stomach did a flip flop and something deep inside of me felt attacked. Nathan either didn't catch Perez's look, or chose not to address it, because his next words were not about me. "Does this mean Dietrich and my mother are in danger?"

"We have already offered our assistance to both—as well as the German government—but naturally, they both denied the help." Nathan swore; the pit in my stomach grew deeper and wider and the snakes hissed louder.

"As you two are the supposed parties to bring forth this prophecy, may I suggest you accept our assistance?"

I interrupted. "What does the full prophecy say?" I croaked out, Jason's words echoing in my mind. *The Bullet can be swayed. The Bullet can be swayed. The Bullet can be—*

"It would seem only your mother and Mr. Dietrich know the answer to this. However, upon reaching out to him again to have him come visit us, his untimely disappearance is concerning."

I gasped.

"So this leaves my mother," Nathan responded, and I could tell he was a raging mess of nerves. I felt isolated with Nathan, as if the two of us were on our own individual islands with a river full of snapping alligators between us.

"From my understanding, though, as those who craft do so in a trance, soothsayers also are in a trance so Mr. Dietrich may not have had any knowledge about what he had said more than anyone else who had actually read what he had transcribed during such a trance."

"Oh, God," Nathan said, sitting back down. I didn't understand. "They weren't alone," he whispered.

"You are correct. Another man was present."

"My father." My mouth formed a perfect 'o'.

"Your father. And of course, he thought it was all rubbish. We have no idea who he may have told."

Nathan deflated like a dying balloon next to me. I reached out to put a hand on his shoulder, trying to comfort him while keeping my own meltdown under wraps.

"I was already alive at the time of the prophecy?"

"Yes. You and your parents were living together in Washington D.C. You all were on a trip to Germany visiting friends, family…and of course, your mother was also working at the time."

Nathan swore under his breath.

"Soon thereafter this happened," Perez continued, quite businesslike, "Your parents split up, seemingly because your mother could not deny her part in this world, and your father could not accept it."

Nathan looked over to me, his eyes dilated. "And then she got pregnant with Grayson." I whispered to him.

"Yes," chimed in Perez, "Your brother came into the picture, and since he was created when your mother was no longer working with us, well, obviously there was nothing we could do."

The snakes jumped out of the hole in my stomach and I made a hissing noise at Perez. Nathan was drowning in his mothers' past, not paying nearly close enough attention to what, and how, Perez was speaking. *Since he was 'created'. 'Nothing' we could do.*

Perez became an impenetrable barrier, sat back in his chair and pulled out another wad of papers. He had his pen poised as he looked between Nathan and me. "Can we assume that the two of you are in an actual relationship now?" His pen paused as he looked for an answer.

The snakes were out of me, and all that remained was an empty hole full of terror. "Look, I know everyone is invested in this crap—for whatever reason—but I'm *really* uncomfortable with my love life being at the front and center of this—I mean—can't a kiss just be a kiss?" I weakly asked, trying to take control of the situation by deflecting with humor.

Nathan was still, and I could tell he was paying attention again.

"I'll take that as a yes." Perez wrote something down in his notes.

It was me who swore after that.

"So now what?" grimly asked Nathan, more deflated than even earlier in the conversation.

"Have you consummated your relationship?"

Perez had another box to check off and the bile rose in my throat.

Having fully caught back up to the present, Nathan flushed like the gentleman that he was.

My flush was rage.

"I"ll take that as a yes." Perez wrote down some more notes.

"Pregnant?"

"God dammit!" I yelled.

Perez looked me up and down, "Hormones? I'll take that as a yes." Wow. What a pig.

"Nathan, let's get out of here!" I exclaimed jumping up, but Nathan blocked me from exiting.

"Does my mother know the rest of the prophecy?"

"She has told us she does not."

"She's coming into town this weekend."

"We know."

"Should she go into hiding?"

"She will not."

"Should we?"

He shrugged.

"All we know is, that the union of your two families is supposed to bring forth a powerful child. Many groups wanted to stop the union, but it looks now that it will come to pass. However, they can still stop the child."

My hands instinctively went to my stomach.

"And they can kill me trying." I growled like a 9-foot tall bear.

"Ms. Moore, I assure you, they will try."

11

"Halloween is soon," Nathan idly said to a pane of glass as I drove us home.

"I know." I murmured, lost in the space between overthinking and not thinking at all.

"Should we do something fun?" He lightheartedly asked, glancing at me.

My hand went to my stomach. "Dress like an acorn?" I muttered.

"Yeah, I could be a squirrel."

We broke out into laughter. It felt good to laugh.

His phone rang and a very one-sided conversation took place. I wasn't sure who he was speaking with, but his responses were very terse. I turned music on low and hummed the rest of the way home.

When we pulled into the parking lot, his mother was waiting for us. In spite of the chaos, her essence always created a calming lull for anyone in her presence, and so I was super happy to see her. I parked and jumped out of the car for a hug, almost before I had even turned the car off. "You're early!" I exclaimed.

Nathan trailed behind me, still tense from his phone conversation.

"My eldest," she said, extending her arm to grab him into a group hug.

"Hi, Mom," he said.

"We were thinking of doing something fun next week to get into the Halloween spirit," I said, optimistically forgetting everything that had transpired. "Maybe go to a party in the city. Nathan wants to dress up like a squirrel."

I saw a look pass between them, and I pretended to not notice. "Come inside, Alexandra," and I left them in the parking lot.

Inside, it was light chatter and an increasing excitement in search of something spooky to do for Halloween. Alexandra said she had some friends in Atlanta that she planned on inviting to whatever party we ended up attending. This odd, impromptu gathering that was coming together with such ease my haunches were hackled.

In bed that night, I asked Nathan, "Why is your mom so taken with this Halloween idea?"

"I honestly don't know, Violet. I don't question her anymore. I simply cannot."

I let out a long, frustrated sigh.

"Grayson is so not going to be down with this."

Nathan laughed. "You are right. He will not be... down with this." I smiled up at him.

"Some of my colloquialisms are still weird to you, huh?"

I fell asleep in his arms.

Sometime during the night I found myself in between worlds as my mother was with me. We were in a land that was made of broken mirrors and realities a la Dr. Strange. She took me through one of the mirrors and we walked upside down until we M.C. Eschered our way to a flat plane. The world had flip flopped. We were walking amongst tall grasses the color of aquamarine. The sky was in hues of violets and pinks, intermeshed in teals, much like aurora borealis.

"Mom," I finally broke the silence. "Where are we?"

As I was awaiting her response, I tried to think of the last time I had seen her. She broke my concentration with an answer. "We are here, we are there."

"It's so lovely," I murmured as I looked around and touched everything. "These colors are so vibrant." I picked up a flower as my mother walked aside me on a newly created dirt path. "Mother!" I exclaimed. "You must taste this."

It tasted like cotton candy and strawberries. "Smell," I continued, asking her nose to join mine.

She leaned over, took in a big whiff, and said, "Your egg should stay in your nest only."

The flower drifted to the ground and disappeared. The tall grasses continued to wave alongside us, but my peacefulness was fading. Her last statement concerned me. I furrowed my brow and looked at the multi-suns setting. "I don't even like omelettes, Mother."

"Keep her safe and hidden. It is the only way."

I turned back to her, and I saw that we were now floating on a raft in a teal and golden sea. "This water is so lovely," I said, running my fingers through the wetness. "It's cool," and as I drank some between my fingers, "Also crisp-tasting."

"The sea is a wonderful place to protect your nest."

"Of course, Mother," I murmured. "I will protect my nest."

"It can get lonely, you know," she continued on the widow's peak of a cottage overlooking the ocean. It didn't bother me that we were no longer in our raft.

"But look at those suns setting. It's so overwhelming." I was overcome with feeling small.

"Yes, Violet, but you must keep her safe. I fear, even from

Nathan."

"What?" I sharply asked, the broken glass penetrating my mind, my mother being pulled away in a torrent of wind on the sea. I was stuck on the balcony of the cottage; alone and unable to get away from it.

"Mother," I screamed.

The last thing she shouted at me was in Norse, and I couldn't quite make it out.

I woke up with a start, heart pounding, drenched in sweat and nausea overtaking me. I barely made it to the bathroom to vomit.

***

Somehow I had fallen back asleep and later awoke to the sounds of voices coming from the kitchen. "I think you should encourage her, Nathan. The sooner we know, the better off we'll all be."

"Mom, please—"

"Everything is falling into place—"

"It's too soon, Mom," and he sounded desperate, his voice muffled. "We've only been together for a few months. This just can't be. It's too soon."

"I know, I know."

I turned onto my side and faced Barnaby's rear end. "Oh, God," I grunted. He turned to look at me with his ever-watchful eye. The noise I made was enough to peak the interest of the pugs, and they came bounding into the room. After many failed attempts at leaping onto the bed, they finally made it, snorting happily in my direction. Barnaby, disgusted, jumped off of the bed and waltzed out with his tail up high just as Alexandra walked in with some tea.

"Good morning, dear, I brought you some tea." She smiled and I sat up, scratching the bellies of the pugs. "It's perfect to fight nausea and nightmares."

I sipped on it and asked, "Nathan told you?"

She just smiled, not uttering a sound, stroking my hair.

Nathan called from the kitchen, "Does anyone want eggs this morning?" I froze.

"Eggs?" I glanced from Alexandra to the empty doorframe. "Did he say eggs?"

His figure took over the doorframe. "Does anyone want eggs?"

I tilted my head at him, giving him an odd look. "I don't really like omelettes."

"No problem. Over-easy? Scrambled?"

"I'm... I'm okay. I think I'll just take this tea into the bathroom and shower real quick. I'll join you both after that."

Nathan gave me a pained look, and Alexandra merely nodded.

***

Time was rapidly speeding up and blurring together. Alexandra was still mum on the rest of the prophecy, but even so, Nathan and I were trying to sort out what to do—if anything. We were trying to figure out who was after us—if anyone. My head was spinning from all of the what-ifs...and my stomach was churning.

I missed the bliss I had previously had.

It was late in the following week, and Grayson and I were sitting on my balcony while Alexandra and Nathan had gone to grab food. We were in a heated debate and I was really frustrated with everything. Not to mention, I had suddenly found myself eating crackers nonstop to keep from feeling nauseated.

"Violet. Stop being in denial. Look at your behavior! Everyone can see it!" He exclaimed, exasperated.

"You're one to talk." I shot him a dirty look.

He left his seat and overlooked the balcony, looking away from me. "Violet, I'm absolutely not in denial. I'm more in love with you now than ever," he earnestly said. He turned to face me, causing heat to raise in my cheeks. Not out of embarrassment, but because his demeanor was so genuine. He reached down, pulling me up next to him, holding onto my hands. "But we are past that now. The three most important people to me are all in danger, regardless of minute details. The last thing we need is to be caught off guard. I know you want me to see Jason tonight—"

"You *should*—" I cut him off, and he dropped my hands.

"Take a damn pregnancy test," he muttered to the trees.

I grabbed my crackers and stomped inside the house, narrowly missing Phang and Mina who were curled up together near the doorway.

***

The apartment was not big enough for the four of us *and* the animals, so that night after dinner, Alexandra and Grayson left our humble abode. I was able to give Grayson a look right before they left, and he imperceptibly nodded. I took that to mean he was going to meet with Jason after all.

For some reason, long after Nathan and I had fallen asleep, I woke up and drifted to the door. Just outside of it I found Grayson with a burgeoning fat lip in disbelief. I closed over the bedroom door and brought him to the guest bathroom, cleaning him up.

"I take it the conversation didn't go well." To myself, I muttered, "This feels all too familiar."

He sat on the toilet, looking dejected. "I don't know what to do, man!" He exclaimed, slamming his hand against the sink. "Jason's not going to let this go, Violet. I don't know what to tell you to do." He shook his head.

"There's nothing *for* me to do, Grayson," I calmly said, draining his blood off of my fingertips in the running faucet. I shut the valve off and sat up on the sink with the door closed over. My feet were covered in Halloween socks and I had spooky pajama bottoms on.

Grayson smiled. "You look ridiculous."

"You're one to talk," I rolled my eyes.

And then I shoved him off the toilet, evacuating a lot of the night's dinner. He ran some water for *me*, and I pitifully looked at him after I cleaned up. "Okay, Okay. I'll take a damn test after the stupid party. We stood up and just stared at one another, trapped in limbo and fear. I reached out and touched his lip, shaking my head, and he took me into his arms and held me.

"We'll figure this out, Violet," he softly said, then left for his hotel room, a mere whisper on the wind.

The following afternoon, I was in bed with Nathan, telling him about Grayson's midnight visit. He was lying on his back and I was propped up on him deep in thought. As he played with my hair behind my ears, I switched gears and suddenly asked, "Did you always know we would end up together? From a vision?"

He paused his motion behind my ear, dropping his hands onto the small of my back. "Any vision I've had of the two of us just means that we may be together in a similar moment. It doesn't indicate a relationship, how we got to that point, or what happens afterwards."

I lied down on him. "So no."

"So, no," he agreed. He leaned over to his phone right before it began to vibrate a message. I flopped off of him and rolled into Mina's sweet face. She opened up her eyes and gave me a snort and a lick. "Grayson's on his way over here to talk about tonight."

"Why are we even bothering going? Halloween itself isn't for another two weeks!"

Nathan sat up, tossed the covers down and stood up, stretching. "Going to take a quick shower and he should be here."

About an hour later, the boys and I were on the balcony,

discussing Jason and the others who sought to, you know, destroy us. "I feel like we've been here before. Are we making a mistake going up to Atlanta tonight? Jason knows you're in town," I added, nodding at Grayson's swollen lip.

Nathan and Grayson exchanged a look which echoed nights of Germany past. Finally, Nathan stood up and spoke, jostling Barnaby with his toe. Barnaby was not amused, and managed to escape back into the apartment before Nathan had even finished speaking.

"Even if... even if someone is present who doesn't belong... there's no baby. Anyone we run into will probably just be lurking around to intimidate us." If you didn't know Nathan very well, you would have missed the slight breath he took after the word baby. With my onslaught of sickness, it was hard to ignore that I actually *may* have been pregnant. It was also possible I was sick to my stomach because the whole situation *made* me sick.

Nathan looked down to the parking lot, and Grayson shot a look to me over his head. I rolled my eyes and stuck my tongue out as response.

A slight smile shaded Grayson's face; Nathan turned and noticed, but didn't say anything.

"Intimidate us so we'll break up?" Nathan shrugged. "Welp," I guess we should start getting ready." Nathan stepped inside but Grayson blocked me before I could follow him.

"You and I both know there's more to tonight than just this party. "

"A vision?" I asked.

"Potentially."

"But it may be Alexandra and not Nathan. She's been really gung-ho about this whole thing." Grayson casually put his arm around me and walked me inside.

"Guess we'll find out. See you guys at the hotel," he said as

he made his way to the door.
I frowned in his absence.

95

12

Here we were, at this inaugural Halloween soiree taking place inside an old, probably haunted theatre in Midtown Atlanta. I was dressed up as an acorn, Nathan was my squirrel. Grayson's hair was slicked back to match his black clothes, vampire teeth and red lipstick he had pawned off an old firefighter friend who was attending the party with us.

Outside of the theatre, Alexandra was dressed up ever-so-elegantly as Veleda, an old Germanic seeress. Her two friends who were dressed in togas and gold jewelry embraced her just outside of the entrance. People were milling in and out of the theatre dressed in modern marvels, superheroes and super random creative costumes which gave you pause as you tried to figure them out. Someone had maxi pads all over them covered in blue ink... I shook my head at Nathan. "A little too much, that one."

He smiled.

Grayson and his friend greeted Alexandra's comrades and then stepped inside. I saw him shoot a watchful eye around the group upon entering. Nathan took my arm and we stepped up to her friends. "Violet, these are my dear, dear friends Maria and Klaus."

I shot a quick look to Nathan. *Klaus?* As in *the* missing Klaus? He raised an eyebrow as I shook their hands. "Nice to meet you," I murmured.

Nathan pointedly looked at his mother. "No offense, Mr. Dietrich, but it was my understanding you had gone missing." He reached over and shook his hand.

I was flummoxed. I *knew* Alexandra had been up to something! Which a thick accent, Klaus spoke. "Ah, yes.. Well, see, being missing merely means absent from where one thinks one should be. It can *also* mean living very openly and freely in the midst of a Halloween get-together." He winked at his wife, as well as Alexandra. "It is my utmost pleasure to finally meet you, Miss Violet," he said, pulling my hand to his mouth for a kiss. Then Maria embraced Nathan and me.

"Do not fret, my dears," Alexandra touched my shoulder as well as Nathan's. "They have been traveling, is all. Let us go inside and have some fun."

The five of us walked inside the first set of doors, and it was like we had walked through an ice curtain. A stinging pain sliced through the bottom left of my abdomen, and I instinctually reached and slid my hand just below the shell of the nut costume. It was slow-motion; without sound. I turned my head opposite my hand towards Nathan but his head was looking straight over the crowd, above hundreds of masked goblins and ghouls in the foyer. Music was distorted; people were dancing, standing, talking, laughing, drinks being sold via various carts on various floors.

If I hadn't been moving like Han Solo's reemergence from carbonite, I would have found myself ambling towards the theatre itself, where the original Nosferatu was supposed to play in about an hour or so. "Nathan!" I trilled, removing my hand from my stomach and seeing blood.

Everything seemed frozen but me as I moved slowly

through the ice. Panicking, looking down at my hand again, I realized there *was* no blood. Sensing I wasn't alone in this in-between space, I pulled my head up and followed the direction of Nathan's frozen peepers to see a hooded figure in the far right corner of the room.

He lifted his scythe at me, and then the world came crashing back into he present moment. "Shit,"I hissed, and Nathan looked down at me. He hadn't seen nor felt a change in the space-time continuum as I had.

"What happened?"

"Time froze and the monster in the back made me think my stomach was bleeding."

"What?" He asked, very confused and instantly looking to the back of the room. Being tall had its advantages.

Grayson and his date came sweeping back by us, handing us small flutes of God knows what. My stomach churned. "I'll pass," I said, looking back at my clean hand. Grayson smirked, then his brows furrowed. Grayson's date engaged Nathan with some random dialogue, but I could tell Nathan was casting a worried eye over at me.

"What happened?" Grayson grabbed me by the elbow, taking me to a less populated part of the room. We left behind a bewildered Nathan, a firefighter dressed as CatWoman, Alexandra and the Dietriches.

"When we walked in, it was like I'd stepped through an ice curtain. Time was frozen and I saw blood on my stomach. There's some creep in the back corner playing games with me. He's dressed like—"

"Death, yeah, I saw him, too. No doubt Vendetta Veritas. Maybe even Jason himself." Grayson groaned, and tenderly touched his lower lip.

"Maybe you need to tell me what precisely happened the other night!"

"All you need to know is, Jason and I are no longer

friends." He grimly smiled.

"Well, why the hell did your mom bring Klaus?"

"That," he said, scanning the crowd once more, "I have no idea."

Nathan and the girl came looking for us, and he took me from Grayson asking for a dance. He and I shrugged at one another, and then I forgot about everything, hungrily getting wrapped up in the magic of Halloween, and Nathan himself.

He made me laugh; he made me feel safe. Nothing else mattered and nothing could change this reality. To hell with the rest of them. Mid-way through the night, I got queasy and extremely emotional due to the music. I had to excuse myself to the restroom and ran into Alexandra and Maria on the way out.

"Are you ok, mein Schatz?"

"Just a little overcome with emotion is all," I smiled. Maria excused herself, and I was able to speak with Alexandra alone. "So why did you bring Klaus here?" I asked without pretense.

"I need you to understand that Klaus is an Innocent. He was not in this life, as we are. He and Maria were simply dear, dear friends of mine, and also of Nathan's father. Nathan's father was always...perhaps, embarrassed, of my connections to the esoteric. And so when Klaus went into that trance in front of the two of us, and recited the prophecy, well.. Nathan's father blamed me."

"*Was* it your fault?" I blurted, as if Alexandra could force men to cluck like chickens.

She laughed. "Of course not. It just *was*." She finished washing her hands and pulled out a paper towel. "This way of life has a way of sneaking up on you. You cannot escape them, Violet, but there is always more, or less, you can do."

Riddles.

Alexandra left the bathroom and I was alone. I looked into

the mirror, seeing that my makeup was smearing and my eyes were drained. I sighed, stepped into a stall and heard someone join me in the restroom. This person did not enter into a stall near mine, rather, she was making a lot of noise by the sink. I flushed the toilet and made my own way to the sink, to wash my hands. I was deep in thought, until I realized the person who had entered the bathroom while I was in the stall was casually resting on the sink, watching me from behind a mask.

I wasn't afraid, but the heaviness of Alexandra's words pierced me. I was tired, and I had barely begun. No matter how safe Nathan made me feel, I would always be watched until I got pregnant. And if I had said child, the child would be watched.

This was enough to make me queasy again. To constantly be monitored, by *these* people...by the Feds...all over the world. I dried my hands and snapped at the girl. "You can tell your ruler that there's nothing here for him."

The girl turned to the mirror, and slowly applied some lipstick as I continued to stare at her. She popped her lips. "I am ruled by none, sweetheart," she said in a long, southern drawl. "The Veritites have decided to simply let you know that we will always be with you, watching you, keeping an eye on you and whomever you bring into this world. Your little treasure can be a treasure to us all. And patience, my friend. We have *all* the time in the world." She jumped down and walked towards me, trying to intimidate me with the slight stature differential. "There are *so* many things to do between now and the coming of age of your little gem." A flash of darkness splashed across this hidden person's eyes, and I saw a flicker of jealousy in that splash.

"Jason has nothing better to do than sic you on me? Please." I stepped up to her, painstakingly crafting each word. "Any 'gem' that I have is herself, and herself alone. *She* won't get confused by your manipulations; *she* won't be afraid of your Vendetta Veritas or any other group out there who seeks to use her for their gains. She will *always* have me to guide h—"

Someone had finally stepped into the restroom, breaking up this little tête-à-tête. "Careful, darlin'," she drawled, stepping to the door to leave herself out. "Your little gem may be all of that, but it appears *you* have some fear."

I was furious.

I stepped out of the bathroom and ran into Nathan. "Hey, Beautiful," he said. "I was beginning to... Oh. I see. What happened *now*?" He asked, exasperated.

Before I could say anything, Grayson appeared at my side and stepped between Nathan and me. "I saw her. I know her. What did she say?" He gritted his teeth. Nathan, again, was cut off from me by his brother and I could see that his congenial attitude was waning.

He asked, "Don't you have your *own* date you should be with?" Nathan then physically removed his brother from me.

Grayson barely acknowledged him as he continued to stare at me, "My date is merely a *friend* who thinks Jason's full of crap, too. She ran into some other people and we parted ways for the night." He reached out to grab my shoulders. "What did she say?"

I told them both, and Nathan quietly took me in his arms, me standing up on my tiptoes for the full embrace. I buried my head into his shoulder for a minute, then peeked out to see Grayson's watchful eyes. The hazel burned into my own blue, and I dipped my head back down into Nathan's shoulder.

"Let's go home," he said. "I'll see if I can grab Mom. She made her point with Klaus; Jason made his point with his sycophant; we've had our fun. It's time." Nathan steered me away from the hallway bathroom and Grayson curtly let us pass. I wouldn't meet his eyes.

On the way home, with my shoes kicked off and a full car, I said into the window, "If I've learned anything from tonight, it's I need to take steps to strengthen me against these psychic attacks. I'm too open. I'm not worried about the stupid intimidation tactics of following me into a bathroom." I pointedly looked at Grayson behind me, who was moodily looking out the window as the city lights faded. "But the psychic stuff of making me see blood, of distorting time and space. I need help with that."

Nobody said anything. "Perhaps one of you could teach me. I'm not sure which one of you is more adept at such a thing, but—"

"Nathan can guide you on ways how to do this," Alexandra looked out at the moon, tracing its image into the window she was peering through. "Fate can be so cruel."

I didn't know what she was talking about. The rest of the ride back to our town was quiet, contemplative, and unsettled.

13

I knew I had promised Grayson I would take a pregnancy test the day after the party, but I did not. Instead, I focused on learning as much as I could from Nathan about protecting myself from psychic attacks, as well as helping to make myself invisible. Grayson left town for the week to do some traveling while Alexandra looked into renting a place for a longer duration. She said she wanted to be near us.

However, by the end of the following week, the missed period, and the other symptoms were too much for me to bear. I felt confident I could better protect myself if need be, but I hadn't yet been willing to check the big unknown.

I had come home early from work in Atlanta, and I pulled the test out. I stepped into my bathroom, and naturally both pugs followed me in. I peed on a stick, wondering why this method hadn't gotten less gross over the years. I placed the stick on the bathroom sink, and stepped out, sliding next to the door while I waited. The pugs parked themselves at my feet, and even Barnaby joined us, curious why I was sitting outside of the bathroom. My watch went off, and I knew it had been long enough.

I was exhausted. I already knew the answer. The positive sign on the test did not surprise me. The strong, protective feelings did. My life, forever, would be changed. It was no longer about me, my needs, wants, desires and fears. It was about this life growing inside of me that I had to protect against all the odds, in spite of who we were. I knew, without a doubt, that *she* was a *she*.

I sobbed for an hour on the bathroom floor. About everything.

When Nathan returned for the evening, he found me curled up on the floor halfway on the bathroom, and halfway in the hallway. "Oh, no, what happened?" he asked, closing the door quickly, dropping his stuff and rushing over to me. I found that I had no voice when I tried to speak.

He scooped me up and held me close to him. "Whatever it is, I will fix it, I promise," he pleaded, feeling warm and safe. I let him hold me for a long time before I finally spoke.

"I'm pregnant."

It was amazing a great chasm in the Earth didn't open up and swallow him whole, but it didn't. He managed to hold onto me, but his warmth was gone. He had grown cold—and it didn't seem to be because he was mourning the loss of *us*, no, it seemed more that it was from fear. "It's yours, you know," I said numbly, trying to make him warm again.

"I know she's mine, Violet." He stood up, and took a full step back from me. "Are you really?" he asked, curious and with a slight tremor of, was it happiness? Pleasure? Satisfaction? Completion? I showed him the pregnancy test and he let out a slow exhalation. "All these symptoms you've been experiencing... queasiness... strong emotions"—I shot him a warning look but he continued—"It's all because you're pregnant."

He sat back down next to me, and smiled. From ear to ear.

I was taken aback, but then my heart started to race. His

smile was becoming contagious. I hadn't let myself imagine the wonderful possibilities with such a fact being true.

"Stop smiling like an idiot," I said.

His smile widened. "I'm sorry, Violet, it's just… I'm just… happy, you know? Ever since I found you again, all these visions, the swirling energy, this prophecy… One thing was always very clear to me. It was that you would be a mother. You were *meant* to be a mother. And trust me, I understand all the probabilities about what a positive test means, but right now, in *this* moment, I'm just so damn happy this is happening, it's *really* happening. And it's mine to behold and be witness. This is all really *mine*." I couldn't help but laugh. He continued, "And I love you. I love you so God damn much." He leaned into my face and fiercely kissed me.

I kissed him back, and for a short moment, he just sat with his face leaning into my neck, breathing me—*us*—in. Then he stood up, pulling me to my feet as well, He put his protective arm around me, and steered me to a recliner. "Oh my God, Nathan, I'm *fine*, really." My eyebrows were raised and he rushed to the kitchen to get me some water.

"I'm sure you are, but"—he called to me from the other room—"you know I'm a traditionalist! It's my job to"—he came back into the room I was in—"take care of you." He handed me some ginger water, and I sipped it, laughing. "Even though you're beyond capable."

He then did the unthinkable, and it took me a moment to catch onto what was happening. He got down on one knee, indicated I should lean over. He pulled off my necklace removing the ring from the chain. This ring had protected me for so long, and now I wore it without a second thought. Sometimes I'd still feel its heat, but it never posed cause for distress.

He slid it onto my finger and mused to himself, "It fits." I was confused. Of *course* it fit. He knew it fit. He had given it to me a long time ago when he had run away from us, and he'd placed it on my finger when he had returned. But I only ever wore it on a chain. He had a larger ring of the same design that he also wore around his neck. He asked me to unclasp the chain, and I did so, handing him the ring.

Then he slid it onto his own... *ring finger*... and it dawned on me what was happening.

"When a craftsman creates something like this, she or he is usually in a trance and doesn't remember too clearly creating the pieces. Mom made three rings, one for one son, one for the son's wife, and the third was, well, we didn't know until we were in Germany this past Spring. But she'd made the third for the child, the one with the gift. Not for the other son."

All was very still.

"Violet..." I held my breath. "Will you marry me?" He held *his* breath.

"I can say no? And you won't be mad?" I asked in the stillness of the moment.

"Of course not," he said quickly. He believed in free will as much as he believed in his visions. He simply just wanted to be with me, more than anything else, above even his honor, his pride.

I slowly exhaled, counting to four, squeezing my eyes together tightly. I looked up at his green eyes which were holding a sober expression; my blue eyes felt soft. "Then I feel I must say...yes. Okay." His eyes lit up, the gold flecks sparking in excitement and the rings created such a heat between our clasped hands, a bright light flashing between the rings when I said yes.

"Whoa," I said, looking down at our hands then back to his face.

"Whoa." His smile was contagious, and I felt myself bubble back in happiness to him. The nagging feeling, of course, was still there, but I wanted it muted.

The crazy shit, the weird stuff, the inexplicable stuff? Never got old. I was enamored with the magic of everything. Well, most of the time.

Sometimes it really pissed me off.

***

"Halloween is next weekend," mused Nathan. "Blue Moon, too."

"Pretty cool, if I do say so myself."

"Should we?"

"I mean, why the hell not? No point of a long engagement. Right?"

Nathan took me in his arms as we overlooked a small lake in our little town, sitting on swings watching the sunset. "Right." He gave me a kiss.

***

Grayson held me for a long moment, his lip slightly trembling as he said, "Congratulations," before he handed me over to my beaming husband. Over Nathan's shoulder, I met Alexandra's watchful eyes underneath the full moon.

Our small wedding ceremony took place outdoors underneath a beautiful gazebo by a large lake just outside of the city. The beams from the moon painted a lovely picture further highlighted by globes of soothing lightbulbs strewn about. Some people were dressed in costumes, and yellow and orange mums littered the grounds.

Nathan and I had our traditional first dance, and then many of our friends who had attended the impromptu ceremony danced alongside with us. Those who could not attend watched an online livestream. We served food catered by our favorite Mediterranean place near where we lived. We had many memories of the restaurant and we made sure they felt like they were guests, not just caterers.

Suddenly, I felt warmth spread from my abdomen up to

my heart, and I knew our daughter was having a good time as well. We hadn't told anyone I was pregnant yet. We knew it would stir up madness. However, everyone knew, because of the impromptu wedding. It was unspoken.

The party was wrapping up, people were leaving and heading toward their lodge rooms. Only a couple of my friends remained, Liz and Layla, and I was sitting with them while chairs were being picked up. The lodge owner came over to us, "Don't worry—you can stay out here all night for all we care. We just need to get most of these pieces up because it's supposed to rain. Even so, we'll leave the lights on the gazebo. Those don't have to come down."

I stood up, "Thank you so much again for accommodating us on such short notice. It's beautiful here."

"No problem."

We had paid quite a large sum of money to get everyone on such short notice, so no worries there. Thanks, Feds.

"So, Violet." I sat back down, knowing I couldn't lie to my friends anymore. I heard some guffaws from behind me, Nathan, Grayson and some men from work I didn't know. Liz took her gentle hands and reached out to clasp mine. Layla had her arms crossed and a no business attitude.

"Spill. We have barely heard from you in half a year and all of a sudden...*this*?"

I slid my hands away from Liz. "The short story is... Remember what happened in Germany?"

Layla leaned in. "How could we forget? You got together with the evil brother," and she shot a look over at Grayson. There's no way Grayson could have heard what we were saying, but I swear, he somehow knew he had been the topic of conversation.

"He's so hot," sighed Elizabeth.

I shot her a look. "You're married. You can't call him hot."

"*You're* married, so why so protective?"

I groaned. "Anyway," I drawled out long, looking over at the brothers, one of them my husband, "Shit hit the fan, right, with that whole," I lowered my voice, "prophecy nonsense. Gray disappeared. Nathan moved to Atlanta."

"And he moved in with you.. Yeah, we were all shocked when that happened," Liz tossed a look to Layla. "Because of... everything y'all had been through. We didn't think it was such a good idea, honey," she said, squeezing my hands.

Layla sat back again and loudly laughed. She narrowed her dark eyes and said, "Obviously we were wrong. Here you are, marrying the guy just a few months later. I was hardly aware you'd even started dating."

"Ugh, I know! I'm sorry," I sheepishly said. "Things picked up after Nathan moved in with me. Their cousin came to town—remember I mentioned her, Blaze—I know I told you about her." The girls nodded. *Phew!* I'd at least mentioned her. "Then we went up to New York and that's when Grayson told us more about the morons after us. Oh, shit," I said, feeling a short burst of cold walking towards us. Slithery, slinking, cold.

Nathan felt the change in the atmosphere at the same time, and stepped up to speak with our new guest. "Oh, gross, is that Jared? Who invited him?" Liz asked. Liz had been on the receiving end of Jared's oiliness when he was trying to figure out who I was. Due to the complicated nature of Nathan and his relationship, we had decided to unofficially invite him to the wedding. He was supposed to be out of town. We stressed that he needn't come. Somehow he had made it.

He smacked Nathan on the back, looked over at me and grinned. All I could see were his teeth, all I could smell was burnt leather.

By the end of the night, we all were exhausted, exhilarated by the kiss of the moon and the magic of Halloween. Each of us tucked inside our lodge rooms.

Nathan and I stepped inside a warm shower, washing off the mud from the barefoot stroll we had taken back to the room. He kissed my naked belly, wrapped me into a luxurious bathrobe, and together we both snored away our first night of matrimony.

14

Even though our lease was not up, Nathan and I decided to purchase a little bungalow in the city and planned on moving sometime before the baby was born. It was a cute cottage-style house with a nice sized backyard, three bedrooms, and an open air kitchen I loved.

However, with each passing day, even as I was able to psychically keep intrusions away, I would see people following me. I was preparing to close my bodywork business down since I was moving away, but if anyone new inquired about an appointment, I would balk. I became spooked, seeing enemies, frenemies, lurking in every aspect of my life. I wasn't sure if it was paranoia or legitimate, but it was becoming unbearable.

I felt like I was running out of options.

***

It was morning, and it was quiet. I was sitting on the balcony, drinking a hot cup of tea as the sun rose. Nathan was oddly enough still asleep, and Phang and Mina were sitting outside with me. I had a blanket wrapped around me, and as I stared off in the distance a plan was forming. It was one that made my stomach turn, but I had never felt so positive about a hard decision in my life.

Nobody was going to harm my baby. I would not allow it to happen, and I would take whatever means necessary to protect my child. My daughter's life was more valuable than any of ours combined.

I heard a light tapping on the door, and I hurriedly walked inside. I had a feeling Grayson had arrived, and I didn't want to wake Nathan. I opened my door with my finger at my lips to Grayson, and went to my bedroom and closed over the door. I made sure to keep my blanket wrapped around me as I stepped back out onto the balcony, half-closing the door behind us.

I quietly asked Grayson if he wanted some tea, and he shook his head as he plopped himself down into one of my chairs. He looked tired—he apparently had taken the red-eye into Atlanta and Ubered himself to our apartment. His dark hair was neat and tidy. It was cut shorter since I'd seen him last. His tattoos peeked outside of his dark grey shirt, and his feet were covered in black flip flops. "Did you just get in from New York?" I asked.

He didn't respond, only cleared his throat before speaking tersely. "I had a vision."

I ignored him, and continued to stare into the sunrise. Phang tried to jump on my lap, and farted.

"There's something *seriously* wrong with that dog," Grayson said with a sigh.

I still didn't say anything.

"Violet." He stretched his long legs out before him, and I finally turned his way, placing Phang back onto the porch. She slid back inside the apartment, and soon after, Barnaby came out.

"What." I stated, rather than asked.

His half-awake eyes turned to me, hazel with green specks.

He stifled a yawn and said, "I know you think you have to do this, but Nathan deserves better, and you know it."

I wrapped my blanket tightly around me, searching his eyes.

"It's the only way to keep her safe."

"No it's not."

"Could I be found?"

He hesitated, and looked over the top of the railing, and just then, the door scraped open and Nathan stumbled out shirtless and in shorts, barefoot, with a head full of messy hair. "Brother," he yawned, walking over to me and kissing me on the top of my head. "I see the lady of the house kindly let you in."

He stood behind me, keeping me warm. I leaned back into him and closed my eyes. Barnaby ran inside, and then Mina came out. It was musical animals at the moment. Grayson looked at Mina and said, "It's like a circus in here," He stifled another yawn. "Any chance you have a nice, warm bed I can crash into for a few hours?"

Nathan gestured for Grayson to follow, and for the briefest of moments Grayson's eyes met mine and held. His breath caught before he bowed out and grumbled a 'see you later'. I stayed outside so I missed whatever conversation the two of them had, but I wasn't ready to let my interrupted conversation be totally dropped. I would ask him again later if it would be possible to find me.

I had to figure out who I could trust with my plan, and Grayson and Nathan were not people I could trust.

***

Alexandra and I were alone at the kitchen table; the boys had gone out for a run. She reached across the table and held my hands as the animals swarmed around her feet. "It's not the only way, you know."

"How did you know?" I asked, tears pressing at my

113

eyelids.

"We can all help. Grayson has ties to the other side. Nathan's gifts…"

"As long as they know where I am—*everyone* is at risk. Once she's an adult… Then there's nothing more I can do. She just has to make it to eighteen."

Alexandra shook her head, and bit her lip.

I hadn't been able to press the issue with Grayson, so I asked, "Could I be found?"

She met my eyes with hers. "Only those who have visions know that a vision will not be enough information to find someone. But… Grayson and I both have seen sand, and the color of the sand can be narrowed down…"

"But only those who have visions can see the sand."

"And those who have visions can be forced to tell *about* the sand."

My stomach flip flopped. I knew Grayson's visions were more powerful than Nathan's, but the thought of either of them being tortured for information made me sick.

The tears began to spill. "I don't want to hurt him, Alexandra. I want him to be in her life. I know he won't run away with me, though. He'll make me stay in plain sight and I can't live like that."

Alexandra's face drooped as she said quietly, "I know you feel that it will be that way. But… Maybe it won't."

"Do you know something?" I asked, hopeful.

She sadly shook her head.

"No. However, I know the entire prophecy."

I perked up, blowing my nose into a tissue.

"How?"

"I was there when Klaus recorded it. I witnessed the whole thing. Sometimes prophecies are merely spoken, but this was different; Klaus's hands and fingers moved of their own accord. He hammered out various runes on the parchment, and then he spoke aloud in a monotone voice. I had moments to try to memorize what he said, convert it to English, and remember what the runes on the parchment implied. So we locked it up in the box, hid it, and lied. The only other person who knew it all was Nathan's father, and obviously he must have spoken about it to the wrong people because word got out about it."

"Why did you hide it?"

"Because my heart exists outside my body."

I looked at her, confused.

"Grayson. Nathan."

"Oh." I waited expectantly.

She pulled her long, dark hair into a pony tail, took a swig of water, and stood up, beginning to pace as she recited, as if she had the words etched into her very being, "The Brothers in youth must be separated to keep The Order or one will perish; The Weapon will bestow upon a brother The Bullet. All will be in peril during these times. Pairing brings forth Peace, or War. Sacrifice leads to Safety. The Bullet must dislodge correctly, or else"—and she broke off, placing her hands on the table, bending down to face me directly—"or else, *All* shall perish. If The Bullet is dislodged upon her Own Accord, Great Peace shall be bestowed at Her Behest. Or, Darkness will permeate Light, and the Conclusive War is fought."

I breathed out, trying to make sense of it all.

She sat back down, and looked at the backs of her hands before speaking. "I understand prophecy is open to interpretation, and only *we* give words weight. Visions are images of what will become due to a current vein of action or thought, which is subject to change once a person doing the thinking alters the projected path. I know all of this. Yet, even I have judged these words and given them meaning."

"What is she? The second coming of *Christ*?" I half-laughed, drily and without any humor, finally vocalizing the insanity of the situation and how it seemed.

Alexandra grimly smiled. "Not exactly *the* Christ, but *a* Christ, if you will. We *all* are Christs—we all have light. We also all have a shadow, our own darknesses. It seems that your daughter's proclivities may be stronger with a reach greater than ours. This is why people want to—well, *control* her rather than *stop* her." I felt sick to my stomach again, and it wasn't from the early pregnancy. Alexandra continued, "I know it sounds like you have to make major sacrifices to keep her safe, but that doesn't mean you need to run away. We can protect her together."

"But if she's forced to accept her fate when she's not ready —or by an outside force—we all will *die*? And Darkness will consume the Earth more than it already does? I mean..." I chewed on my hair. "What does *Great Peace shall be bestowed at Her Behest*? She won't have to put herself at risk, will she?" My hand immediately went to my stomach.

"Oh, mein Schatzi," Alexandra said. "As she grows, you'll realize, painfully so, that we have such very little control of anything at all. In which respect, we are frankly lucky to have been chosen for such a noble cause."

Nathan and Grayson returned. I did not betray Alexandra's secret.

***

Several weeks later, as the first hint of a bump began to show through my clothes, Nathan and I returned from our late honeymoon to an apartment stuffed with gifts and cards from our friends and family. A small package sat in the middle of the pile, addressed to only me. Nathan respected my privacy, and did not inquire as to what Grayson personally had written to me.

***

I was six months pregnant and had complete leave from

work. I had been doing very little for the government anyway; mostly I had just been doing bodywork, leading private yoga lessons and even teaching a Reiki class. My clients were under the impression I was moving into the city, so they had come to terms with me closing up shop.

Layla, Liz and Sam knew what my plan was, and they were helping me along the way. I did not let Tollie or Janine know my plan, as they were agents of the government, which of course I could not trust. However, I suspected they were suspicious. Alexandra mailed me protective gemstones, candles, powders, resin, and books. This was another private, untouched package Nathan did not inquire about.

At times I thought he was clueless. Other times I thought he was playing along so he could stop me, or playing along because he *couldn't* stop me. One night, with our upcoming move looming on the horizon, we were in bed and he had his hands on my stomach as she kicked. He looked up at me, and put his hands around my face, green eyes with gold flecks boring into my blue ones.

I furrowed my brow and asked, "What?"

He searched my eyes and said nothing, but kissed me instead. Afterwards, he held me so tightly I almost couldn't breathe. I fell in and out of consciousness, but was pretty sure he was silently weeping at one point.

Pretty sure anyway.

***

The time had come. Everything was boxed up, and most everything was in a U-haul. A few things, however, were in *my* car. Necessities, things I told Nathan I wanted easy access to once we got to our new house. Grayson had flown back into town to help us move, and he and Nathan were talking by the U-haul while I stood alone in the apartment looking around at its emptiness.

Eventually, Grayson came back inside, alone. He turned to

look at me, and said, "So this is it?"

I held my breath. "Does he know?" I whispered as I exhaled.

"He has not told me that he does. But as you know, this family likes secrets." He hesitated. "I know Alexandra told you what the Prophecy says."

I looked at him in shock. "Does anyone else know?"

"No."

I started shaking as he walked over to me. He tilted my chin up, and asked again, "So this is it? I don't see you, for eighteen years?"

My heart pitter-pattered, increasing its rate tenfold. I couldn't think like that or I wouldn't go through with it. I couldn't let the fear take hold. I couldn't let the guilt crush my heart.

"You won't even recognize me," I whispered.

"I'll *always* know you. *And* her," he pointed at my stomach. "Does she have a name?"

"Nathan wants to call her Amara."

We walked out of the apartment, and I softly closed the door behind me. We paused, standing in the breezeway of the apartments. "Goodbye, Violet. I hope… I hope you find what you're seeking. We will always be a phone call away if you change your mind. And just so you know…" He searched my eyes, becoming more quiet. "He will never stop searching for you."

"Goodbye, Grayson." We gave one another a quick, emotionless hug, but as he turned away, his hazel eyes were on fire with emotion. We walked down the stairs to the parking lot, and he walked over to Nathan. I watched him say something to him, then get in the driver's seat and slowly drive the U-haul onto the street.

The plan was for Nathan to follow Grayson to the city after helping me place the animals in my car. From there, some of our friends were supposed to meet us at the new place and help us unload. I had to go to my former massage shop to grab some last things before leaving, and turn in the key. Therefore… I was supposed to be about thirty minutes behind the boys.

Nathan put the animals in my car, and after closing the door, pulled me into his arms, placing his chin on top of my head. He then looked down at me, and seemed to be choosing his words with care. Unless, of course, I was imagining things.

"Violet…"

"Yeah?"

"You are my life. You have always been my life, and you'll always—no matter what—be my life. So in life, is death. So in *death*, is life. Our bond is beyond this three dimensional existence, and nothing will ever change that. Just… please remember… I'm always here for you. Your needs are my priority. Always. I never realized how much I wanted… no, *needed*, this family." His voice had turned mournful, and he had to catch himself from tearing up.

I looked up at him, and met those damn green eyes, those damn green eyes with gold flecks. His gaze was more intense than Grayson's, deeper, piercing and finite. "Nate," I looked down, "Nothing would make me happier than being in our new house, raising our daughter together. Nothing." I looked back up at him.

He held onto me tightly, and gently kissed me before turning to walk to his car. As I climbed into my own vehicle, instantly driving off without pause, his silhouette with his hands in his pockets, silently watching me, burned into my retina and memory.

At the studio, Layla stood by with a screwdriver and changed my license plate. Three more random plates were located inside my car. Liz took my cell phone from me, and handed me a new one. She gave me a piece of paper with login information. She said she didn't know what the phone number was, and once I changed the address and login information, she'd have no access to the account. I planned on changing the number and service once I got to my destination. Sam handed me a bank bag with thousands of dollars in cash, as well as debit cards under an alias to a bank account that her and everyone else had transferred money.

I was leaving a note with them to give to Nathan saying to pay them back. Layla gave me a P.O. Box number in a small town in North Carolina. It was a solid three hours from where I planned on going, and it was a P.O. Box that they knew I didn't plan on going to for several months. Once I got to my destination, I had plans to open up another box an hour away from where I was moving.

The girls looked at me, my car, and the animals. I looked back at them. My face was a canvas of wetness. Layla kept her emotions in check; Sam seemed terrified; Liz's tears were freely flowing. She grabbed me by my shoulders, searching my eyes. "Are you sure?"

I swallowed loudly. "Mmhmm," I said, falling into her arms as she held on tightly. She passed me to Sam whose fear I tried not to consume. Sam passed me onto Layla.

"You can always change your mind. At any point. We will not think less of you. Nobody will. I don't think any path will be easy, but we will *always* support your decisions. Don't forget that."

I merely nodded, took a deep breath. "I'm doing this!" I shouted, raising my hands towards the heavens. I turned my back on the girls, and without looking back—I couldn't handle another permanent image burned into my brain folds —left.

As I drove through the city, my animals in the car with me, my child in my womb, the car loaded with luggage and boxes of essential items, I could barely see, the tears were blinding me so. The animals were terrified by my screams and sobs. But by the time I drove into South Carolina and ditched my newest plate for another one—this time a North Carolina tag—my face streaked and puffy—I was calm, determined, and ready for my new life.

Sacrifice was going to lead to safety.

Amara was going to grow up being loved, cared for, but above all, *safe*.

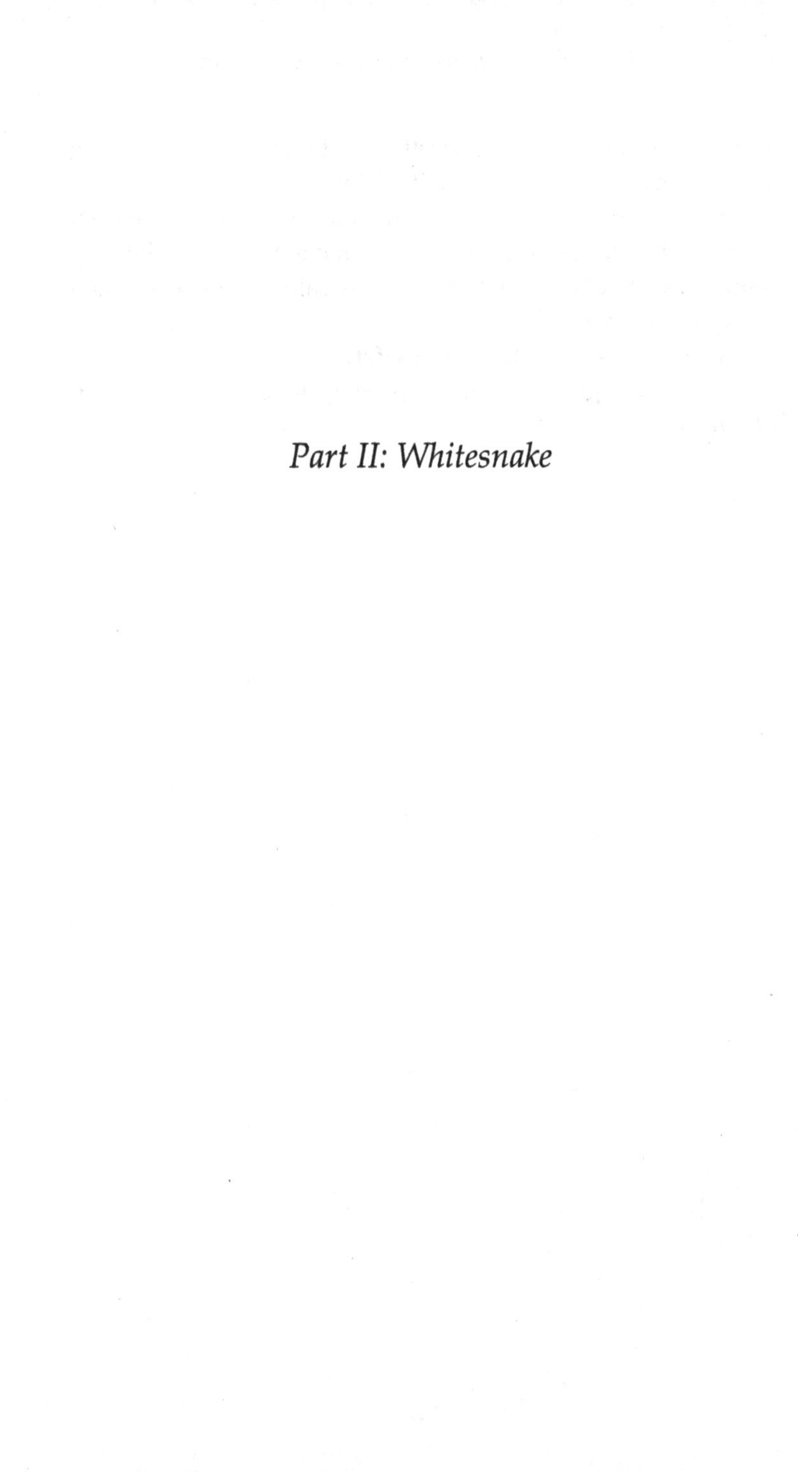

Part II: Whitesnake

The Brothers in youth must be separated to keep The Order or one will perish; The Weapon will bestow upon a brother The Bullet. All will be in peril during these times. Pairing brings forth Peace, or War. Sacrifice leads to Safety. The Bullet must dislodge correctly, or else All shall perish. If The Bullet is dislodged upon her Own Accord, Great Peace shall be bestowed at Her Behest. Or, Darkness will permeate Light, and the Conclusive War is fought.

Here I Go Again

15

I found myself in a mainstream hotel off of Interstate 85 in Somewhere, North Carolina. It was 9 PM and I was in bed with two confused pugs and one annoyed cat. I had unceremoniously sneaked them into the room with me. Luckily they had been quiet while I had done so.

At the moment, though, as I contemplated how I was technically homeless while seven months pregnant, the pugs' snorting noises brought me comfort. Even Barnaby, with his ever watchful eye was curled up at my head and gently making a buzzing sound.

I wouldn't exactly call it a purr, but something close to it.

***

I had fitful sleep that night. My dreams, or rather, nightmares, consisted of green and hazel eyes, enemies, Darkness, and faceless pursuers. I dreamt of being in a wedding gown, fully pregnant, stepping off of a cliff while holding Nathan's hand. The dream that made me wake up in a cold sweat, though, was of my daughter as a little girl, beautiful chocolate hair covering her shoulders, dressed in a filthy, stained white dress, wielding a sword. Men in dark cloaks bowed at her feet as white light swirled around her head with lightning crackling within. She turned to face me, green eyes sparkling and blood dripping from her smile.

It was terrifying.

In the morning I took a long, hot shower, and opened the blinds. I grabbed a postcard that the hotel so generously had gifted me, and quickly scribbled a note to Layla. In the note, I reiterated that if they wanted to mail me anything, they could send word to the post office box she had set up for me. I also reminded them that there was no set timetable for when I would check the mail, other than, presumptively, before my due date.

Layla and I had created multiple codes regarding whether or not I was fine. She was the only soul in the world who knew the codes. The code I chose for the postcard was *Rotting Cherry*. It meant that I was okay, but dying on the inside. More or less.

I also wrote an additional note to Nathan, letting him know that in spite of my absence, we were forever married in my heart and mind. I paused before sealing his letter, but quickly felt my resolve harden my body. I knew that there was literally nothing I could say to Nathan in that moment to help him. He was on his own. As was I.

So many thoughts rushed through my mind as I got prepared to take my car further into my journey. It was easy to focus on the fact that I was leaving, running scared. It was easy to let the panic take over, the fear of doing the wrong thing. The fear of being alone. It was not as easy to think that I was running smart, or that I was doing the right thing.

But as I eased my car back onto the interstate, this time heading in a reverse direction than I had originally traveled the previous day—this method supposedly throwing off any scent from my current track—I forced my thoughts to be on something else. On *other* unsolved mysteries in my life—not just that of my unknown future.

My mother walked across the stage of my thoughts, and I pondered how she was still such an enigma. She had passed when I was just about to enter high school. It was only recent times I had understood the inconsistencies from my childhood actually meant something. My life had turned upside down when I realized that not only did both of my parents have some sort of psychic prowess, but perhaps my mother had been hunted down for her gifts.

And killed.

I was not sure I'd be able to continue exploring my history since I was now officially on the run, and hiding not only from my husband, his family and the government—but other nefarious parties, too. It was frustrating. But I knew that, at the very least, I'd have to keep quiet and not stir the pot about my curiosities and incessant need to know whatever truths were to be discovered. Maybe I'd be lucky and everyone would forget about us and stop hunting to find us.

Of course, I believed Nathan never would. Or Grayson for that matter. Alexandra and I had set terms for the future; they were tentative, they were mere whispers of barely spoken acknowledgments.

I sighed, realizing where my mind had drifted. I had to do this. I had to leave. Everyone was after my daughter, my beautiful, awe-inspiring yet-to-be-born Amara Dawn.

***

I exited the interstate and turned left onto a lonely road headed East towards the coast. I found a small, empty rest stop. It had a couple of tree-shaded picnic benches, a small outhouse type building, and a trashcan. As it was isolated, I felt safe enough to eat lunch and let the animals walk around.

I let the dogs out first on leashes, and then returned to Barnaby. He did the typical cat thing: flattened out like a pancake and looked at me with frightened eyes wondering what the hell I was trying to do to him. I put him back inside his kennel, and got on my phone, calling Sprint. I told them I needed a new number, and the city I was moving to. They told me my new number, and I wrote it down. I changed my password to my account and my login information to a new email address I had set up the night before in the hotel, and that was that.

Every so often a car would speed down the barren stretch of road, but nobody ever even looked my way. I took a deep breath, and quickly changed my license plate for the last time. Well, at least until I officially registered it in my new home. I looked back at the plate, with all of the doors to my car open and the pugs wrapped around my feet.

The plate read California. I didn't even want to think about how Layla had come across all of these random plates for me! I slid the pugs back into the car, slamming the doors behind them. I got behind the driver's wheel, cranked on the air conditioning to cool the car back down. A giant blob of rain fell onto the windshield. I looked up, and saw clouds rolling in. They were mainly white, so it was bizarre that rain had somehow found me. I continued to listen to a short lived rain shower as it hit the car, just staring out the windshield towards the highway. The rain stopped, and sun peeked through a hole in the clouds.

I closed my eyes, counting to ten, and looked over to the dogs. "Okay. Let's go." Barnaby mewed, and I pulled back onto the highway, looking East. The sun had already arced overhead, and I could tell the direction I was heading was settling into early afternoon.

That was it. I was now essentially off the grid from my previous life. I looked at the ID Layla had created for me. I had kept my first name as my middle name, and turned my middle name into my first name. It wasn't particularly clever, and I hoped it didn't bite me in the ass. I planned to go by

Violet, though. My last name was now apparently Wood, a nondescript name. I had a feeling it was paying homage to Harry Potter.

Layla did love those wizards and witches.

I drove through little towns and areas of vast nothingness. I saw gas stations that looked like they'd been around since the 1970s, and were actually still *in* the 1970s. I finally left the mainland while driving across a long, low bridge. It was still a few hours from dusk, and I rolled down my windows, letting the evening salt air in my windows for a taste.

Finally. *Finally.* The Vitamin Sea was just what I needed to relax. I took in a long, deep breath and slowly exhaled. I had been quiet for a long while, just listening to podcasts and music. I turned the sound off, and spoke to the animals. "Well, guys, here we are. Home. Hopefully for the next eighteen, safe and incredible years."

I turned onto the main drag in town, and eventually drove past the little stilted bungalow I was going to move into. It was hard to pass by it, but I knew I couldn't go straight to the house and just move in like a normal person.

I was *not* a normal person.

I continued north and drove through all of the beach towns, taking in the sights and sounds of each area. I passed by the beautiful elementary school Amara was going to attend some day; I passed by local eateries and major tourist junk mills. I turned east and headed towards areas less crowded. I pulled into an area covered by trees and wooden walkways.

A Hair Cuttery was one of the shops. I walked the animals around, letting the dogs do their business and gave Barnaby a few moments in nature. I had parked far away from other patrons, fully covered in the shade. I left water for the animals with the AC blaring on. I would be quick. I locked the door to the car, praying nobody would peek inside and see the animals and freak out.

I had already checked in online for my haircut. It was going to be easy; chop it all off, dye it a dark auburn. The lady raised her eyebrows at my demeanor, but obliged.

By the time I left, my hair was dark, short, and I now had bangs. I didn't look like me at all. I looked into the rearview mirror and sobbed as I got back onto the road. I had planned it perfectly; nighttime had officially descended and the neighborhood streets were relatively quiet.

I could move in essentially unnoticed.

I parked in front of my sweet, little beachfront cottage as the darkness overcame the coast. I could see that bags of food that I had ordered were resting on the doorstop—good—I wouldn't have to leave the cottage for a few days if I didn't want to leave.

I turned off the car, not wasting a minute. I grabbed the animals out of the car and threw them into the house. I put a cat box down, water and food. At first, Phang, Mina and Barnaby sat in the naked kitchen, looking at me hesitantly. "Guys!" I exclaimed, finding my voice. "This is your new home. Explore. Eat. Barnaby, this is your bathroom. Pugs—if you want me to set up a litter box for y'all, I will, but for now —keep it inside of you!"

They slowly began to disperse, recognizing that they were able to roam and inspect. Barnaby slunk down as he passed by me, giving a long, uneasy mew. "It's okay, buddy," I said, jabbing my toe at his leg in a comforting way.

The house was sparsely furnished, having been set up prior to my arrival. While the animals began to explore, I went to the front door and grabbed a screwdriver out of my bag. I changed the locks. I made sure to go to every door, changing Every. Single. Lock. I checked all of the windows and made sure they were properly closing themselves. I dropped my screwdriver onto a boring, bare coffee table in the living room, and patted my belly.

"We're home, Amara Dawn. We're home." I ran to the bathroom, and tried not to look into the mirror while doing so. When I came back to the living room, Phang was happily snorting on the couch with one of his blankets that I had brought him from the car. Mina was sitting on his foot, drooling with her eyes closed. Barnaby ran up to the cat condo I had waiting for him. While it didn't smell familiar, it gave him a clear view of the kitchen, dining and living room areas. It also had a window into the side yard, where he was able to see whatever creatures lurked in the dark.

I stepped outside to grab the rest of the items from my car. I locked it up, and stood on the front balcony, looking around at my new neighbors. Lights were on in most of the houses nearby, all with cars parked in the carports. I assumed most of the people were tourists, but also suspected some of the homier looking ones, with potted plants underneath the light of street lamps, had locals living here full-time, or at least the duration of the summer.

I sighed, opening the door one last time for the night, using my feet to push the rest of my bags inside. I shut and locked it, pressing my back against it. I closed my eyes, exhausted. *California.* I had come from California, some little town near Sacramento. I had moved to California for college. Yes, the weather was great. Yes, I was sad to leave it. But I had grown up on the east coast, and missed it. This town in North Carolina appeared to have small town charm with access to larger cities. No, I had no family anymore. No, I was not running from a bad relationship, but yes, I was very pregnant and couldn't wait to meet my daughter, Dawn.

I walked over to the couch, opened up some Chinese food I had gotten right after I had cut my hair, and dumped it onto the table. I was too tired to unpack or even make it to the bedroom. I didn't care. I put on some happy reruns on the TV, grabbed a blanket and felt my eyelids begin to close. I felt safe, at ease, and exhausted. I could worry about unpacking tomorrow.

131

16

Day Three. I woke up early, feeling stiff as a board. I probably shouldn't have fallen asleep on the couch. The sun hadn't quite risen, and the morning was quiet. The animals were roving around, sniffing this and that. I tried to meditate by listening to the sounds, but found that my anxiety was at an all-time high. The earth seemed uneven and my feet were unstable with my legs full of jelly. My heart rate seemed stuck on high and my breathing was shallow.

My mind was so overloaded with thoughts, yet I couldn't think anymore. The walls of the cottage began to close in on me, so I stepped outside onto the balcony with the pugs, quietly telling Barnaby we would be back. I took the dogs down to the ocean to try and calm down. My hair was so short, the wind blowing through it was ticklish and annoying. I hoped that by the time fall and winter rolled around, my hair would be grown out enough to cover my neck again.

I had scoped this area out beforehand, so I knew that there was a path down to the beach that had public access. Sure enough, I found a sign agreeing with what I thought I knew.

Phew. That would have sucked had I been wrong!

The dogs hadn't seen sand before, and I wasn't sure they could comprehend the ocean on any level. In spite of everything, though, I found myself laughing. When we walked onto the beach, Mina found joy in the sand and pounced like a cat. Phang, however, seemed confused and kept trying to shake it off his paw. The ebb and flow of the waves soothed me as I tuned into them, turning on Reiki channels and expanding my energy into the ether itself. Luckily the sea water was quite warm as it enveloped my feet.

There were people on the beach with me, but they were not close enough to try and pet the dogs. I was happy with that. I wasn't sure I was ready for interactions just yet. Once I walked back onto the streets, people who were walking, biking or riding skateboards mostly acknowledged me with a nod of the head, or slight wave as they passed by. I couldn't tell tourist from local, and the anonymity further soothed me.

I turned into my own driveway, and determined to keep the implosion of space away, opening many of the windows. Barnaby immediately jumped up onto a window sill, sniffing at the salty air. The dogs started to kick off the sand at the front door, and I realized my life was about to become very sandy. I decided I needed Roomba to help out, and walked into the kitchen, putting it on my list of to-gets.

The baby kicked, and it jolted me into a mini-panic. I looked down at my size-increasing stomach, placed my hand onto her and felt tears pressing into my eyelids. "We are fine. We are safe. You are loved." I took a deep breath and with resolve, felt that I needed to continue to do something—I couldn't just sit there and think.

Unpack. I was going to unpack.

I had never minded the quiet before, but this was positively stifling. I cranked on some tunes, the pugs nestled onto my couch with their eyes closed. I felt my eye twitch slightly at the prospect of sand on my new couch... but I reminded myself, my new life came with new issues.

Like sand on the couch. And that was totally okay.

I felt slightly giddy that I was annoyed by something so simple. By the time I was finished, it was late morning. At least the place felt a little bit more like a home. I went to a window nook that was in the kitchen. It was perfect for some cushions and plants; I would have to get something to place inside of it. I scattered some of my crystals across the landing and placed my hand on a beautiful, small, fluorite box.

Connection was painted on it in gorgeous, magical blue ink. It wasn't in English, of course, but rather, runes. Alexandra had sent it to me after she realized what I was doing. Naturally she didn't want me to leave her son, but... perhaps, as a mother herself who had made some difficult decisions concerning her own children, she understood. The box was to keep its contents safe and without the ability to make a dangerous connection to me. Or Amara.

I felt a steady hum from within the box, and I looked out my window to the small backyard. Just beyond the tops of the trees, in the distance, I could make out the ocean. I dared open the box, just for a moment. Instantly a flash of light jumped out of it, erupting into rainbow colors on the sea blue colored walls. I was mesmerized.

Barnaby mewed, breaking me out of the reverie, colors being blinked away. I fingered the chain and ring that was on the link, gave it a quick squeeze as it warmed under my hand, no doubt making a connection to one of its other counterparts. In a hypnotic daze, I let it drop. I slowly placed the lid back on the box, placing it far out of reach in the window.

I found my notepad, and began to make a list about things I had to accomplish, least of which was find a good doctor to deliver my baby. I would call around the following day for that. I filled out my online documents to start the distance job I had decided was going to make me money, and eventually I got tired of that, too.

I pushed all of the paperwork aside, pacing for a few moments in the kitchen while the animals slowly began to wake up from their slumber, looking for some treats. It was quiet again, and my mind was contemplating that I would return to my massage work at some point, and I needed to figure out how to get licensure in North Carolina. I was not quite sure how to go about that with a new name, other than taking a licensing test again.

Ugh. That didn't sound fun.

I spoke aloud to the pugs, and decided I was going to drive around my new town, scoping out coffee shops and cafes, and maybe even a little space where I could eventually rent to resume my bodywork practice.

I got into my car, weaving my way out of the neighborhood to a main drag. I found a cute little space near a holistic grocery store that would be perfect to practice... assuming it was still available after Amara was born. I parked my car, and went into a kitschy bookstore selling coffee, conversations and trinkets. Since it was just after midday at this point, it wasn't too crowded. I ordered an iced decaf sweetened drink, and while I was waiting, looked through a stack of local authors' books.

One in particular caught my eye with the author's name of M. Liam. The title of the book was *Protection of the Sea*. The back cover said it was about a young woman who, against all odds, survived a harrowing ordeal. Mysteries were plentiful, but the sea always offered her the protection she needed. But what happened when she realized that the sea was actually also a man?

I chuckled to myself. "That is a superb book," said the

barista as she handed me my drink.

I felt stiff responding, but I knew it was necessary, "You've read it?"

"I've read all of Liam's books. He loves writing about Nordic magic and damsels who kick ass."

A shudder rippled through my body. "Ah, maybe I need something lighter, then." I grinned, trying to cover my discomfort.

"For real—it's so *Gucci*. My family owns this store—so I'm serious—I know books. Take it. For free. You'll love it."

"Oh, wow—thank you so much." *Gucci* I thought, eye twitching. *What the heck are the kids these days saying?* I took my drink, my new book, and wandered outside to the little outdoor seating. A gentle ocean breeze caught my short hair, and it was cooling and lovely. I couldn't focus enough to read past a couple of pages of the book, but the barista was right— it looked like an easy, gripping tale from the start. Maybe after I felt more settled I could read it.

Nighttime began to fall, so I walked across the parking lot to grab a sub at a sandwich place before heading home. Once I pulled into my driveway, soft light left some areas of my new house. It looked cute; it looked safe. It needed more personality, but the butt of a pug in the window and the grimace of a cat in another one was enough garner a small laugh. With as much bravery as I could muster, I got out of my car and walked up the wooden steps to the balcony.

After a quiet dinner and letting the dogs use the bathroom outside—to which I discovered there were little cacti all over the yard—I plopped down on the couch with a blanket. I turned on old cowboy movies and drifted in and out of sleep for hours before finally dragging myself to my empty bedroom. Luckily I was so tired, the empty bed did not bother me.

Day Four. The following morning the sun streamed in

through the poorly closed curtains, waking me up. Barnaby was on my head; the pugs were nowhere to be seen. I stumbled into the restroom, brushed my teeth, and opened up the blinds in the kitchen and living room area. Oh, it was a beautiful morning indeed. I could clearly see the ocean in the distance, slowly crashing onto the sand. Clouds lazily drifted across a cerulean painted sky. I opened the windows, and closed my eyes, listening to the gulls.

A girl could get used to this.

I put on a pot of water to have some herbal tea. I let the pugs out back to use the restroom, but they quickly came back in. I took several burrs out of their paws, realizing I was going to have to make the backyard safe for them. I opened up some smelly food, spoiling all of them with the wet stuff. Listening to their happy sounds as they all ate, I took my tea to a little bistro table by the deep window sill. I looked past the crystals and plants out to the sea.

The world was waking up; I began to hear children in the background, cars honking their horns, general traffic and even a siren off in the distance. It was no longer as peaceful as it had been. I turned on NPR and began to prepare breakfast for myself.

After it got late enough into the morning, I put in a call to a couple of doctors and found someone who was willing to work with me. My appointment was for the following day.

I had my backstory ready to roll if need be, but my intention was to be as mum as possible about what had brought me to this little town. I glanced at my silent phone on my teeny, tiny coffee table, feeling empty.

Nobody would be contacting me.

I had found a dog park the previous day in my travels, so I decided the dogs and I would go visit it. I watched them explore the park and sniff other dogs' welcome centers. Yuck. A good looking twenty-something kid approached me using total lifeguard surfer-dude speak. In the following weeks, I would come across his messy, curly headed self a lot, eventually meeting his girlfriend who always inquired about the baby. It was nice to have unassuming people talk with me. They were nonjudgmental and never pressured to find out more information about me.

Although, I assumed if I continued to talk with them, I would have some answering to do.

Day Five. The day after the first time at the dog park, I found myself at the doctor's office. The rooms were cozy, painted in calming colors of the sea. They had comfortable chairs, real curtains and an assortment of things to drink along with pre-packaged snacks. A midwife and doula were both on staff.

Everyone was very friendly, and caring even as I was a stranger. Questions were asked about the father, but nobody seemed prying. You could tell they were concerned, though, but they never made me feel uncomfortable. I had found the right people to help me birth her.

They gave the option to birth at home or in the facility. The facility was state of the art, full of everything from birthing balls, pools to traditional beds. However, I figured it was probably safer to do the birthing at my house. I also didn't want to be away from my animals for too long since there was nobody there to watch them.

17

I eventually lost count of days and began to count time by my pregnancy again. I was eight months along, and I felt as large as a strip of townhomes. My ankles were swollen; my wrists were swollen; I looked like a pale, out-of-season watermelon. The indigestion alone was murderous; everything I ate, I ate twice. I was more than ready to *not* be pregnant, but, according to the midwife, I was also nowhere near ready to give birth.

I was told to settle in for the long haul. I was not amused.

I joked about my plight with Nancy, the girlfriend of the dog park kid, Sid. Impossibly, those were their names, and they were the cutest couple. Nancy had a blonde pixie cut, streaked with red and orange. My own hair had started to grow out, and she constantly asked if she could dye it a different color for me. The incoming roots drove her crazy— she worked part-time as a hair dresser. She always massaged my wrists and hands for me when I'd waddle my way to the dog park. She was certainly an angel placed before me.

I hadn't let Sid nor Nancy know where I lived, but they became insistent on helping me out as the baby's due date got closer. I finally acquiesced and let them into my living space. There were no reasons not to trust them.

They loved the chakra flags, the Buddhist statues, the crystals. They laughed and said I had to be the only person who had five different yoga mats. Nancy fell in love with my flag that read *Peace. To bring peace to the Earth, strive to make your own life peaceful.*

One day, Nancy had ridden her bike over to my house offering to take the dogs out for a walk. "Oh, my, God, Violet! That box is *gorgeous*! May I?" she asked, reaching to grab the little fluorite box out of my window.

"No!" I inadvertently shrieked in terror as she reached for it. I took a deep breath and winced, waiting for a reaction, but Nancy was smooth as anything.

"No problem, Vi. Hey, Phang! Get your little tail over here," she calmly intoned, grabbing harnesses and leashes.

I placed the box inside my underwear drawer after that.

A lovely elderly couple lived on my street, and I would see them sometimes in town or while walking. The lady in particular, Gladys, would invite me over for tea. I stopped in once or twice a week to visit with her. She knew a lot about the people on our street, some about the people in our "neighborhood", and a little bit about people in town. She was kind, trusting, and I definitely used her to get more information about the people I had chosen to live near. The most interesting person on our particular street, other than me, of course, was a man in his fifties who also lived alone. He was at the end of the street, with trees in his backyard and apparently a direct path to the beach. He mostly kept to himself, primarily because he was a writer. Gladys said he lived in New York, except for when he was actively writing a novel.

Mysterious, but at this point, not nefarious. I'd only seen him a handful of times, and he'd merely nodded at my waddle.

Mostly, the houses that were on my street were full of vacationing families who were spending a week or so at the beach. The majority of the families were from the northeast, but some came from as far west as Michigan. Everyone was always super friendly. One family had a tween, red-headed little girl who was as fiery as her hair. She reminded me of a younger Blaze. This girl's name was Gynnifer, though, and whenever she would see me and the dogs piddling around the yard, she would run across the street. Phang and Mina loved her, and were sad to see her go after two weeks of her family's vacation. They promised to stay at the same house the following year, and couldn't wait to meet the baby.

I started to recognize more faces as time went on, especially when I was in town. Owners of stores and restaurants seemed to enjoy speaking with me, inquiring about the baby. If I was at the dog park or just walking around town, the same faces asked to rub the dogs' bellies.

I was Violet, the single, pregnant lady with the dogs.

***

Close to nine months pregnant, I found myself pumping gas into my car. My midwife had given me the go-ahead to leave town for the day and I was about to drive to the original P.O. Box Layla had set up for me. I was more than a little nervous and had to do many ritualistic grounding exercises before even getting to the gas station to leave.

I was afraid of being accosted by a multitude of persons— be it Tenebris on some rogue mission to control me and the baby; the German group who attacked Grayson, Nathan and me on Sylt before the baby had even been conceived; the government themselves; Grayson; or, God forbid, Nathan.

To boot, these were just the people I *knew* who were interested in me and my baby.

I mean, logically I knew they could not possibly camp

outside of that post office 24/7, even if they *had* caught wind of where Layla had set it up. My plans were to drive southwest first, though, and open a new P.O. Box in another small town. I was going to set up P.O. Boxes in random directions and angles from where I lived, so nobody would be able to pin point my actual location. At some point I would be brave enough to open one in my own town. But not just yet. Once I got to Layla's post office, I would retrieve whatever packages/letters I had, and then send off some letters of my own.

I took a giant breath in, closed my eyes while the hum of the gas entered my vehicle. I exhaled, and found that I wasn't alone. The local Sheriff, who was probably in his late fifties, early sixties, nodded at me from across the pump. I had seen him around town; he was tall and physically fit, dark, greying hair, serious, and always quiet. I was surprised when he spoke in a slight southern accent.

"You headed out of town today?" he asked as he walked over to me. For whatever reason, his demeanor made me even more anxious.

"Yes… I've got some errands to run in neighboring towns."

"Gloria gave you clearance to leave? It's safe?"

I cleared my throat and looked at him surprised "You know Gloria?"

He bit his cheek, and a hint of a dimple was exposed. "She's my wife. Small town, and all… I sort of figured you were one of her patients. Sorry—didn't mean to pry or anything."

"Oh," I relaxed. I could see that any attention from a stranger would always add a shake to my ground. I audibly sighed. "Yes. She said the baby wasn't ready to come anytime soon."

"I'm off in an hour if you'd like company? I can take you wherever you need to go."

The sun started to peek over the horizon. "Oh, no, that's alright. Thank you, though, Sheriff Derek. I really appreciate that."

"It's Garrett."

I smacked myself on my forehead and finished pumping the gas. "Sorry—pregnancy hormones. They make you forgetful as hell."

His smile widened. "Have a good day, ma'am."

He walked back over to his police cruiser with his coffee, and slid into the driver's side.

***

Forty-five minutes away from Layla's P.O. Box, I stopped at an unassuming gas station for some water and to stretch my legs. I had already gone through my water bottle by the time I'd reached the first post office, but had immediately gotten back in the car to head towards the *other* post office. I needed a refill. I took my time inside the little store, perusing the rows of junk food and odds and ins, half-listening to the conversations of other people in the store. Their southern drawls were thick.

I got back into the car. Ten minutes from the gas station, though, I pulled off onto an empty stretch of road to change license plates. I just needed to remember to change it back at some point before I returned home.

An hour or so later, by mid-afternoon, I pulled into the parking lot of the small post office. This one was slightly larger than the ones I had already been to that day. My hand was shaking as it held the key. I opened up the box, pulled out several letters, and several notices of packages too big to store inside. I went to my car and looked at the letters—they had all came from Layla's address, some of the envelopes bigger than the others. I opened the large ones, and could see that multiple letters were inside of them, different scrawls on many of them.

I decided that I couldn't read them until I was safe at home. It was just too emotional seeing everyone's different handwritings, and there was too much to sort through. I felt stripped naked, unsafe and vulnerable.

I shoved the envelopes underneath the passenger side mat, and then pulled out my own, prewritten letters from my bag. One was for the girls, one was for Grayson, one for Alexandra, and one was for Nathan. They were not sealed, so I scrawled an additional 'thank you' to Layla's, letting her know I had received their goodies. I told her I was about to grab the packages and would be in contact before the year's end.

A lump formed in my throat. That was almost six months away.

I reiterated that they were not to use that P.O. Box anymore, and there would be no future way to contact me until I contacted *them*. Layla had had orders not to send me anything past a certain date.

Everything I was going to read was already dated by a month. *Don't think. Don't think.*

I instead looked over at the other letters, and didn't feel the need to add anything to them, but I did pause at Nathan's. I pulled the simple card out. It had a heart inscribed in gold filigree. The inside was blank, save for my own handwriting which read *I love you*. A tear fell from one eye, smudging it. I hurriedly wrote *I miss you*, closed it up and sealed it. After a beat, I thought to myself: *enough*. I needed to go back inside, get the packages and mail these letters off. *Don't think. Don't think.*

I stepped back inside, handing the clerk five slips of paper stating I needed to pick up my packages. She had black hair, sparkly brown eyes and a smile that was contagious. She yelled to someone in the back whom I couldn't see. "Henry! Henry! Our mysterious Violet is here to get her packages!"

Her accent was thick. Henry, an older man with a beer belly and crazy looking mustache, pushed a red cart out from behind the back and peered at me over thick bifocals. "Anywhere I can help place these packages for you, Miss?" My eyes about popped out of my head. It was five *very large* packages, three of which had the Target logo emblazoned on them.

That made me sad. There wasn't a Target anywhere near me now.

"Oh my gosh, I had no idea there would be so many!"

The lady's eyes twinkled as she helped me. We closed the P.O. Box. I handed her my mail and paid for it, and then "Henry" walked my boxes to my car. I was extremely suspicious of him; something seemed off. He didn't seem like a Scout, but something wasn't quite right. He definitely seemed like a plant of some sort.

From which party, though?

It made me super glad I had changed my license plates at the last minute. It also meant, unfortunately, that I was going to have to take an extremely long way home. I sighed, annoyed. Since I was on high alert, I easily caught him memorizing my plates.

Sure—no problem. I was gonna ditch those babies in about fifteen minutes at a local Walgreens. *Go ahead and memorize them, buddy.*

Ugh. I felt a sharp stitch coming from my abdomen, and doubled over for a brief instant.

Unfortunately, dear old Henry caught me in action. Oddly enough, his concern seemed genuine.

"You okay, Miss?"

"Just groovy. Thanks so much for your help, *Henry*."

He narrowed his eyes just a bit, and wiggled his fake mustache at me. "You take care, Miss."

"Will do."

I tried to drive away as if I didn't suspect anything, but as soon as I pulled into the back entrance of the Walgreens, making sure no cameras or people were around, I hurriedly changed my plates to another set of random ones provided by Layla. I tossed the plates the man had memorized into a dumpster. As I eased back into the traffic, looking at my backseat covered in boxes that wouldn't fit in the trunk, I breathed a sigh of relief. I exited onto the interstate... heading the wrong way, of course.

I was impatient and really wanted to get home, though, so I only went north for about thirty minutes before turning around and heading back to the cottage. I stopped one last time for gas, snacks and a plate change. By the time I pulled back into my new hometown, it was pretty late. I was tired, dirty, frustrated, hungry, and needed to pee. I pulled into my favorite local sandwich establishment, and guess who was there?

Officer Garrett.

Unbelievable. I had a knack for attracting people I didn't want to attract.

18

"Just getting back from your day of errands?" he smirked, as he opened the door for me into the restaurant.

"Thanks—*Officer Garrett.*" He winked. "Yes, it's been a long day. I want to get home, eat and sleep for days! Only—"

Again, I doubled over in pain. He reached for my elbow.

"Are you okay?" he asked, and the silver-haired owner of the sandwich shop, Mandy, quickly rushed over.

"Is it time?" she asked excitedly.

"No…" I grumbled. "I've just been having some pain off and on today. I'm okay."

Mandy, looking concerned, said, "Well alrighty then. You just want the usual, then, hon'?"

"Yes, please."

I reached for my wallet, but Garrett shushed it away. I thanked him, and while we waited, he asked me if I thought I should contact Gloria. I shook my head no. It had just been a really long day, I assured him.

He walked me to my car, and helped my big round belly inside. Since he was a sheriff, his sharp eye couldn't help but notice the status of my car. Letters were scattered all over the back, packages piled and stashed in every nook and cranny, trash strewn about, and a screwdriver. If I didn't feel like I was about to push a tiny human out of me, I may have felt worried, or even embarrassed by such an insatiable mess. But I didn't, and I wasn't.

I drove home, pain coming and going. Nancy had stopped by and taken the dogs out for a walk about an hour ago, so I knew it was safe to go inside, eat dinner, and pass out. I pulled out my sandwich, making sure it was high enough from the furbabies so they couldn't reach it. But then I switched gears and decided I wanted to take a quick shower first, so I abandoned my meal for the time being.

As the pain seemed to increase as the warm water rained down on my body, I began to think that maybe something *was* wrong and that I *should* contact Gloria. Shit. *Shit.* SHIT! My hand slid off the bathroom wall as my stomachache made me stumble. I wasn't sure if I had spontaneously gone into labor, or if something was wrong, but I desperately needed to call her. *Now.*

My wet hair was in a heap at the base of my neck, shower water dripping down my body as I slid towards the hanger for my robe. I pulled at it, but it wouldn't come. I had to hold myself up on the wall for a moment until the pain subsided again.

I took a deep breath to steady myself, messily piled up my hair on my head, and finally was able to grab the robe. I dried my feet as best as I could—I was afraid of falling—and I walked down the small hallway to get to the kitchen table to grab my phone. I forlornly looked at what it was sitting next to—my uneaten sandwich.

Barnaby was keeping a watchful eye on me from the couch, and the dogs were both a noticeable distance away from me, watching. Alert.

I dialed Gloria's phone number and held my breath, trying

to use logical thought to balance the pain. I knew better—I knew that pain wasn't as bad if you continued to *breathe*. However, it was like my mindfulness training was being thrown out the window and stamped on by a herd of elephants. It didn't matter. It couldn't help.

Gloria picked up the first ring. "I'm on my way, I'll be there in about thirty minutes. Garrett is closer; I'm going to send him over now. Yes, he already called me to tell me. If I have to meet you at the hospital instead, I will do that. But try to set up whatever you can; as long as nothing is wrong, Garrett will do the rest! He may not be a doctor, but he is highly trained. Don't you worry about a thing, okay? Just relax as best you can!"

I blinked, trying to take in everything that she had said, but let out a loud yell, dropping the phone. "Oh, God," I screamed. The dogs dispersed and whimpered in a sort of hollow distance; Barnaby came up next to me and started to mew and rub his head against my leg. But I was numb to anything going on outside of me. I just felt the pain, the dull, aching pain, and tasted the terror like it was a giant, bitter pill on my tongue.

I heard a loud banging on my door, but I couldn't get up off of the floor to get it. I tried to whisper for Garrett to come in, and just couldn't. The contraction hit me moments later, like a blow of multiple fists to the abdomen. I must have yelled for Nathan, because after Garrett knocked my door in, his immediate question to me was, "Who the hell is Nathan?"

He lifted me up and brought me over to the couch to rest. He grabbed me a cup of water and I was able to sip on it between contractions. "I'll get you new locks as soon as Gloria gets here."

"Okay," I gasped, as another contraction came on.

After it passed, I asked, "Is this just labor? Or is there something wrong?" My lip trembled violently. Garrett reached out and touched my hand, comforting me.

"I believe it's just labor, but I am no expert. I can bring you to the hospital if you'd like, or we can set up here for a home birth and await Gloria. I think you overdid it today, and your body threw you into a tizzy. It may even be false labor—you seem to have gotten better since I've arrived."

That made me start to cry, and Garrett looked slightly awkward. "I'm so scared!" I wailed, starting to hiccough. Phang and Mina had ventured a little closer to me. Barnaby, however, didn't trust Garrett so he was near the hallway, watching us.

"Honey," Garrett said, "Don't you have *any*one at all I can call for you? Family? Close friend? Nathan?"

Hearing Nathan's name sent a shockwave through my body. If only Nathan was there... He would know how to calm me down. I thought about Nancy, or Gladys, but decided I didn't want to bother either of them. It was almost 9 PM and Nancy had already helped me that day. Gladys? She was probably in bed asleep.

Sadly, I shook my head. "There's no one I can call," I whispered.

Just then Gloria arrived. She was a good ten years younger than Garrett, and so very different from him. She had long, silky black hair peppered with grey strands which she often kept in a ponytail; tattoos on her arms, and a giant phoenix on her leg. She was small and muscular, with brown eyes, yellow skin, rosy cheeks and dark pink lips. I loved her. I thought she was beautiful.

In this moment, though? I'd never seen *any*thing as beautiful as her.

She calmed me down, and convinced me to go see the doctor. When I got to the hospital, the doctor told me the same thing Garrett had said—I had just worn myself out. They decided to keep me overnight, and the following day I was going to be put on bedrest. Garrett and Gloria promised me they would make sure the animals were okay, and that I was in a good hands.

I felt a presence that night, and I was pretty sure it was my mother. Usually she came to me in dreams, or the hazy space between sleep and being awake. But as I was so sleep-deprived and over-tired, I was truly wide awake when I saw her. She sat at the edge of my bed, a white outline of a glowing Angel. I felt slight weight from her hand being pressed on my leg, and I promptly fell asleep.

***

It appeared Garrett had been appointed my keeper, because he was the one who pushed me in a wheelchair to his police cruiser the next day to be brought home. He walked me in, showed me my new door and door locks, and lent an arm to get me inside. Gloria had kissed me on top of my head and told me to keep resting, and that she'd check in later.

I was about two centimeters at that point. And it could still take an entire week or more to be fully ready for labor. I was not happy about this, but I was glad that nothing was wrong. Garrett got me nice and cozy on my couch, put a sandwich in front of me, and eyeballed the boxes and letters scattered about my house.

"Do you want some help opening these things?"

I shook my head. I assumed it was baby items, but I wasn't totally sure. I had already purchased a ton of baby things myself, of course. But since I had missed out on a proper baby shower, I had a feeling Elisabeth had taken care of it remotely for me.

"Here—I'll bring two of the boxes next to you, along with the letters. That way you can open them if you feel up to it. NO heavy lifting, NO moving things to rooms they belong in, okay? Just get up to use the restroom and that's it."

I smiled, pulling my hair back into a ponytail. "Yes, sir."

He patted me on my head as he stood up to leave. "You'll be alright, Violet. Call me or Gloria if you need anything. I've already got that spitfire Nancy dropping dinner by for you, and I gave Gladys a key to come in here in a few hours and walk the dogs."

My mouth dropped open.

"Small town, Violet."

I nodded, grateful he had been placed before me.

He left, and I flipped through the TV channels, trying to find something to watch. *Harry Potter* was on, but I wasn't in the mood. *Twilight* was on—just what I needed, some edgy, high-angsty teenage drama to help me drown my sorrows. I drank my raspberry leaf tea, and pulled out my first letter.

It was in Layla's handwriting, and she had written it the day I had left. It made me very sad to read it as she had described, luckily not in great detail, Nathan's reaction when he realized I had left. Elisabeth had written weeks after I had disappeared, and just wrote about gossip of our mutual acquaintances. She told me she couldn't get any deeper than that, because she was just so saddened and scared for me. She sent her love. Sam sent me an envelope full of confetti shaped like baby items. It made me laugh.

Alexandra had sent a letter, mostly in runic language. She reiterated the mostly unspoken terms she and I had agreed to —that Amara and I would visit sometime in the future. But nothing would be set in stone until after Amara turned two. And maybe not even then.

Grayson had sent me nothing. But, I still had the letter he had given me when I returned from my honeymoon. I imagined that was more than enough.

Nathan's letter was short, and it was only in English. "I will never stop searching for you two. I love you. Always."

Ah. Another *Harry Potter* reference, whether he knew it or not. I touched the script he had written, trying desperately to feel something from it, some connection to him, and I felt... nothing. I lifted it up to my nose, my mouth, seeking a scent, a sensation and...dead air.

I slid the scissors alongside the first two boxes that were next to me—from Target. It was loaded with baby supplies. Oh my goodness, I loved my friends so much. They were amazing. Baby books, blankets clothes, burp cloths, diapers, music boxes, teething rings, medicine... They had thought of it all.

And that was just the first two boxes! I had three more to go through, plus a small one that I had a feeling was more for me than the baby. I pushed everything aside, clutching Nathan's letter to my chest as I ate half of my sandwich before falling asleep.

19

About a week later, I was startled by the sound of Phang barking. I noticed a small pool of water coming from a region of my body that was no longer visible to my eyes. It was dribbling onto the floor. *Crap.*

One way or another, I was having this baby in twenty-four hours!

I calmly started my text chain. I contacted Nancy and Gladys. They were to be on animal-duty for the next couple of days, with one of them due to come to my house in the afternoon to walk them. I texted Gloria and told her my water had broken, but that I wasn't having any contractions yet. She told me to hang tight, take it easy, eat something small, and she would send Grace, the doula, over as soon as possible.

I was to text both of them as soon as the contractions started.

I slowly walked to the baby's room, grabbing a beautiful hand-knitted blanket from her grandmother. It was rainbow colors, swirling around in amazing patterns, and super soft. I grabbed a stuffed animal of a giraffe that the girls had sent me, and an adorable baby cap that read "daddy's girl" from

Nathan. The newborn onesie I had prepared for her to first wear? That one said *I'm my uncle's favorite.*

There. Everyone was represented for the birth.

I took some chux and placed them on my couch as I sat there, cradling the one box left that I hadn't opened from my crazy post office day. I also had a pad of paper. I was going to write my thank you cards, and detail the events of the birth for Layla to do with what she pleased.

But first, the small box. I murmured comforting sounds to soothe myself, and opened it.

Inside was a book, a book I hadn't known Nathan had made for me. He had written a brief note, saying the intent of the book was that of a housewarming gift for the day we moved into our new home. His now empty and quiet bungalow, for which the silence was stifling and suffocating. I could relate—things had been the same for me.

My heart snapped in half, and that was enough to trigger my first contraction.

It really hurt, much more than I thought it would. It didn't last too long, though, and another one didn't come for twenty minutes or so. It was enough time to get a start on the cards and birthing tale. Nathan hadn't been cruel with his letter, just matter of fact. He told me he was going to move out of the state, and back up to DC by month's end. He knew he wouldn't find me before she was born, and he wanted to move forward with his life without us.

He did mention that there had been visions of her as an older child—but not as a baby. This made my stomach turn. He did not go into detail about what that meant, or who had had the vision.

He told me to stay calm, chant, and have a beautiful birth experience. He was full of sorrow that he was missing the arrival of his one and only child. He joked about the child line on his palm that I had once read—the one that suggested he would have the one child.

He ended the letter with the word *committed*.

The book was compiled of pictures of the two of us from over the past couple of years. Pictures that I had forgotten had even been taken. Some were crappy cell phone quality, but some were beautiful depictions of our wedding day, and of my ever-growing belly. I was deeply touched, and deeply saddened.

Finally, Grace, with her hair behind her ears and no-nonsense attitude, arrived. She saw my pile of things for the baby and didn't bat an eye at the "daddy" or "uncle" clothing pieces. She just told me to rest easy while she set up the birthing tub. It was green and bulbous and reminded me of that terrible phase when we as a society thought it was a good idea to have blown-up furniture from Spencer's. She hooked a hose from the tub to my washing machine outlet. She said once my contractions got closer to one another, she would start to fill it. The animals looked at me with wonder.

Why was this giant green float in the living room?

Grace pushed all of my furniture out of the way, and sat with me. She quieted down with each contraction, held my hand when I needed, spoke to me in a quiet voice when it was called. We talked about nothing, we talked about spirituality, we talked about the weather. Eventually Nancy showed up to take the pugs out for a walk. She merely winked at me without impeding the whole birthing process.

I had been told that every person added to the mix would slow it down for another hour. I wasn't sure I bought into that, but I was also aware that I was so deep within myself that I probably hadn't even nodded to Nancy.

I started to murmur chants with my eyes closed. I went back and forth between Norse and Sanskrit. Grace had obviously never heard the runic sound before, but said it was beautiful. She joined in with me when I used the more familiar Sanskrit chants.

We had a nice hum going on.

My contractions still weren't that close together, so Grace suggested we go for a walk. She made sure I was comfortable, helped me down the stairs from my porch, and we shuffled down the road to the beach. Once there, though, I couldn't very well walk on the sand with ease, so we just stood at the end of the walkway, breathing in the hot air, feeling the sun on my skin, feeling the salt stick to my face and enter my lungs.

It felt amazing.

We had passed the quiet writer on the way, and it was really the first time I got a close look at him. He was younger than I thought, maybe not even quite fifty. He was stepping out of his car, holding a canvas bag of food. His curly brown and grey haired self turned towards me, and his light blue eyes sparkled a bit as he spoke. "Today the big day?" He asked in a deep, rumbling voice.

Wow. Not what I was expecting. In spite of the state of my mind, I recognized that while he was good looking, his eyes held a tinge of sadness in their depths, mixed in with the sparkle. It piqued the interest of my curious nature, but then a contraction hit.

I tossed up a finger, begging for a moment of his time to wait, then smiled. "Today's the day! And so far, believe it or not, it hurts like a bitch."

He laughed, wished me good luck, and then Grace and I continued our walk to the beach.

Time passed, slowly. Hours passed with not much happening. Just contractions, agonizing pain, then stillness. At some point Gloria had arrived, and her and Grace chatted in low tones while I kept to myself. The animals continued to stay near, but not close.

The midwife and doula had filled up the semi-transparent

tub and told me to sit inside of it. I had no recollection of when they had filled it. The water in the tub was amazing. It calmed me down; felt warm and comforting. It took the pain away. It was so soothing, that in that moment, *for sure*, I knew a water birth was the right decision for me.

Apparently, though, Gloria and Grace were not too pleased with my progression *or* comfort, so they dragged me out of the tub and put me into my bed. My bed was covered in plastic and chux, just begging for the goo of childbirth to explode out of me. My comfort was gone; pain returned, discomfort reigned king. My blood pressure spiked upwards.

Things got a little messy and gross—let's just leave it at that. But it became apparent, after over thirty hours of me laboring, something wasn't right. The baby's blood pressure dipped every time I had a contraction.

Unfortunately, I was headed to the hospital for a transfer. Grace was going to clean things up and make sure the animals were okay while Gloria drove me to the hospital. The hospital was about forty minutes away.

I asked if I could take a quick shower before going, and she was okay with that. Even though the kid appeared to be stuck, it wasn't a major emergency.

And then, *it* happened. That warm water relaxed my body and I just started to scream. The contractions fell on top of one another with no pause. Gloria was encouraged, and told me to push like crazy after I stepped out of the shower. I squatted in a daze—I just wanted this damn thing out of me.

Then a big fat *nope*. The baby was still stuck and not going to come without additional help, so into the car I went.

Everything was a blur. I was mentally drained and physically exhausted. I was dissociated from my body. Things were happening to *her—Violet*. But that wasn't me. I observed. I felt the pain, but that wasn't real.

It finally occurred to me that even though I had put in all

this love and work for this baby, there was sadly no guarantee that the payoff would actually *be* a healthy baby. I was hoping that once I got to the hospital I would be able to relax, but that wasn't the case. Gloria pulled up to the hospital, and patiently waited outside while I screamed one more time in the car. Grace wheeled me into the labor and delivery unit and it was a flurry of chaos. She continued to speak with me in a low murmur, telling me what was happening. I closed my eyes, yet still saw the energetic imprint of all the people.

Gloria arrived about the same time that the doctor came in. The doctor apologized the whole while, as if it were her fault that Amara didn't want to come out. One of the nurses told me how to push, and then when the doctor wasn't quite ready, on how *not* to push. I had heard of that before, nurses or doctors telling the patient not to push.

What a joke.

My body was doing the work without me at that point, so she was nuts to have asked that. The doctor applied a suction cup to the baby's head, and pulled with all her might while I pushed and screamed and apologized for being such a drama queen.

The labor had been quiet until the shower broke something within me.

The nurse on my left ripped my oxygen mask off of me and sat me upright as the doctor was finally able to retrieve my beloved Amara. After the head finally broke loose, it felt like a mile long of this inhuman rubber doll with tentacles being pulled out of me. It was only by hearing the cries of the baby that I realized she was really there, on Earth, with me. I felt comfort in that.

I also fell into a mini-state of shock from the violence of birth.

The nurse smiled at me, and Gloria squeezed my hand,

tears in her eyes. The doctor whisked Amara away, and they started voraciously scrubbing her. I was too tired to protest—the umbilical cord had already been cut in the chaos—again, not what I had intended—but Amara was crying and breathing and looked healthy. They barked out Apgar numbers, but I couldn't care what their significance was.

"She's a girl—did you know that?" asked one of the nurses.

The doctor appeared at my feet, and proclaimed, "I'm *so* sorry. We have to get the placenta out now." And wouldn't you know it? Not only had the baby been stuck, but the placenta was stuck, too."Trust me, you need the drugs for this." I had had no drugs until then, but I decided to listen to the doctor.

Grace whispered, "It's a good thing we transferred your for the birth—we would have had to transfer you anyhow! At least now you can be together."

The placenta eventually came out, and had I not been so exhausted, the looks on Grace's face would have made me laugh. The doctor let me look at the brains that had been feeding the baby. It was wild looking; inexplicable. Disgusting, foreign.

Amara was placed on my chest, asleep, skin to skin. The nurses kept saying how important this was. *Of course*, I thought to myself. *Why wouldn't I want my baby on my skin?*

Gloria encouraged me to breastfeed when she saw Amara rooting around with her dark, alien eyes. It was a weird feeling, this latching on by her tiny little mouth…but then she began to feed. Then she fell asleep. And fed… Then fell asleep.

We all laughed in giddiness. And then it was quiet.

I was alone. They had yet to transfer me to another room, and all machines were turned off. It had been a long night, so Gloria and Grace left me. I was told that Garrett was going to stop by later, as well as Nancy and Gladys.

While sitting partially upright, I held my curly, dark-maroon haired baby, and dozed off.

20

We were home. The dogs thought Amara was *also* a dog so they nibbled on her feet whenever I wasn't looking. Barnaby stayed at her head on the bed most of the time, except when Amara and I were co-sleeping in my bed. I had all sorts of amazing knick-knacks to place her tiny body into when it was bedtime but since she woke me up every two hours for a feeding, I found that sleeping in my bed was the easiest for both of us.

Safety be damned for those who naysaid.

I was in and out of reality and consciousness because I was so tired and scattered. I was damn lucky to have Nancy, Gladys, Gloria, Grace and Garrett keep tabs on me. Hell, even the writer stopped by with gifts and casseroles those first couple of weeks. Since I had to breastfeed so often, I was limited in what I could do. I'd go for a walk up the beach, having her tiny body tucked into a wrap, and then have to feed her when I got there. I'd shuffle the dogs down the street to find somewhere to poop, and we'd have to turn around to head home so she could feed.

I ordered take out a lot, or ate whatever meals the

wonderful people I had met brought me. Gladys came by once a day to allow me the luxury of a steaming hot shower while the baby slept or cooed or pooped on her. Gladys was in love and cooed right back.

As Amara got bigger and I had to feed her less often, everyone started to come around less as they returned to their lives. I began to see each of them maybe once a week, although Gladys came by every day for a cup of tea since she lived so close. Nancy got really busy with work, so she wasn't able to help out with the dogs anymore. She had given me the name of a friend who was a dog walker for a living, and Keith was amazing with the pugs. They seemed like they were starting to love him more than me.

I felt badly for neglecting the fur babies.

Eventually, Amara's naps began to get longer, so I was able to take the baby monitor outside while she slept. Sometimes I'd sit out back by myself with the dogs, and other times I'd go out front, hoping to catch a neighbor on the go.

This is when I became closer with the writer. As it turned out, his name was Morgan and he was from the northeast. His wife had unexpectedly died from a terrible bike accident, and he didn't suppose he would ever stop mourning her. I gave him no specific details about why *I* had ended up alone where I was. He never pushed to find out what had happened. He let me tell him what I was able to tell him, and I did the same for him.

Pretty soon, he became like an uncle to Amara, playing with her, reading to her. Gladys would come by and prophesy that he and I would eventually get together, and I would always sadly tell her no, it wasn't like that. Morgan chose to extend his usual writing schedule deep into the fall and winter months after she was born. Usually he would return to the northeast mid-summer, but he stayed behind that first year, primarily because of the baby.

He asked if he could write a book loosely based off of what he knew about us. It made me uneasy, especially if it would be widely published. Once I saw that all of his author biographies listed his location as New York, I gave him permission. I told him I was heavily amused he thought we'd be good fodder for a novel.

Amara's alien eyes had eventually turned the most amazing shade of green, with gold flecks. Just like Nathan's. Her eyes, however, were shaped like mine. Her bottom lip was pouty like mine, but her upper lip was a perfect cupid's peak like her father's. Her skin tone was the same shade as mine. Her maroon hair eventually turned chocolatey brown, with hints of auburn hiding in the curly mass.

She was simply perfect.

Everyone just loved her.

She'd toddle in front of my house and neighbors on the way home would pull over just to talk to us. The vacationers all came by, too, and Gynnifer, from the previous year, actually played with her quite a bit. Amara's first birthday came and went, with her smushing her blue icing into her face with squeals of laughter in our front yard as everyone stopped by to say hi.

She was old enough, and we were secure enough now, in our lives, that it was time for me to work outside of the house. I had done bodywork, inside of my house, during her naps after she'd turned about six months old. Morgan had also gotten me a part-time job working for an online company. But it was time for me to have an outside location, and get her into a daycare of some sort. I still had some time to kill before I could enter her into a preschool, but luckily for me, Nancy had a friend who did an in-home daycare for really cheap. It was within walking distance of the space I rented to do the bodywork, and the space I rented was just a short bike ride away when the weather was nice.

Life was good.

It was around this time that I traveled to one of my P.O. Boxes to send a letter to Liz and Layla. I sent copies to Elizabeth and the originals to Layla—just in case one of them had moved. I gave them the list of the P.O. Boxes I had, and told them I wouldn't be checking any of them for several months. I told them that since I wasn't sure which one I *would* be checking next or when, they should send responses at their own risks. I told them I would get back to them as soon as I could. I made sure to enclose zero pictures of Amara, which was incredibly difficult.

But I described her in beautiful, vivid detail.

Morgan had ridden with me to the P.O. Box, never questioning why we had to go hours out of our way so I could send two letters to two different addresses.

After Amara turned one, Morgan couldn't put off attending to matters anymore back home, so he left late that summer. It was a good time to part ways, and we missed him terribly when he left. He told us he would keep in touch, and that he would send copies of his book as he finished each chapter. He also promised to be back in his house the following Spring, but if we felt like heading to visit him in the winter, we could visit anytime.

Naturally, I was too afraid to take him up on it.

When Amara was about a year and a half, I retrieved the letter Grayson had sent me at the time of my honeymoon. Inside of the envelope was a yellow string connected to incense. I was to burn the incense and chant certain words until the yellow string burnt out, and from there, I was supposed to concentrate to connect to Grayson. I inhaled the sage scented mix while Amara napped, aggravating Phang and Mina with the smoke. Barnaby glared at me from the couch with his one eye as I waved the smoke to and fro like Grayson's instructions had indicated I should do.

When the string burnt out, I felt a rushing connection happen, and it abruptly stopped inside the deep recesses of my mind where I felt...Grayson himself. *Gray?* I probed hesitantly.

Violet! It worked! I was afraid you'd gotten rid of—

No. I just wanted to wait until she was older—

How are you doing?

I paused. *Very well, actually, but—*

I know. Nathan's been scouring the beaches of Georgia and South Carolina looking for you. We recently sent packages to one of your P.O. Boxes—

Good to know. We'll go within the month to check them out. I paused again. *Is she being hunted?*

Not right now, no. Everyone knows she's been born, but there's no trace on her—or you—you've hidden yourself well. But know that—

There was a crackle, and I was losing my concentration talking to him.

I'm losing the connection. Gray? Grayson? Are you okay?

Know that they'll never get up, especially once she's older—

Can you still sense me? Grayson?

If you see Alexandra, you and Amara need to take caution—she's being watched all the time and—Violet? Violet?

I could still sense him, but he couldn't sense me. The connection was broken.

***

Over the next couple of years, my circle of friends began to shrink as people moved away, or got too busy in their own lives to worry about the single mother at the beach. Gladys and her husband had moved to Florida. Sid and Nancy had moved to Charlotte, gotten married and were pregnant with a child of their own. Garrett and Gloria were busy with their grandchildren and end-of-careers, but I saw the sheriff in his town car on occasion. We also tried to get together every couple of months or so for a potluck.

Mina abandoned Phang, going somewhere into the Great Pug Oblivion that only Mina could know about. Phang initially became depressed, but eventually became my shadow whenever I was home. Barnaby just got older and grouchier.

At about this time is when I found that I had an active, talking two year old. Not only that, but I was about to embark upon an intercontinental flight to Germany with said two year old.

It was late summer, and Morgan was extending his stay at the beach until the following Spring. His book was in editing, and the book he had released after Amara turned one kept him busy with book tours around the country. He made sure when he wasn't touring that he was relaxing at his cottage. He had a very full, busy life, and Amara loved him to pieces whenever he was around.

She called him Uncle Morgan.

He repeatedly told me he would come with me to Germany, and I repeatedly told him it wasn't necessary. He didn't question one iota as to why I was visiting my mother-in-law but not her son, and he drove us to the Charlotte airport, giving us both a kiss as we turned to walk to security. He looked slightly concerned as we walked away, but when I turned to glance back one last time to wave goodbye, he had already disappeared.

Sometimes he seemed more like an angel than a real person.

I was a nervous wreck boarding the plane, and I was dreading my stopover in Atlanta. I quickly found, though, that people were much kinder and not as pissed off at me for bringing a two year old on a plane like I thought they would be. TSA and the flight attendants were actually more than amazing.

Once we were on our last flight, Amara looked out the window, making all sorts of *oohs* and *ahhhhhs* much to the smiles of nearby onlookers. I gave her a piece of dried mango chunks to chew on to help her ears pop, and off we flew into Hamburg. Amara was asleep when we landed, and lethargic as hell when I grabbed our luggage. We popped over onto a train, which mystified the little one as outside whooshed by so quickly. She started to get crabby, and I gave her a sweet treat and brand new story book to play with.

She fell asleep soon thereafter, and an elder gentleman with lilting English spoke quietly with me. He was traveling with his wife who was also asleep. "Taking the wee one on holiday?"

"Something like that," I smiled.

"First time to Sylt?"

"No, actually, I've been here a few times. It's the first time for her, though."

"What's her name?"

I had recently taken to calling her by her middle name. I was afraid Amara would yield too much interest, and I wanted it to be something she would respond to and not question.

"Dawn," I whispered.

"Beautiful name."

"Thank you."

***

It was nighttime when we arrived, and I was starving. I was staying in Keitum, which was not the area Nathan's mother lived in at all. I was slightly terrified of being tracked. Even though my necklace was heavily covered in salt and protected, and Grayson had implied that there was no trace on us, I was still worried about being discovered.

Speaking of being discovered, there was a feeling, deep in my gut, that Grayson was going to show up. Honestly, I was desperate that he would. I was completely comfortable with Alexandra, and I knew Amara would love her. But a part of me selfishly wanted to see Grayson because he would bring me comfort, but also, due to his direct connection to Nathan.

They were brothers.

What could be more connected than that?

The beautiful little cottage-like motel I was staying in was perfect and ready for us. More amazing than that? The woman who checked us in had handed me a delivery menu of food. It was if she could read my mind. She offered a delicious muffin and banana when we checked in, and Amara, strung out on airplane and train food, was all about that whole food banana.

We got into our rooms, and she began to bounce on the bed. She peered in drawers and cabinets as I unpacked our belongings and made a quick call to Morgan. He was happy to hear that we were well and had arrived at our destination. He again offered to make the trip to Germany, but I declined. Although I generally felt like he was an angel, sometimes his attention caused a stir of unease in me.

Amara fell into a soft slumber after a mutual bath we had taken, and she looked like a seraph with her hair falling at her shoulders, her rosy lips slightly parted. I knew I should sleep, too—it was four in the morning—and God only knew what time she would be awake and be ready to roll—but I sat in a chair, looking out the window at the amazing night view.

My phone beeped, and my heart jumped out of my chest.

It was not a number I recognized, but I answered it.

"Hello?" I whispered.

"Do you want to see me?" he asked.

"Are you here?"

"Yes."

I felt my heart race. I drew in a haggard breath before continuing. "Dawn is asleep."

He paused. "Dawn?"

"Dawn."

"Look to your left, if you're sure." I clenched my eyes shut for a beat, then opened them and looked to my left. A shadow of a man was standing in front of some hydrangeas. The lighting was dim, the stars blinking brightly without me. My breath caught as I recognized an oh-so-very identifiable outline, and I heard *his* breath quicken as he hung up. I made sure the door was unlocked as I stepped out.

He came up to me, and stood several feet away. I couldn't raise my head to meet his eyes. He closed the gap, and gently said, "It's okay to look at me, you know. I haven't all of a sudden become a monster to look at."

His attempt at humor was enough for me to be brave and look up and meet his eyes. His hazel eyes were clear, and determinedly set to show no emotion. My eyes, however, held no resolve and instantly teared up.

"Violet," he murmured, trying to convince me it was going to be alright with a single intonation of my name. He reached out to hold me, and I let him. His auburn hair was short, and he was greying more at his temples than from the last time I had seen him. I breathed him in, I breathed in my crazy past, my hopeful future.

He seemed lighter in spirit than before, or at least my three-second assessment told me that. Perhaps the Darkness had finally lost its grip. I wondered if me leaving Nathan had somehow changed him. Maybe it had made him feel more secure in his own life to know that perfect Nathan's life wasn't as all together as it seemed.

My love for Grayson remained, but it was no longer a forbidden love, or a love that had gotten away, or a love that never was. It was a love that was maybe even stronger than what I had with Nathan, because it was a love that allowed my daughter, Amara Dawn, to be seen by him.

He walked into the room and looked at her.

He inhaled her soul, his nostrils slightly flaring at the sight of her. I closed the door behind us and made sure the blinds had snapped shut, too.

"When did you get in?"

"Yesterday."

"Does Alexandra know you're here?"

"Yes… After you contacted *me*, I contacted *her* and she told me the general time of your arrival. I hope you aren't angry with her… But I can offer protection that she can't."

"I know," I said quietly. "I'm not mad. I'm also not surprised. I had a feeling you'd be here."

He hesitantly smiled. "Nathan—"

"I know he doesn't know. And my heart breaks every time I…" I broke off, staring at my hands folded in my lap. Grayson pulled his chair up to me, and grabbed my chin.

"You don't have to do it this way, Violet. You know that."

"But…"

"But," he sighed. "I unfortunately continue to agree with you, and although Alexandra will never admit it, she does too."

"So… There's that."

"There's that."

I yawned. He nodded at the bed where my angel slept, and approached her.

"What are her gifts?"

I wrapped my sweater around myself and slowly made my way to the bed. I leaned down and pulled her hair back behind her ear and she grumbled. I turned back to Grayson. "I'm not sure. I'm not going to keep anything from her, but I certainly haven't encouraged anything, either."

"You're lying," he said quietly.

I didn't say anything. I wouldn't even let the thought enter my mind.

"Grayson… I can't go there. It's just too…"

He paused, turning towards me.

"Go get some rest. The sun will be up soon."

"Will you stay?"

"And sit uncomfortably in a chair the rest of the night?" He laughed. "Of course."

I pulled out a chaise lounge that had been hiding in the corner and threw some sheets on it. "Amara—I mean, Dawn —knows her Uncle Gray may be here, so she will not be surprised finding you sleeping over there when she wakes up. Now go to sleep yourself."

I grabbed him in a quick hug before sliding in next to my daughter, falling into a darkness of pure exhaustion before my head even hit the pillow. I didn't even see if Grayson had moved towards the lounge or not.

21

I woke up the following morning to the sound of toddler babble, and a wet pillow underneath my head. I smacked my lips together and wiped drool off my face. I rolled onto my back and stretched out from head to toe as I yawned. "Mama, up!" Amara excitedly said to me, staring at Grayson for the first time. "Mama, up!"

I sat up and rubbed my eyes, trying to straighten out my pony-tail. I saw Amara tugging on Grayson's hand. "Amara, it's okay. I Know Grayson is here," I sleepily said.

"Uncky Graysh!"

I smiled, trying to pull my eyes apart from the glue that wanted to keep them shut. "Yes. Uncky Graysh."

He looked over at me, a five o'clock shadow clearly visible, one that I hadn't noticed just a few hours before. Amara climbed onto his chest and started to touch his face. He laughed, and then she covered her nose and said, "Stinky breath, Uncky!"

We both laughed. "Come here, Dawn, let me change your diaper."

"Pull-up, Uncky. Me have pull-up." She was indignant.

I changed her pull-up and cut up apple slices for her to eat while Grayson started up some coffee. I yawned while opening the blinds, and looked out the window. I curiously found myself looking upon people dressed up in 18th Century garb. Amara was happily chewing on her apple watching *Cookie Monster* in German as I continued to look out the window.

"What are those people doing?" I inquired.

Grayson handed me a cup of coffee as his gaze followed mine. "It's something they do here, reenactments. This bunch is probably going to some festival, and they just dressed up for the part. They're not locals—see? They're leaving the hotel." The women in their dirndls and crazy pom-pommed hats were followed by men in lederhosen or vests. They somehow managed to stuff themselves like clowns into several cars before departing the hotel.

I sipped the coffee, and let the blinds snap close.

"Do you think it is safe to see Alexandra today?"

"Tomorrow, Mommy."

"I—what?" I was shocked. I thought she was watching her show. Grayson and I both turned to look at the kid sitting in front of the television. Her back was to us.

Grayson raised an eyebrow. "Why's that, Am—Dawn?"

"Bad men." She pointed at Cookie Monster and screamed in delight, "Leibkucken!"

"Dawn, who told you there were bad men?" I walked over to her, demanding attention.

"Grandma. She told me. In my head." She pointed to her head, squealing with laughter as Cookie Monster smashed cookie bits into his face.

My mouth dropped open and fully stunned, I whispered, "Mental telepathy. I wonder how far it reaches?"

Grayson kneeled in front of Dawn and asked her. "*When did she tell you?*"

"When the sun woke up."

"Have you heard her voice before?"

She looked at him with curiosity, and reached her tiny hand out and touched his face, holding his cheek in her palm. "Just today." So matter of fact.

He stood back up, and I walked next to him. I hesitated. "Are you sure it was Grandma?"

"Yes, mama. She said come moomorrow. Can we have pancakes now?"

I looked to Grayson and asked, "Is it even safe for us to go out to eat?"

Grayson wandered over to the closet, reaching for a bag he'd placed up high out of reach. "In short—I never got another firefighting job. I joined a private security firm. I'll take this extra protection with us."

My mouth gaped open as he put the gun into a concealed holster on his hip. Sure—I had been around magical weapons of sorts, but I had never been around weapons that harnessed the power of a *bullet*. It made me extremely uncomfortable. "Grayson—"

"You can't always fight with peace and love, Violet. You know that. Have you forgotten the last time we were here together?" He sighed, reaching out, taking my chin, forcing me to meet his eyes. He held my gaze for a long moment, and the horrific memories of the last time we were in Sylt came crashing into the forefront of my mind.

When a group of people had taken to beating the piss out of Nathan to get their hands on information, Grayson had channeled the Darkest manifestations I had ever witnessed to help us win the fight. I had such terrible injuries that Nathan's powers of healing weren't able to help mend me as quickly as his norm. Of course, he had almost been killed... It was really a wonder we had walked away as put-together as we had.

I swallowed loudly and forcefully turned away. "Where can we go eat?"

"There's a place we can walk to."

***

In ways, it was totally surreal walking around Keitum with Grayson at my side as my daughter chased butterflies and seagulls. In other ways, it felt perfectly normal. And yet in even other ways, it was devastating it was Grayson, and not Nathan.

"Mama," she suddenly turned and walked back over to us.

"Yeah?" I asked warily, wondering why the sudden seriousness.

"Gramma just talk me."

I scooped her up, placing her on my hip as the breeze gently carried her hair off of her face. I looked to Grayson, and he put himself on high alert. "What did she say?"

"Safe to come now, not moomorrow." Innocent.

I raised an eyebrow to Grayson, and he shrugged. "Do we really continue to trust the two year old?"

She haughtily put her hands on her hips and said, "Ma-maaa. You trust me."

This is how I found myself inside the rental car with Grayson in the passenger seat and Amara carefully latched into a carseat. The drive of long, curving roads to where Amara's grandmother lived was not particularly lengthy. The landscape was beautiful. We passed by serious shades of green on one side of the road, and pristine beaches far below the other side. We drove through little towns, houses with thatched roofs, long wooden walkways down to the ocean, signs for cafes, bars, hiking.

I pulled into her cottage driveway, suddenly feeling very unsure of myself. Seeing Grayson was one thing—in spite of our past, I felt safe with him. I felt like he could protect us if needed, I felt like he was a single entity who couldn't hurt us.

Extending my daughter to Alexandra was a whole other step, one that would change everything. Not only would it be another person from my past knowing my daughter, but it was also clinching an unspoken agreement of sorts that we would *continue* to keep this beautiful little girl from her father.

I was just about to say how I couldn't do this when Alexandra rushed outside of her front glass door, wearing long, linen pants and a white tunic. "Oh! Mein Schätze!"

I looked over to Grayson, and he gave a short, small smile before opening the door. "Hi Mom," I heard him say as I busied myself with Amara's seatbelt, muttering. Alexandra opened up the backdoor of the car, and reached her arms out for the baby. Amara willingly and happily went, as if they already were old friends.

I awkwardly walked over to Grayson. He glanced back to me as Alexandra fussed at Amara. I grasped for his hand, clinging to his fingers. They felt safe; solid. Alexandra put Amara on her hip, turning back to us all smiles. Amara opened up her little arms for a group hug, and we all obliged, me fighting back tears.

Slightly shaky, I pulled back, still holding onto Grayson. "Please call her Dawn. Just to be safe."

"Of course!" Alexandra continued to dote on her grandchild as she let us inside. She hadn't changed a thing, the cottage looked as open and as inviting as ever. "Grab yourselves something to drink and come back into the den. We have a lot to discuss." She dumped a basket full of toys out for Amara onto the floor without another glance towards us. I was in shock.

Grayson grabbed my elbow and turned me towards the kitchen. I could hear Alexandra and my daughter chattering in the background.

"Do you know what she wants to talk about?" I asked, still

shaky.

"Nope. But do you want some tea?" He asked, rummaging through her cupboard. He seemed comfortable at her house now, and that made me feel an inkling of satisfaction. The last time he and I had been there together, he had been an outsider of his own making. It was apparent that he had visited her during the years we had been apart.

I stifled a laugh. "Sure, tea sounds great."

"What?" he asked, half a smile etched into his face.

"It seems unlikely that we would be in a situation so normal as you asking me what type of tea I'd like."

A full smile flashed across his face before he turned away. "I feel like we've had discussion about this in the past."

"Ha—that's for sure."

I stood next to him as the tea kettle heated up. "I also remember that morning here with you—" he started, but I stopped him, blocking him with my hand from speaking any further.

"Not going there, Grayson." I bit my lip.

"Sure," he lazily responded, turning his back to me again as he began to pour the tea.

That was most definitely a conversation I was *not* interested in having, especially as I was *married* to his brother, still in love with his brother, and of course, had a child with his brother. Even so, a flash of his naked body egregiously entered my mind before I could stop it.

***

Amara was asleep in Alexandra's arms on the couch, and Grayson was snoozing on a recliner, his legs stretched out in front of him. I was leaning up against the recliner with my arms crossed, touching Grayson's legs, rather comfortably.

"Strange, isn't it," she stated, rather than asked. "It's almost as if you three were the family, and not you, Dawn and Nathan."

I closed my eyes, squeezing them tightly. "I miss him so much," I whispered.

"I know," she said lightly, and not judging.

"Why hasn't he been able to find me?" I opened my eyes and looked at her.

She looked down at Amara, brushing the hair off of her face. "Whether you intended to or not, you've put impenetrable protective barriers around you two." She looked over at Grayson. "To everyone, but Grayson and I. We can sense more or less where you are located, but to Nathan, and everyone else, they could drive right through your town and have no idea you were there. It's as if..." She trailed off.

"As if he can't pierce the bubble." I sighed. "Well. That's good to know. And feel terrible about."

"It's okay, mein liebling."

"No, it's not. He should be raising his daughter."

"All I meant was, is that he understands. But he will never quit looking for you. If you should ever let your guard down with him, he will find you."

"Considering I'm not even sure how I have my guard up, I guess I have to wait and see what happens. But I'm happy that all the precautions I feel like I'm taking are keeping her safe from everyone else. Because if I let it down for him, I'm assuming everyone else can get in, too."

"I think it's safe to assume that, yes." She seemed to choose her next words carefully. "There's been another prophecy." She let out a long sigh. "Interested parties have not forgotten you."

I sat up erect, and Grayson stirred to being fully awake, too. "What do you mean?" growled Grayson, clearing his throat. "You didn't tell me—"

"Grayson, calm down," she said. "You, nor Nathan, know everything there is to know about these things, and you cannot pretend that you do. *Yes*, I keep secrets. It's to protect you all. And you should not judge me anymore than you *do not* judge Violet about what's going on between her and Nathan." She smiled motherly at me. "No offense."

I shrugged. "So about the prophecy…"

"It was uttered to me in the darkness of the night. I am not aware that the person who uttered it knows he said it."

"He? Who is *he*?" asked Grayson crisply.

She pressed her lips together. "Nathan."

"What!" I exclaimed, jumping up, frustrated and surprised. What *couldn't* this family do? "When did you guys start prophesying? I didn't think that was one of the gifts this family had!" I looked from Grayson to Alexandra.

"We come from a long line of seers, Violet. I'm not named Alexandra by accident. It's just that I had never prophesied anything of this importance. None of us have. Until now."

"Well, what did he say? Or write?" Grayson pulled me to his side as we faced off with his mom, his mom who was still seated, cradling my baby.

"If you recall, the English translation of the last part of the prophecy was *or else All shall perish. If The Bullet is dislodged upon her Own Accord, Great Peace shall be bestowed at Her Behest. Or, Darkness will permeate Light, and the Conclusive War is fought.*"

"Right, and everyone gave those stupid words meaning and now Ama—Dawn, *The Bullet*, will bring forth a battle that will give total control to either side."

"The battle for control will never fade, Violet. You understand this is the continuous struggle throughout all times, even without our own personal stories within the struggle. And while sometimes it's cut and clear who is right, or wrong, other times it simply is not."

"Yes, I get that, but—"

"And remember, these are translations from words spoken from a man who wasn't even aware of what he was saying—

he never wrote anything down—he was channeling Old Norse."

Grayson cleared his throat, interrupting, "Mom, what the hell did Nathan say?"

She paused, folded her hands in her lap and recited, "*The Bullet and The Arrow meet. Until after time passes, a one-time defeat.*"

I slumped back down onto the floor. "Fantastic."

Grayson squatted in front of Alexandra and looked at Amara. "That's it? That doesn't really mean much, to be honest."

"There's more."

"And?"

"*But shall they join, Thurisaz.* Translation not needed there."

Grayson growled, I hushed him. "The baby," I furiously whispered. "Don't wake her!"

He hissed at his mother, "We are just pawns in this mess! *Always* pawns. It never ends. One generation after the next after the next after the—"

"Yet we must keep trying, son. Love is worth the fight. The fight, for us, is worth it, even if others know nothing about our endeavors. We are protectors of the people."

I tiredly ran my fingers through my hair. "So this *Arrow* is another person. It could be anyone at any time." I grimly looked at Alexandra, "So basically... I can't let her have any friends or they'll consume existence with chaos. She needs to be locked up like Rapunzel."

"Now, Violet—" Alexandra began, but I continued.

"We have the upper hand, I get it. Nobody else knows about *The Arrow*." I stretched out my legs. "I'm only kidding about locking her up in a tower." I sheepishly smiled.

"Theoretically, couldn't someone else prophesize about this, too?" Grayson sat back down into the chair, glancing between the two of us. I placed my hand on his knee, trying to help him keep his cool.

Alexandra shook her head. "I don't think that it works that way, but I may be wrong. I do not believe prophecies happen so often. This is why they are so powerful and highly sought after to control. Again, it's simply a way to control fate. But —"

"Free will or not, if you fight fate, you acquire *more* problems. Yeah, I know. It's best to flow."

Grayson bitterly laughed. "Best to flow. Sure."

"Just keep doing what you're doing, Violet. Guide her, protect her, love her. I have great faith in her *and* you. Dawn is manifestation of pure joy, pure light, pure love. You will continue to do wonderful things for her. Your sacrifices are for the greater good."

I started to feel panicky, and removed my hand from Grayson's leg. "You said you and Grayson could essentially see where I am hiding her. You two can't *ever* come visit us— you just *can't*."

"We will not, will we, Grayson?" She shot him a sharp look.

He refused to look at her at first. "What?" I asked, my voice high pitched.

He finally met her eyes. "I promise, I won't." He said softly.

I had a feeling someone had a vision about something concerning me and Grayson, but they likely weren't going to share it with me. I didn't need to be psychic to trust my intuition about whatever fantasy Grayson had probably concocted in his mind. And of course, having him around would be...but... This was for me to do alone.

I leaned back against Grayson and the recliner, shutting my eyes again. "It's settled. Only I will contact *you* when it's time for a visit."

22

A couple of years more or less peacefully passed. Amara was in preschool full-time, and I had focused on my bodywork business, making decent money between that and my online work. Morgan had finally moved away for good; it had gotten to be too much for him to keep up with his multiple residences. He moved up north and stayed, always offering us a place to crash if we visited the city.

Amara's preschool friends' families would venture to Disney World, or other theme parks nearby, but I was too hesitant to let her too far from our protective bubble. I didn't have any real fear that someone would attempt to kidnap her —that wasn't it. I really just didn't want anyone to make contact with us. I was hoping our absence would make them forget.

I knew, however, that that peace wouldn't last forever and I was going to have to let her venture out of our safe little haven. I made a couple of friends in the energy world—other bodyworkers, owners of a couple of yoga studios. All were just on the fringe of magic, just grazing right up next to it without really realizing it was truly there.

As it turned out, it was really no different than it had been in Georgia. People were essentially the same anywhere. We all had our similar wants and dreams, our similar fears and dislikes.

I started sharing space with a woman named Kassidy who was roughly my age and very similar in personality and style. She had two children, one daughter and one son who were both a few years older than Amara. Luckily the kids all got along well together and they became a pseudo-second family to us. Kassidy was a go-to in a pinch, and vice versa. While she was married, her husband worked long hours and night shifts. We fulfilled the empty spaces we each carried with us.

At certain times throughout the years, she and her husband would try to set me up with some of his co-workers. Every time I had to fight hard to get them off of my back. Eventually they stopped trying to set me up, and let me do my own thing.

After Barnaby and Phang eventually passed, Amara and I got lonely. We adopted a german shepherd named Malcolm, and Kassidy and her kids were the ones who were going to take care of him while we flitted off to Germany.

"I don't understand, Vi," she had said, petting Malcolm on the head as he lied down and looked at her with his soulful eyes. "You guys never go *anywhere* outside of our bubble—I can't even get you to run into Virginia Beach with me most of the time. Yet somehow, at the moment, the exact moment Amara turns 5, you're taking off to *Germany* of all places? To see her *grandmother*? Why haven't I ever heard—"

"It's for the best. I promise. It's not safe to share—"

"Yes. I know, Violet. You're in hiding. I get it. And I've never *asked* you to share more than what you've felt comfortable or safe enough to share—but—*Germany!* I can't even!" She threw her hands up in exasperation.

"Let's go. We've got this couples' massage we need to get

to." Her long, curly, dark red hair bounced as I tried to playfully push her.

"You're not going to meet some dark, romantic lover I know nothing about, are you?"

"Ha! If only."

She narrowed her eyes at me as we walked down my steps. "What's Amara's father's name again? Nathan?"

I glared at her and marched on ahead. "Let's go!"

"Fine," she said mournfully behind me. "You know all it will take is a tequila or two and I will get you to secret spill *allll* over the place!"

***

Amara was running around the fire pit chasing Alexandra's cat, Juni. It was the three of us, and as Amara *was* five years old, she was extremely aware of what was going on. My guess was Alexandra had reached out to Amara as soon as we landed in Germany. That answered *that* question from years prior—Amara had to be relatively close to her telepathic counterpart for it to work.

"She's got much power, many gifts," mused Alexandra. As I looked closely at her, I realized that perhaps Alexandra's health was starting to dwindle.

"Are you doing well, Alexandra? You look frail."

"Nothing to worry about, meine Geliebte. I'm not moving on anytime soon."

But I gave pause to worry anyway.

We stood watching Amara, and she suddenly stopped mid-stride and yelped, "Mommy!"

I rushed over to her, Alexandra hot on my heels. "What, honey?" I asked.

She turned to me, and then froze, her eyes clouding over and her face expressionless. "Alexandra?" I asked, voice up an octave.

"It's a vision," Alexandra whispered, moving up next to

me.

I kneeled before Amara, clasping her hands, trying not to shake while she looked so distant. "Mommy," she said calmly.

"I'm right here, Dawn, what is it?" I managed to choke out, pretending the calm that I wasn't.

"In my head... I see... I see a man... *Daddy*," she said with certainty. She looked up to her grandmother who nodded in response, yet pursing her lips, not offering up whatever secrets she kept. *How did she know what her father looked like?* I had deliberately kept pictures of him away from her, afraid she may run up to him if she ever saw him. "And Daddy is next to a stone. A stone with writing on it. I can't read the words, though," she pouted.

In spite of everything, I had to laugh. It was funny when she got pissed off at not being able to read yet. "And you are sure that it's Daddy?"

"Yes. And he's *really* sad, Mommy. He looks older. He's holding a hand. Yours?"

Alexandra shrugged her shoulders at me. I picked up Amara and tried not to sweat about it. "Come on, honey, let's go inside."

Alexandra followed us into her house, with Juni racing ahead of us through the sliding glass doors. "Is this the first time you've ever seen anything like that? Something in your head that wasn't being seen with your eyes?"

"Just once, mommy." She took the juice box I handed to her and began to sip it, her feet dangling off the chair as I moved her closer to the kitchen table.

Alexandra sat opposite of her at the table, her long hair piled into a loose bun at the nape of her neck. It was almost fully grey hair at this point, with very few dark chocolate strands intermittently remaining. I really looked at Alexandra, long and hard at that moment. She *did* look frail, I thought. She had really aged since the last time I had seen her. More grey hair, deeper wrinkles, and just not as full of vigor as usual. Tired.

"What happened in the vision?"

"It was you and Uncle Grayson."

My eyebrows about popped off my face. "How long ago?"

"Ohhh, mmm, I don't know? Weeks and years?"

Damn five year olds and their sense of time.

"What were they doing, Dawn?" asked Alexandra.

"They were walking in a park, and I was riding my bike. It was warm and I saw a snake on the path and got scared."

"How old were you?"

"Oh, mommy, you're silly." She sipped her juice, and I bit my lip.

Alexandra smiled. "Psychic five year olds. Who would have thunk it?"

I plopped down on the third chair, and begrudgingly agreed. "Well, I guess I'll be seeing Grayson at some point."

***

When we returned home, Kassidy picked us up, grabbing Amara's bags while I grabbed mine. When she pulled into the driveway, Amara made a big point to show Kassidy what a big girl she was by bringing in one of her backpacks on her own. It seemed like it was a little heavy for her to carry, but she was insistent about carrying it. She ran into her room and slammed the door shut as she unpacked. I figured I'd follow up about the whole thing later.

Kassidy looked at me with questions in her eyes. "I have no idea," I said as I slumped down onto my couch, with my the bags at my feet.

I reached over into one of my smaller bags, and pulled out a small wrapped gift for Kassidy. "Yay!" she exclaimed. "Presents!"

I rolled my eyes. "Of course I brought you something. Hey,

Dawn—get your butt out here and see Kass open up her gift!"

"Coming, Mom!" Amara said as she left her room, running into the living room, tripping over Malcolm. "Malcolm!"

"He's happy to see you, honey."

He licked her face.

"Mommy."

"Yeah?"

"Malcolm was there with the snake, too."

I looked at Kassidy and laughed uncomfortably. "A dream she had."

"Not a dream, mama, you know that. I—"

"Hush."

Kassidy started to look confused, so I gestured for her to open up the gift. Amara sat on my lap, and in my mind I was thinking about how I was going to need to start covering up Amara's undeveloped gifts. "Oh my gosh, you guys, it's *beautiful!*"

She pulled out a lovely, ornate necklace designed by a local artisan we had found in Keitum. It had tiny orange and green stones meshed into a silver hand-designed angel. She took the silver strand and tied it around her neck. "Oh, thank you so much."

"I'm happy you like it."

She gave me a big hug, kissed Amara on the cheek and said, "We will catch up later. I know you two are pooped! I already have *Moana* in your DVD player ready for you two to watch tonight. And..."

As if on cue, someone knocked at the door. "I've got a pizza entering your house right now so you two can eat something."

"Kassidy. You're amazing."

She opened the door to the pizza guy, did a curtsy and said, "I know."

She moved my bags to an opposing wall, opened up the pizza box for us, turned the TV on and left.

After we ate, Amara stretched out and said, "Mommy, I'm tired." She closed her eyes, and I found that I watched the rest of Moana by myself. After I turned off the TV, I got Amara into bed and then collapsed into my own bed, fully dressed. Malcolm leaped up after me with a low whine as I fell quickly asleep.

***

The weekend before Amara started kindergarten, I felt compelled to go inland for the day to go shopping for some school things. Amara was used to me exchanging license plates just outside of town, so she didn't question it as I did it. There. We were from Kentucky now.

Once we arrived at our intended destination of an indoor mall, I got the feeling that we were being watched. I hadn't used any of my *own* supernatural gifts in eons, so I was slightly surprised to be sensing someone's energy from across the way. I didn't think the person was a foe, though, but she or he was definitely watching us. I wasn't sure if the person was connected to that world or not, or perhaps, someone literally just watching us.

Any which way, it had me on edge, wondering if I was being too lax in my travels.

We went into the center of the mall to order vegetables and rice from a Chinese restaurant. "This is mmmmmmm good, Mommy." She said as she fumbled with her chopsticks. Her chocolate hair was pulled into a ponytail, and all of a sudden she paused mid-bite, looking behind me.

"What, baby?"

"Someone in a hat is watching us." Her voice got excited.

"Behind me?"

"Yes."

"Okay. Do exactly as I say, okay? Like we talked about?"

"Yes, Mama."

"Put your chopsticks down. Scoot your chair back and put on your coat, okay? Don't look at the person in the hat, look at me the *whole* time, okay? Can you do that?"

"Yes, Mama. But—"

"Please just listen to me," I desperately said, trying to remain calm as I stood up, grabbing my coat and pleading with her by my eyes.

But I was too late, because as I grabbed my bag, still making eye contact with Amara, I heard a man hiss at me. "Sit back down, you can't be seen, I'm grabbing lunch and I'm going to eat here with you. You're safe."

Amara had a huge grin on her face, still with her chopsticks in her hand. "Can I look at him now, Mama?"

My hammering heart had jumped out of my body when I heard the voice, and I replied, "Okay, but then look right back at me."

I sat back down and rifled through my bag as if I was looking for something and heard Amara's little voice squeak out in excitement, "Uncle Grayson!"

"Hey, kiddo. Keep eating, I'll be back," and he walked away towards the same Chinese place we had grabbed food.

Amara happily scooped some food into her mouth, grinning wildly as I warily watched Grayson's back walk towards the food. *How had he found me? What did he mean by I couldn't be seen?*

My appetite was long gone as I anxiously tapped my fingers on the faux wooden tabletop awaiting Grayson's return. "Mommy," scolded Amara. "You aren't eating." She put her hands on her hips. I took a sip of my tea and smiled.

"You're right. But I'm anxious to talk with Grayson. I haven't seen him in…"

"Years. I know, Mommy. Do you miss him? And Daddy?"

I looked back at her, my brow furrowing. "Of course," I

said softly.

Grayson came back and sat perpendicular to us, facing into the mall whereas she and I had been facing opposite ends of the food court. "Ladies. I am super happy to see you both. How are you?" He looked straight ahead as he spoke with us, and Amara looked at me in confusion.

"Honey, if he looks at us while he talks to us he may appear as a crazy person. Somehow we're invisible?"

For just a moment his eyes made full eye contact with mine, and my heart skipped a beat. Even though it had been several years since I had last seen him, he was aging like a fine wine. *Damn he's still so good looking.* Inward grown. *But haunted. His eyes...* "Not to everyone," he smirked.

I casually stuck out my tongue. "What are you doing here?"

He ignored my question and responded instead, "You haven't written any of us in awhile. Why is that?"

I took another sip of my tea and Amara said, "Yeah, Mommy. I've got drawings to send to Daddy and Grayson and Grandma and what's her name? Auntie Elsa—"

"Not Elsa, Elizabeth."

"Yeah, her." She stuffed more food into her mouth, looking at me with wide eyes.

"Honestly—we've just been busy. Nothing insidious. I promise. We're fine. And apparently mostly invisible." I glanced over at him, then quickly looked into my food.

"We're worried about you. You've got to do better—"

I raised my eyes to his. "Grayson. We *just* saw Alexandra a couple of months ago! And beside—it's not that easy. I've got a double life going on. Have you ever even considered what that's like?"

He raised an eyebrow then looked into the distance. "Yeah, I do actually know something about that."

I looked up again, this time my gaze behind Amara and

froze. I felt like I've been punched in the stomach, and my hands went to my face in fear. "What is *he* doing here?" I barely managed to gasp out.

Grayson slowly looked to his left, as if wading in water; luckily Amara had gotten bored with our conversation and was swirling her noodles on her plate. "Dammit," he cursed. "I can't believe he came back in here. You're safe, Violet, I promise. Just be calm and he won't pierce the veil. He thinks I'm alone."

Nathan. Oh my Gods, Goddesses, Thors and Lokis, *it was Nathan. In. Real. Life.* He looked taller than I remembered, and thinner. His hair was long, curling at his ears. He was only about five hundred feet away from me. I felt my aura start to reach out to his, and I couldn't stop it. Grayson hissed at me to cease all extension, but I couldn't.

I had never felt so drawn to anything or anyone as I did to Nathan—not even Amara. In horror, I felt the connection between us spark to life. He had stopped outside of a Starbucks, shaking hands with someone he had run into. The man departed, heading out of the mall, and Nathan, with his hands in his dark jean pockets—I'm sorry, it had been awhile, and *boy* did he fill out those jeans well—slowly turned to face Grayson. Grayson casually waved at him in greeting.

There was a pause; I stopped breathing entirely as destiny hung in the balance. Amara had stopped playing with her noodles and looked at me curiously. Nathan's demeanor changed, and he put his hand to his heart, almost as if in pain. Amara slowly began to swivel her head around towards him and I silently bellowed at her *NO NO NO!* Amara looked shocked as she stared at me—I had a feeling she had heard me. Nathan half-waved at Grayson, one hand remaining in his pocket and the other still at his chest. He furrowed his brow a bit, shook his head as if to shake out cobwebs, and as Grayson looked back into his plate, stepped inside the

Starbucks.

The world came crashing back down in a cacophony of chaos. I began to panic. "Oh my God, we've got to get out of here, Dawn!" I half-stood until Grayson kicked the chair.

"Sit down, Violet. You are safe. I've got him blocked from coming over here, too, and it will work as long as you *stay calm.*"

"Mommy? Bad men?" Amara looked alert, finally dropping her chopsticks.

"No… A good man. A very good man," I dully said into my food, heart pounding.

Grayson carefully placed his hand on my hand as it nervously tapped the table, yet again. "Violet. I promise. He cannot see you. He sees me sitting alone."

"He knows I'm here," I whispered.

Grayson squeezed my hand, then placed it back on his lap. "It doesn't matter. He may sense something's off, but he won't be able to figure it out."

Nathan walked back out of the coffee shop with his cup in hand, and again waved at Grayson. A lone tear slipped from each eye as they followed his backside as he left the mall. He half-turned one more time, the black sleeve hugging his tattooed arm—it appeared he had gotten new tattoos since I'd last seen him—and his eyes literally met mine, green with hazel flecks on blue. As he looked through me, I felt another tear try to escape, but I wouldn't let it.

Yet again, I was without him.

Amara and Grayson were both finished eating, and I assumed I would never be hungry again, so we decided it was time to leave. Grayson grabbed Amara's plate, put the cover back on mine, and said, "Come on. You guys can ride with me. I'll take you back to my hotel where we'll be safe to talk. I assume your car is nearby?"

"Yes," I said, looking into my hands. "We can go with you.

We have some time."

As we gathered our belongings and began to walk out, I said, "Wait. She needs a car seat."

"I have one," he said.

He held the door open for us, me holding Amara's hand as she skipped next to me, and his hazel eyes meeting mine without hesitation.

"You have a child?" I asked, shocked.

The door closed and he put his arm lightly around my shoulder, and whispered in my ear, causing me to shiver slightly. "No. I have a car seat. I knew you were coming."

23

"Grandma!" exclaimed Amara as soon as we entered Grayson's room, or, as it turned out, Alexandra's room.

"What is going on here?" I asked, hands wrapped tightly around myself, feeling uncertain. "Family reunion?"

"Did she see Nathan?" asked Alexandra, ignoring me completely as she squeezed the hell out of a super happy Amara.

"Yeah," Grayson half-growled. "He must have felt the pull at the mall. He was supposed to be heading back to his room but he came inside to grab a coffee. Is he supposed to see you again before he leaves?"

"No, we already said our goodbyes. I made sure of it for you and Violet." She raised an eyebrow.

He crossed his arms across his chest and said, "Mom, stop it. Don't imply—"

"I'm implying nothing. Fate is never written until time has passed."

"Um, would you guys stop talking *around* me and tell me what's going on?"

Alexandra released Amara and came up to me and gave

me a hug. "After our last visit, I caught a glimpse of you with Grayson. I knew I had an opportunity to seek you out stateside. As it turns out," she continued, gesturing to a bag full of surprises for Amara, "The boys already were going to be here anyway, so I assumed this is where we would find you."

Amara pulled out several presents, and looked at me, grinning. "Can I open them, Mommy?"

"Of course."

While she immersed herself in Bluey and Little Mermaid toys, and Alexandra played with her, Grayson and I sat at a table crammed in the corner of the room. "Why were you meeting Nathan here?"

"I wasn't. *He* had a meeting about, well, *you*, with his superiors, and I just wanted to know what bullshit they were going to feed him, so I joined in." He smirked, sarcastically saying, "Hilarious how you're right under their noses and they have no idea."

"How did you know I'd be safe?"

"Just a hunch."

"Pretty big risk, for 'just a hunch'."

"We'd love for you guys to stay the night," interjected Alexandra. I hadn't known she was listening.

"I have a dog back home." I called to her.

"I'm sure one of your friends will watch him," said Grayson.

"Nathan's still here? What about the government goons?"

"They're not staying at this hotel, and like I said, I already said goodbye to Nathan." Alexandra turned to Amara again.

"What about you, Grayson?"

He shrugged, and looked out the window, pausing for a beat. "Whatever you want, Violet." I saw the clench in his jaw as he looked away from me; I saw how close his hand was to mine. I felt the heat that remained. In spite of time. In spite of everything.

I just didn't want to deal with it. Any of it. There were so many reasons why I had left. Seeing Grayson years ago had been a comfort, a blessing. This felt much more dangerous. Multi-level dangerous.

Unfortunately, Amara had been listening in more than I had given *her* credit. She came up to me, and hugged my leg while holding one of her new dolls. "Please, Mommy? Let me stay with Grandma!"

I looked at my watch, my knee beginning to jump. It was already late afternoon, much later than I had intended to stay. I didn't have to work the following day; it was a Saturday. I sighed, and grabbed my phone out of my pocket, searching for Kassidy's name in my contacts.

I stepped outside to ask if she'd watch Malcolm, and she of course, agreed. When I came back inside, Amara was practically bouncing off of the walls. "Mommy! Let's go for a bike ride, you brought it, remember? Let's go to that park so I can show Grayson and Grandma how good I am."

Alexandra smiled, and I rolled my eyes. "The damn vision."

"The vision."

Grayson perked up. "There's a lovely park nearby," continued Alexandra.

"Dawn had a vision about this in Sylt."

"She did, did she?" He laughed, and held the door open for all of us as we walked out. I glanced back at him, narrowing my eyes, as we all piled into *his* car to go back to the mall to get *my* car because it had the bike in it.

"How did I get so lucky to get involved with a bunch of vision-having nut jobs?"

"Mommy, don't say that word."

"Sorry, honey."

***

After we came across the snake from her vision, and Amara was in Grayson's arms as I pushed her bike along the path, it was decided that it was time to order pizza back at the hotel. I pulled into the parking lot with Amara in her carseat, tired and almost asleep.

"Honey, wake up. We're getting pizza, remember?"

As we ate the pizza, Amara asked us all a question. "Malcolm wasn't with the snake like before. How come?"

I looked to Alexandra to answer the question; I still wasn't entirely sure how visions worked. "Oh, meine Liebe, at some point your mother chose not to bring him with you, to keep him at home. That was a vision, not a memory. Always remember the difference."

Amara did her best to raise her eyebrows at me, but it looked silly on a five year old, so I laughed. "I'm learning as you learn, baby."

Alexandra demanded we stay in her room and not get our own, so I grabbed my bag of just-in-case-items. Due to my paranoia, I always had a bag of clothes packed in our car, with a stash of money, just in case. Grayson came through the adjoining room to share dinner with us. I got Amara ready for bed, and once she settled in with her cartoons, her eyes instantly closed.

Alexandra announced that she was going to turn in for the night herself, and so Grayson stood up to return to his room. I shook my head, grabbed the rest of the beers and followed him into his room after kissing Amara on the head. "Not that easy," I said, closing the door between the rooms half-way. "You've still got to tell me what they said to Nathan about us."

Grayson opened up two more beers for us, and stood dangerously close to me as he said, "To Amara." I looked up at him, not flinching, repeating what he said, and took a long swig of my beer.

They call it liquid courage, but it's really liquid stupidity when your inhibitions drop and you find yourself giving in to your desires. I hardly ever drank anymore, and when I did, it seemed to hit me rather quickly. I could feel the alcohol humming through my veins, making me ill at ease because of my *increasing* general ease.

I placed the beer onto the small table in his room. Grayson was just quietly watching me as I fought internal battles. I was positive he could hear my racing thoughts. He came up behind me, placing his beer onto the table next to mine. "What is it, Violet?" He softly asked.

I warily looked up at him, mere inches away, yet not touching one another. I met his eyes, hazel with green flecks melding into my blue. I exhaled, closed my eyes, and counted to four. When I opened them, I found my arms wrapped around his waist with his mouth against my neck. Everything in my mind was screaming no, but my body was responding and I was helpless.

I turned my mouth into his, and electricity sent shockwaves through my body. I reached my hands up to his head, pulling him violently towards me. He broke away first, with a panicked look in his eyes. "We can't," he huskily said, flushed in the face.

I met his eyes, and bit my lip to shake myself out of this dream state. "We aren't," I agreed.

"Don't do that," he whispered, stroking my lip with his thumb. The color of blood on his thumb tip shocked me.

I looked away from his hands, and forcefully removed myself from his embrace. It was like pulling two of the strongest magnets on earth apart—no easy feat. "We won't," I said flopping myself onto the mattress, covering my face with a pillow and giving a short scream into it.

I felt the mattress give next to me, and a nudge at my side. I sat back up, and took the beer he offered. I took another swig, dangling my feet off the bed to the floor.

Our breathing had mostly returned to normal, and when I glanced back up at him, his panicked eyes were no more. Steely, they were. "So. The meeting."

"The meeting."

"What did they say?"

"They told Nathan they were closer to finding you guys."

"Oh, really? Is this true?"

A slight smile pursed his lips. "Of course not. They think you're in Virginia Beach or on the Eastern Shore somewhere."

"Ugh. Why do they even think I'm coastal?"

"I'm assuming the post offices you frequent suggest you're coastal rather than inland."

"Well, sure… Who the hell wants to drive further inland than they need?"

Even now, Grayson always had an undercurrent of menace about him. He lifted his beer up to me and we both drank. "So why *did* you come here this weekend? Did you know—"

"Grayson," I interrupted. "Don't. I just wanted to go shopping for Dawn's school. She's starting kindergarten." I walked towards the vanity outside of the bathroom, looking at his distorted image through the mirror.

"I know," he responded quietly. "Nathan mailed some school stuff to her to one of your boxes. You should really get it before she starts school." He stood up and bent down on the other side of his bed.

"Okay," I sighed. "I will hit them all. Did they tell him anything else?" I asked across the room.

His backside called out to me, "Just that Amara was a valuable asset to our government."

"Bollocks." He snorted in response. "She's my fucking daughter," I continued. Grayson still wasn't responding, but I heard him rustling into one of his bags. "She's not a weapon. She's a human being." I turned to face him in the room rather than the mirror. "Gray!" I exclaimed, exasperated.

He walked over to me with a devilish grin, and handed a shot glass to me. "She's a fucking human." He poured some bourbon into it, and lifted it up to me. "To Amara," he said for the second time that night.

I toasted my daughter, his niece. "To Amara." Leaning against one another, we took our shots and then slammed them onto the counter. I could feel his breath on my face, and smell the whiskey from his mouth. He grabbed my wrists in one hand, and walked backwards towards the bed.

He gently pushed me down, the angst replaced with a yearning. "I know it's wrong, but I don't fucking care anymore," he said earnestly, pressing his body on top of mine, sliding his knee between my legs.

"Good," I breathed, pulling off his shirt.

I woke up a couple hours later to his light snore. I watched him in the dim light, his hair falling across his forehead, one leg sticking out from underneath the covers. I sighed. I had officially cheated on my husband. With his brother. *What the hell was wrong with me?* I half-choked, half-laughed to myself, sinking into my pillow.

I turned onto my side, and draped myself across Grayson, waking him up. I just had my t-shirt on; his body felt warm underneath me.

"I need to get back to Dawn," I said quietly. "I don't want her to wake up without me." He shook himself out of his sleep, and glanced at the clock. It read fifteen minutes past two.

He pulled me close to him. "I'm not ready to give you up just yet, Violet," he said softly. "Please don't make me," he pleaded, looking deep into my eyes and taking my breath away.

He brushed my hair behind my ear, and I placed one hand on his chest. "You know I love you, right?" I asked, as I peered down at him in the dark. "I have no idea why, but I do." I smiled tersely.

He kissed my forehead, and reluctantly pushed me off of him. "Go on. I'll see you in the morning."

He looked sad, and it broke my heart. My lip wobbled like crazy, but I knew it wasn't fair to him to rely on his strength anymore. Our time had passed, and I was back on my own.

I slid out of bed, grabbing my pajama pants and pulling them on. Grayson was sitting up, sleepily watching me. He must have put his grey sweatshirt back on at some point, because just then he took it off, and tossed it to the foot of the bed. He looked damn good there, shirtless and sleepy. He was still in good shape, but for once I knew he wasn't trying to seduce me.

"I got hot," he said, answering my unasked question.

"Perfect," I said, grabbing the sweatshirt, and holding it close to me. "Mine now." I impishly grinned, and walked towards the adjoining doors, pausing for a moment, waiting to see if he would call me back.

He did not.

I stepped through the other side, and stood with my back to the door, breathing in his scent from the sweatshirt. I tiptoed to the bed where my daughter peacefully slept, and I slid under the covers with her, exhausted. She exhaled once I was in bed, and turned towards me, saying 'Mama' in her sleep.

My poor baby.

***

It was early and chilly. Alexandra had said her goodbyes and wished us well. Amara was strapped in her carseat, and I was standing outside of the car, wearing Grayson's sweatshirt with an old pair of jeans, my hair messily placed at the nape of my neck. The bright light of the sun was peeking out from beneath the clouds.

"It looks better on you," he said gruffly, placing one leg between mine as I leaned up against the car. I tilted my chin up at him, feeling raw, feeling exposed.

"Take care, Gray."

"You, too." He reached into me, and held me tightly, clearly not caring if anyone saw. I wrapped my arms around him in response, feeling his bare skin against my hands. He lightly brushed his lips from my neck to face, pressing his mouth into mine. "I love you, too, Violet," he breathed into my ear before eventually letting me go.

He stepped back, and I nodded at him before getting into my car. I tried to soak up that image of Grayson, as well as some of the others from the night before. I knew that this would be the final time spent with him like that.

"Mommy. Why are you wearing Grayson's shirt?" she asked as soon as I got in the car. "Why did he kiss you? I thought mommies only kissed daddies or other mommies, but Grayson's my *uncle.*"

"Life is complicated, sweetie," I said, catching her eye in the rearview mirror as we drove off. "And I liked his shirt, so he let me have it."

"You smell like him."

"I know."

"Mommy?"

"Yes, baby?"

"I'm happy we got to see them, but I sure wish we could see Daddy."

"I know. Me too. I miss him *so* much." My heart snapped in half again.

***

On the way home, we passed one of our post office boxes. Luckily it was the correct one with packages from her father. As we got closer *to* our home, Amara pointed out that I hadn't yet changed the license plate. I shook my head in disbelief—it was so easy to get sloppy.

Once home, we unpacked all the goodies, and started to organize the items she would need for school. Once she was in bed, Kassidy came over for a little while to catch up. She walked in, tossing a toy towards Malcolm without looking at me. "I left this in my car earlier. Here, boy," she exclaimed quietly, knowing Amara was down the hallway asleep.

I was sitting in the kitchen with a tall whiskey, wearing Grayson's sweatshirt, still full from the warmth of him. Finally Kassidy looked up at me as she dropped her bag onto my couch, and the look that crossed her face was almost comical. I was idly stirring my whiskey with my pinky, as she entered the kitchen, giving me a slight shove.

"You had *sex*!" she shrieked.

"Shhhhh," I hissed, indicating my sleeping daughter in the other room.

She whispered loudly, "You had sex!"

I laughed in response, tossing my head. "How do you do that? How do you know?" I hugged myself as if it were Grayson hugging me.

"Ooooh—that's his, isn't it?" She leaned in, her curly hair bouncing off of her neck, taking a whiff of the sweatshirt. "Oh, he smells *good*!"

I laughed more lightheartedly than I should have laughed.

"Well? Who is the mystery man? Are you going to see him again?"

My smile faded. "No." I got up, and wandered into the den with my drink. I nodded my head towards Kassidy, suggesting she could grab a drink too, if she wanted.

"Why not?" She immediately followed me, though, too wrapped up in my story.

"Because he's Nathan's brother?" I kicked my feet up on the coffee table.

A hush fell across the room. "You *dog*." A confused smile

ripped across her face.

"I know," I half-laughed. "But to be honest... I don't really feel as awful about it as I think I should. If that makes sense."

"I wonder why that is?" she asked, plopping onto the couch next to me.

"I know, right?"

There was a pause, and she carefully chose her words. "Did you know you were going to see...?"

"Grayson."

"*Grayson* when you left?"

"I had a hunch."

"And Nathan?"

"He was there, too."

"Whoa. The plot thickens."

"He didn't see us," I said quickly.

"Hm."

Another pause. Kassidy crossed her arms across her chest. "You know, you can trust me, Vi. We've known each other for years now... Our kids are growing up together... I've *seen* some things..." She looked at me meaningfully. "Remember that time Amara levitated your hamster?"

I snorted. I remembered. We had had a hamster in between Malcolm and Phang and Barnaby, and there was this one afternoon Amara had straight up levitated the damn thing in front of Kassidy. I had played it off, of course, and Kassidy had narrowed her eyes, but she'd never made mention of it. Until now.

"I know that... I know that you and Amara are...*special*. I know that being apart from Nathan—and now that I know about Grayson, I think him, too—I know that it kills you. I know that you left not because someone was hurting you, or because you didn't want to be with someone anymore... I know it was to keep her safe, somehow, by keeping her away from them." She reached out for my hands, her fingers feeling warm against my now-chilly fingers. She continued, "I promise to not judge you. I promise to keep you protected. You know, I've had enough weird things happen to *me* to be foolish enough to not believe what your real story is. Your *full* story." A huge, comfortable smile spread across her face.

My heart began to pound and I was terrified to think I was about to spill the beans. I wanted to. I desperately wanted someone within my circle to trust. But the prophecy about the *Arrow* heavily weighed on me. Maybe I could share some things…

I drank the whiskey down straight. "This shit is really nasty," I said, and laughed.

"Whatever you tell me, it's between us and only us. I have a feeling nobody would believe us anyway. *Even* in our little group of weirdos." She smiled, and grabbed the whiskey. "Guess I need some of this shit, too, eh?"

24

As the years rolled by, I knew I wouldn't be able to avoid my past forever. I knew it all would catch up to me, but I just hoped I could at least get Amara out of high school before it happened. She had gifts, she had amazing gifts. Gifts that superseded mine.

I neither encouraged nor discouraged the development of these gifts. Well, at least I *tried* not to. I had a feeling I came off a little standoffish sometimes when she would excitedly tell me something new she'd discovered she could do. I validated that these supernatural skills she had were in fact real, but I also warned her to be careful, to not share the mystical part of her life with her friends. I think for the most part she listened to me.

When Amara was about ten years old, she was outside fishing with Grayson. Alexandra had come stateside for the summer and rented a little cottage on a lake in the mountains of Tennessee. She had hoped that we would be able to see her, and we did, for two solid weeks. Grayson was able to spend a week with us there as well.

I was frustrated and felt blocked. As Amara had gotten

older, I'd become more comfortable with looking into finding out the truths about my family. By the time of this particular visit in the mountains, I'd been looking for information concerning my grandparents and mother for several years at this point. Unfortunately, I had not found anything of substance beyond what Nathan and Cox had shared with me all those years ago.

I believed I was missing something, something obvious. Alexandra sensed my frustration with the whole situation, but also with her, herself. I couldn't shake the feeling she had information she was keeping from the rest of us.

I looked out the window of the cottage down a large hill, seeing silhouettes of Amara and her uncle down on a dock by the lake. Alexandra walked up beside me, gently brushing my shoulders. "I have something to share with you," she said softly, indicating I should follow her into the next room. I tensed up, but followed her.

She held a file folder in her hand. I raised an eyebrow in question, clenching my hands up against my chest. "These documents answer some of your inquiries. But know that the deeper you delve, the more questions you may have. And some of the answers you seek may not be satisfying at all. This is truly *all* I have about your mother's family. I've collected the information ever since Nathan found you in Atlanta and marked you as *The Weapon*."

I dropped my hands down at my side, indignant. "He didn't *make* me *The Weapon*, Alexandra. I was already marked —"

"Were you?" She smiled faintly. "Read this. Memorize what you can, and then destroy it before we leave this place. I would not let Amara see it, and letting Grayson know is up to you. It shouldn't affect him one way or another."

I took the file from her, and she started to slip out of the room. "Be sure you really want to know, Violet."

I glanced at my phone, wondering if I had time to read through all of it thoroughly before Grayson and Amara came back inside. Once I heard the screen door slam shut as Alexandra left, I figured she was giving me enough time. I grabbed myself a soda and sat down at the little kitchen table overlooking the long backyard towards the docks. I opened the file, and the very first document was a copy of something printed a long time ago.

It had the old school "Top Secret" stamp inked onto the top of the document. My mind instantly painted it red, just like in the movies, but it was a faded black. Parts of the copy were faint and illegible, but I instantly realized what, or should I say, *who*, it was about.

<u>For Immediate Release</u>: Albert Seelish. 1985 15 Dec.
Albert's body arrived encased in a solid silver tomb. Transport provided by US Army under direct supervision of the Commander-in-Chief. Now at Hoover Dam for secure storage. Ada Seelish's whereabouts unknown ATT. Enclosure expected to be opened at 1200 hours 17 December.

There was a photograph attached of what I could only assume was my grandfather's coffin. The picture was black and white, but I could clearly see that the inscription on the tomb was probably made from that specialized blue ink that Nathan's family used when creating magical objects.

Wait... Did this mean Alexandra wrote the inscription on my grandfather's tomb? I racked my brains to figure out where Alexandra would have been in the 80s. I was pretty sure that's when she was still with Grayson's dad. I had been under the impression that she hadn't lasted long with Nathan's father.

I flipped to the next piece of paper, and it was dated 1944, and unfortunately, was written in German. I recognized my grandfather's name again, the Nazi emblem and Adolf Hitler's name. The next few pages were a packet that had been stapled, ripped again, and stapled back together. There were photographs upon photographs of various odd shaped objects; men with weird contraptions strapped to their heads, some lying down on a table, incapable of moving; a man in a chair... *No, wait, not just any man, my grandfather!* He had a metal contraption on his head and sitting across from him, on an aluminum-looking table, was a bent spoon. *What the hell?*

A handwritten note was the next page, written in cursive English on wrinkled notebook paper. Instantly I recognized it. It was in my grandfather's penmanship.

March 16, 1986.

My Dearest Ada, The Asset is watched. Protect The Asset at all costs. My use dissolved a long time ago, but it is not my time to go. The Asset has the information that is sought, information that even I do not have. She can keep The Weapon safe, but if she is taken, then The Weapon will be lost. Perhaps indefinitely.

Tears pressed at my eyes, and I stood up quickly, trying to catch my breath. I looked out at the water, saw Alexandra and Grayson talking behind Amara as she cast her line out again. *My grandfather had known about the original prophecy!* It sounded like he had somehow pieced it together that this *Weapon* was *me! My God, what else had he known?*

Violet, Violet, I thought, chiding myself. I was missing the most obvious thing, getting lost in the story and not just the *facts.* This current letter was dated *after* my grandfather had beens shipped in a tomb to Hoover Dam! I flipped back to the original piece of paper to reread it quickly. I could see that they were packing things up down at the river and in turn, heading back into the house.

My God, I was right. My grandfather was probably alive

when he had been delivered in the metal tomb back in 1985. Was he in hiding? Had he somehow got a letter to my grandmother?

I grabbed the last piece of paper in the envelope, glancing at it quickly before the others made their way back into he house. It was my grandmother's handwriting, addressed to Albert, dated 1987.

The brothers were separated. All will come together in time as it should, but my darling, we will not be around to witness it. All guidance will be given by our daughter, unless she has to go away like you did. I can only hope that all of the sacrifices we have made will be for the greater good of all, that we, as a people, will somehow thrive after the End of Times, and that dear Violet's daughter doesn't perish in the fight. Violet is a spitting image of Imogene at this age—knows her own mind. Dave has taken a job with the feds, which is fine—it will protect Imogene and Violet. I have fears, though, that hiding Violet from her true nature may backfire... But again... all will come together in time as it should. I miss you dearly, and cannot wait until we reunite in death, dear Albert. I hope this finds you with warmth. Eternal love, Ada.

Somehow I made it through the evening without hinting to Grayson, or Amara, that anything was going on. But after Amara fell asleep, and Grayson was sitting outside alone in a rocking chair, looking up at the stars, I knocked on Alexandra's bedroom door seeking answers.

She patted the bed next to her. She was awake, reading a book. She peered at me from over her glasses, and gave me smile. "Nathan sends his love, by the way."

This took me aback. She and I rarely talked about Nathan when we got together—I figured she assumed it was too painful for me, that it wasn't safe, or hell—maybe she just didn't want to bring it up. But yet here she was, mentioning his name without fanfare. "How is… How has he been?"

"He's okay, mein Schatzi, he's okay. He still misses you, but gave up the hunt long ago. He assumes you'll come out of hiding at the appropriate time, so he's just living his life now."

I bit my lip. "Oh." I looked down at my hands, fanning them out on my lap. I hesitated and began to ask in a small voice, "Does he—"

"Of course he still loves you. He's never going to be with anyone else, Violet."

"Oh."

"Alas, this isn't why you come to me tonight, to discuss either of my sons, is it, no. Although, you know Grayson has started to see someone, yes?"

"Yes, he told me." I paused. "I'm happy for him. He deserves someone who can be there, someone who can be present for him."

She laughed, "Yes… You mean someone other than you?"

I wanly smiled. "Of course." I certainly didn't feel like going down that road, and she let the subject drop. It had been a great many years since Grayson or I had even mentioned that last night together.

She closed up her book, and reached across the nightstand for a glass of water. She knocked it over, spilling some. I jumped up and grabbed a washcloth and dried it off for her. As I stood there mopping up the mess, she began to speak again. "Your grandparents have been deceased since the early aughts."

I squeezed the water out of the washcloth, lying it across the countertop. I came back to her. "So my grandfather, when he "died" when I was a kid… He wasn't really dead?"

"No."

"Did you know him?"

"No, but I heard about him. The government wasn't

funding much in the way of studying the supernatural in the 1980s, but there was one name that kept popping up, one name that was still an active member of what was left over from the Cold War. Seelish."

"While I'm obviously extremely interested in all of this, there's one thing that's just not sitting well with me. My *mother's* death. I mean, I've hallucinated, or had visions of her during moments of life or death. Or moments of undue stress. But sometimes I wonder, I mean… Is she alive?" I rushed the question. This new information really sent me into a tizzy about the things I didn't know.

Alexandra was leaning back in bed, arms crossed and muttering something to herself. She popped open her eyes and said to me softly. "I know not the answer you seek. I am sorry."

25

Kassidy had my back over the years. She sometimes would ride with me during my crazy day-trips to mail off things letters and pick up packages. I eventually felt comfortable enough sending her to my P.O. Boxes in my place. I had told her…enough…but still not everything. In particular, I didn't tell her about the prophecies around us. I merely shared that these *gifts* that we had, the *gifts* that Kassidy had seen in action, were on the radar of government agencies and enemies alike.

She forced me out of my comfort zone at times, dragging me out-of-state with the kids to go on vacations. There was one time in particular that I was miserably nervous. She had convinced me to stay in a rented cottage for a month in Florida. I just felt *watched* most of the time. I could never figure out why, but the feeling had been very real and only dissipated once I crossed state lines.

When Amara was in middle school, she had the opportunity to go with other classmates to New York City for a multi-day field trip during Spring Break. She really wanted to go; I had the money. There was no reason to deny her this luxury. The kids were going to see an Off Broadway play, visit the 9/11 Memorial, walk up to the Statue of Liberty and check out Times Square. And so in spite of my worries, Kassidy talked me into letter her go. Primarily because her son, Marcus, who was a couple of years older than Amara, was going to be going, too. Obviously there would be chaperones, but would they be packing heat? Would they be able to bend the will of the elements in their favor if need be?

During those years, I had learned how to to use and carry a gun. Grayson had taught me. I may have been full of magical mystical power, but Grayson's schtick of never bringing a knife to a gun fight muddled my stomach. I couldn't very well ride on Amara's bus with her while carrying the weapon, and so I didn't let her know that I was going at all.

I used it as an excuse to finally visit with Morgan who was going to be in his Midtown apartment during that time. Kassidy shook her head at me in disapproval, but let me go without too much of a fuss. Amara had plans to meet up with Morgan herself at one point, but he had promised he wouldn't share that I was staying with him. No—she was her own creature in time in space, finally free from the tyrannical rule of her mother. She was beyond excited, thrilled to be independent and grown-up.

I knew that Amara would sense me if I tried to put up any defensive walls, and so I merely stayed visible in plain sight. I wore a dark, short haired wig, and simple clothes that blended in. I painted my face in makeup and I had to admit, staring at myself in Morgan's bathroom mirror—this person looking back at me didn't resemble who I though I was.

The rest stops on the way to New York? I was there in a rented car the whole time behind the bus. The ferry ride to Staunton Island? Yup, I was on it surrounded by a rowdy bunch of horny middle schoolers who were so involved with one another, they paid no attention to me. The subway stops, the hand holding, the singing, the pizza place, the restaurant in the hotel? I was there the whole time, observing anyone who paid too much attention to the kids.

At one point I was afraid one of the chaperones had noticed *me* watching them—not as Amara's mom who was on a field trip she wasn't supposed to be on—but as a stranger who could be a potential threat. I ducked out of the train at the next stop before he could get any other ideas about me.

Morgan convinced me to have dinner with him a couple of the nights, to let the kids go off on their own. He had published several books over the years, and I noticed a changed in their tone and subject matter. There was always a single woman, without a backstory, caught up in the action. Sometimes she had a child, sometimes she had a cat, but it was always the same type of character with no past.

Over a glass of wine, I asked him about it. "Well, Violet," he said, raising his glass to me, "You have made quite an impact on my life. You and—"

"Dawn," I hissed, interrupting him, totally spooked. The shock on his face wiped clean after a brief moment. He had forgotten. A sad smile crossed his face as he placed his glass back on the table.

"Yes, you and *Dawn* made quite an impact on me. It has stayed with me, even plagued me a bit."

"What does that mean?" I warily asked. I was happy to see him—he really had been so good to us during those early years. While I had never had any sort of romantic feelings towards him, I was not so sure that I could have said the same about him. However, it had never been a topic of conversation.

"Let's just say, writing has helped me cope with your absence. As it did with my wife."

I looked down, swirling the wine in my cup. I took the bait, "Are you seeing anyone now?"

He laughed, looking out the window. "As a matter of fact, I am. She's out of town right now, otherwise I'd have you meet her. You would like her."

"Well that's good, Morgan. I'm happy to hear that."

"And you?"

It was my turn to look out the window. "You know, it's only ever going to be Nathan for me." I bitterly smiled into the glass pane.

"To lost loves," Morgan lifted his glass again.

"To lost loves," I repeated.

The night following the lunch Morgan and Amara had together—to which, he reported how smart she was and how beautiful she was becoming—Morgan couldn't keep me in. For one, the kids were off to see a play that I also wanted to see. For two, I hadn't seen Amara in days and I was starting to feel sticky. Even though Morgan had reported she was fine, even though she had spoken to me on the phone just a few blocks away sounding like she was having the time of her life —I needed to see her.

This is how I found myself, incognito in plain sight, yet again. This time I painted my face a little more mildly and wore a nice looking dress to go out. Of course, I was still in a wig, and tried to cover up obvious, identifiable tattoos, but I looked pretty good. Morgan let out a low whistle as I took to the stairs.

I grinned at him, and pushed off. The kids had all settled into the middle of Orchestra seating; I was off in Mezzanine, directly overhead. I had the perfect view of the top of Amara's head, and she was easy to pick out. Not just because of the colorful clothing she had on, or her dark, shiny hair and sparkly ribbons—no, she had a significant aural haze about her. My God, she was stunning. Much too stunning for a tween, but what could I do? My little girl was growing up.

I could hear the kids being rowdy as they settled into their seats. The lights went dark, and the play began. As fascinating of a show as it was, I found that before intermission, I needed to use the restroom. I wandered away from my seating and went into the upstairs foyer to search for the it. I adjusted my wig, touched up the makeup, and headed to the wine cart.

All of a sudden, I felt a certain heat signature. It was something I hadn't felt since my Scout-hunting days in Georgia. Even though it had been almost fifteen years, it wasn't anything that I could ever forget. *How could I have ben so stupid? Why had I let Amara go out into the world unprotected while in the dark about who she really was?* I knew that some of the old players had ties to New York—I should never have let her leave the beach.

As the panic began to consume me, I grounded myself by counting my breaths. The world came back into focus, and I continued towards the wine cart trying to get a grasp on where this energy was coming from. There were people in front of me in line, and I took the opportunity to slide the menu up to just past the bridge of my nose to track it.

Lo and behold, almost fifteen years later and with much more of a gut than I remembered, was *Jared*. He looked as oily and seemed as dark as I remembered... It was this sickening feeling I always had around him; I couldn't shake it. He played the middle field like it was nobody's business, and because of that, I didn't trust him. He wasn't good; I wasn't sure if he was bad. He was a disgusting opportunist.

He was with two men I didn't recognize, and my stomach did a deep dive when I saw the third man he was with. *Jason.* The same man who Grayson had been so devoted to during the darkest moments of his life. Head honcho of Vendetta Veritas, the man who had threatened me before Amara was even born. Nausea crept up from my belly. Seeing the two of them together meant we were not safe. And may never be again.

It was my turn to order the wine. I made sure that I felt the small gun tucked behind a strap on my thigh, and so kept my bag close. I knew I wasn't recognizable and that my tattoos were covered—I had just been in the restroom. I also had my wits about me after the moment of panic, and my powers of cloaking, however they worked, was still switched on. I could only hope it was enough to protect Amara who was unwittingly a sitting duck.

Jason glanced in my general direction before walking quickly downstairs with the other two men. I stood over the balcony casually sipping my wine as they left the building. Jared had disappeared into a restroom, and just then, a loud noise erupted from the theatre as apparently Intermission had just started. Doors swung open; people piled out. I stayed where I was, my eyes on the entrance as well as the bathroom. I could see some of the kids step out into the foyer below me, and I prayed with every essence of my being that Amara didn't wander away from her friends.

Jared left the bathroom, and walked up to the alcohol vendor next to the wine cart. Luckily, there were a ton of people milling around at this point, so even if I hadn't been in disguise, there's no way he would have seen me. I kept my position. I saw my daughter swirling around below me, dancing with her friends, Marcus clearly keeping an eye on her. I breathed a sigh of relief, and then stiffened. The men who had left without Jared appeared to be long gone.

Jared ordered a bourbon and was on the other side of the carts, looking down onto the floor opposite me. If he were to glance up, he'd see a woman of nondescript characteristics doing the same thing he was doing. I hoped anyway. I could see him searching the floor, searching the kids below him, trying to find an inkling of my daughter.

There was no way it was a coincidence. He was here. For

us. For her. Somehow he had known. I racked my brains—had I made mention to Grayson or Alexandra about this vacation? Had it been intercepted somehow? Did I mail something to one of my friends talking about this upcoming trip? The feeling in my stomach felt thicker. *Was a plant living at the beach with us?*

The lights flickered to indicate that the show was about to re-start. I watched as the kids grabbed their drinks and snacks and began to filter into the theatre again—or at least they disappeared out of my line of view, and I assumed that's what they were doing. I didn't want to get caught outside of the seating area in the bright light, so I tossed my empty wine glass and walked directly past Jared as he was headed the other way. We were so close, as I looked straight ahead, unbelievably able to detect the bourbon on his breath.

Before I went down my aisle to my seat, I took one look back. Jared was rapidly walking down the stairs. I couldn't help myself; I abruptly turned around and rushed back to the balcony to see what he was doing. I startled the people who were behind me, and muttered a sorry. Jared rushed out of the entrance to the theatre, and I sighed an audible expression of relief. The liquor dealer glanced at me, and I could tell was about to ask if I was okay, but I quickly went back inside to my seat.

Well that was that. She was never going to New York again, and maybe not even a day trip with her classmates. I shuddered as I sat back down in my seat, any wonder coming from the play lost.

That night, Morgan couldn't get me to calm down. I used his phone to immediately call Grayson and in spite of it being an odd number, Grayson had felt compelled to answer. He told me he was going to see Nathan soon, and that he would tell him and they would look into it. He told me we were safe.

Needless to say, I was thrilled to get the hell out of New

York the next day. I followed the bus back into my town, quickly dropping off the rental car before getting my own car to retrieve Amara. She had had the most amazing time, New York was beautiful, Morgan was so happy, and she couldn't wait to go back.

We only ever saw Morgan again when he was driving South for a road trip with his new wife. After that I continued to send him emails, or send him memes via text. I continued to read his books, and I must say, everything he wrote from then on seemed to have a happier tone than when he had written about mysterious women who were hunted and haunted by their pasts.

26

It took a couple of months, but Grayson finally contacted me about Jared. Unfortunately, he, Nathan *and* Alexandra had come up empty. They all agreed it was no mistake; they all agreed they had been looking to make contact with her—not me, *her*! They all agreed that they hadn't seen either of us, and that, by all means, we were still safe. It never sat well with me, and I figured it didn't with the others, either.

I would go to the library and type in Jared's name looking for information. I searched archives surrounding my grandparents and my mother. I traveled to nearby cities while Amara was in school, searching through books, computer systems. It was always a dead end, and so eventually I let it go.

As Amara grew older, she pieced together some facts of her own. I never lied to her when she would question me, but I never offered more information that I thought she needed to know. She knew her father and uncle had not grown up together, but she didn't know why. She knew I kept her from her father to protect her from other people. She didn't know why. She knew she wasn't allowed to speak with her father, but she didn't know why. She knew her father would sometimes send me mail, sometimes send us gifts, but rarely would I mail him anything.

She knew she was not allowed to mention her missing father to her friends. He was just "out of the picture". She knew she was to go by Dawn if we were ever outside of our town. She knew her father, her mother, and her grandparents had all worked for the government exploiting these gifts. She knew that Wood was not my original last name.

Ultimately, she knew we were in hiding from people who were after us; some bad, some not-so-good, others, like her father, good. She knew she somehow had "super" natural gifts that were nothing like what her friends could do. She knew her family also shared these gifts. She knew she'd be able to meet her father once she graduated high school. If she was angry at me about these things, she never shared it. However, she *would* share her sadness sometimes, as I did in return.

***

Amara was entering high school at summer's end. She was fourteen, taller than me, and unfortunately easily drew attention with her glowing personality and gorgeous features. She took after her father with quiet intelligence and inhuman beauty. From me, she had a keen sense in music and a thirst for knowledge.

We had landed in Germany and were taking the train to Sylt to see Alexandra. Grayson, and as it turned out, his girlfriend, Helena, were also in town. I hadn't even questioned whether or not he might be there, and so I was surprised to find him at the train station to greet us.

We had our backs to him, standing outside of a restroom and I felt a presence come up behind me. Amara turned around first, and a wide smile imprinted on her face. "Eeeeeeee!" She exclaimed, rushing up to him and jumping on him like a Wildebeest. "Uncle Grayson! It's been too long!"

"Whoa, kiddo, good to see you, too! Look how much you've grown!" Over her shoulder, he mouthed 'wow' to me. The last time he had seen her she was still very much a little girl. In the past few years, she had almost become a woman…

After I got over my shock, I laughed. A feeling of unease settled into my gut, though, after I realized I had perhaps been letting my guard down. Now that she was older and more physically capable, I knew she wouldn't just wander away with a stranger because of a lollipop. I didn't imagine she could use her gifts as a protective measure, but I also didn't want to find out.

I needed to do better. She was still a child.

"Helena is back at the cottage with Mom. I told them that after I grabbed you we would run errands and bring some food to cook back home."

"Whoa, what? You brought Helena?" The knot in my stomach grew. I didn't like the thought of being introduced to a new person so far away from home. Some of the safety I had felt all of these years was because our little group of four stayed just that—Alexandra, Grayson, Amara and me.

Grayson caught my tone, and gave a slight shake of his head. Amara slid her backpack on, and began jumping like a bunny. Grayson let out a laugh. "My God, is she always this way?"

I slid my backpack onto my back and grabbed the luggage and began to pull it along. "Just when she's excited." I paused. "So yes, almost always." She bounded ahead of us. "Anyway," I started, but Grayson cut me off.

He quickly spoke, "Look, it's fine. Helena knows enough to know enough to *not* ask questions—"

"Wow, that's rude—"

"And anyway, it's safe. I would never put you two at risk." He paused. "Ever."

I furrowed my brows as we caught up to Amara. We placed our bags inside of the trunk and got into the car. Amara leaned forward from behind us. "So tell us about Helena! Is she pretty? Where does she work? Do you love her? Are you going to marry her?" She leaned back into the carseat. "I guess you're too old to have babies, huh."

"Amara Dawn!" I exclaimed. "Watch it."

"I wasn't being rude, Mom. Y'all are just old."

Grayson and I looked at one another and burst out laughing. The laughter put me at ease. It made me feel normal. I often forgot that, in spite of the prophecies, the gifts we all had, Amara was still just a *normal* child going through normal, human events.

"She is beautiful in *my* eyes. She's in research and works at a museum in D.C., and yes… We are already engaged." He quickly glanced my way before returning his gaze to the road.

"Yaaaay!" exclaimed Amara. "Mom, we *have* to go to the wedding."

"Dawn, you know we won't be able to go." I looked out the window as the seagrass and sand blurred together.

"Moooom—"

"No." I said firmly. "But Grayson—congratulations." I reached across the seat and squeezed his hand. He smiled a sad, happy smile in return.

"At any rate," he said, pulling up into a parking lot of a little corner market, "You're both going to love her."

Sure enough, Helena was a hit. She, Alexandra and Amara were playing cards in the den while Grayson and I were in the kitchen talking, making tea. "You look really good, Grayson. I am so happy to see *you* this happy." I impulsively gave him a hug.

"Yeah, I think I am, Vi. I'm in a really good place. Helena and I did the long distance dating thing for such a long time, that when we finally moved in together, it didn't even cross our minds to get married. It wasn't until the past month or so that we realized we should get married."

I laughed, pulling the kettle off of the stove. "Helena is so lovely. Funny as hell."

I poured the hot water into five tea cups. Grayson's voice dropped a bit as he hesitated, "We were close to Nathan for awhile, but he ended up moving into a condo so we don't see him as much." My face must have taken on a sour look, because he then said, "Don't look at me that way."

"Fine. Tell me more."

"He still works for the government, just not fieldwork. I think he's crunching numbers now, it sounded dreadfully boring." He poured some milk into his tea. "We never talk about… anything anymore. Although, he did see Jared about a month ago."

I froze. While life had simply become life over the past couple of years, and it was ever more easy to pretend Amara and I were a mother and daughter team who lived on the coast, there were certain things that would creep back into my psyche. The image of Jared's oily smile and smell of his bourbon still burned into my memories. "What the hell did he want?" I asked sharply.

"For some reason Jared stopped by his office and spoke with his boss. He's apparently come into some money and involved in real estate. Said he'd gotten out of the game long ago."

"Well that's the biggest bunch of bullshit."

Grayson spread the mugs of tea about the table, standing in the doorway. "Tea's ready!" He called out to the others. He turned back towards me. "Yeah—Nate didn't believe it either."

"You talking about dad?" Amara asked, as she stepped into the kitchen with Alexandra.

Alexandra caught my eye as I looked past them down the hallway. "She went to the bathroom," she said quietly.

The four of us sat down at the table waiting on Helena. "Yeah.. I was just talking about your dad."

"Grandma said he just left?" She hesitated and looked at me.

My eyebrows shot through the roof. "He was just here?" I hissed. "First an outsider—"

"Hey," Grayson warned.

"And Nathan *just* left? What the hell were you thinking?" I stood up at the table heart pounding.

Alexandra innocently sipped her tea, but Grayson had the decency to look guilty. "I"m pretty sure he saw you guys at the train station"

"What?" Amara's eyes were huge; she appeared breathless.

"At least from the cryptic text he sent me."

I walked behind Amara, placing my hands on her shoulders. I could tell she wanted to cry, and I squeezed her to try and keep her calm. The last thing I needed was a huge episode about all of this with Helena just down the hall, so I quietly said, "I never would have agreed to come here had I known all of this was going on—"

I was visibly shaking; Amara was visibly upset. Alexandra reached her hand out towards Amara's hand. "You're right; I should never have allowed it. Please forgive me. Dawn, I am so sorry." A single tear slid down Amara's face, and she gulped.

"I'm okay."

"Are you sure he's really gone?" I tersely asked.

Grayson said, "Yes, he's gone. His plane leaves from Hamburg this evening. He had to leave as soon as you got here. He's gone. I promise."

Helena came into the room just then, and we all sat down for tea. Even so, when I retired to the bedroom for the night, I opened up all the drawers in the room, looked through the closet. Now that I knew he had just been there, I suspected he had left something behind for me.

For Amara.

I found nothing. I felt empty.

27

High school turned out to be mostly uneventful, save for the normal drama of a young girl growing up. The years catapulted forward, and I found myself looking at my reflection in the bathroom mirror. I had on a dark navy skirt cut to my knees and a white tank top blouse with giant navy flowers on it. My hair fell loosely around my shoulders, streaked with grey, matching my crow's feet and worried blue eyes. I wore navy flats, and saw some of my blue inked tattoos peeking out from the front of my blouse. I applied chapstick, and pulled a small purple knapsack over my back.

My skin was tanned from the newly approaching summer, and my cheeks were a natural shade of rose. I had taken the time to polish my nails a light pink color, and I took a deep breath, turning away from the mirror in my bathroom.

"Mom, c'mon, we have to go!" called my beautiful daughter from the other room.

She was a sight to be seen. Her long, dark auburn hair was almost to her waist, curling at the tips. Her face was tanned, her green eyes vibrant and alive. She wore a green A-line dress with thin, yellow flowers on it, which enhanced her slender frame. She wore dark burgundy flats, her white, shimmery graduation gown over her shoulders, but not zipped. In one hand she held her white cap which she had decorated with the silly phrase "to infinity and beyond" by use of fancy masking tape.

I saw a glimpse of her wrist before it completely became hidden by the gown, and a blue tattoo showing the runes 'Gebo' and 'Jera' flashed back at me. I had a matching tattoo near my collarbone. It meant eternal love, and while of course it wasn't in magical ink, they were still magical in their appearance.

"You're being ridiculous! Don't be so nervous. You look beautiful. You *are* beautiful. If Daddy can somehow come today… He is going to find you stunning." She had resorted to using her baby voice, something she used on me whenever I was feeling down. She came up beside me and gave me a hug.

"Amara Dawn, I don't want you worrying about me. Or your father for that matter. Today is about *you* and you only, okay?"

As we pulled up to her high school parking lot, students being dropped off to prepare for their graduation march, a lump formed in my throat. We had done it.

I had done it.

She was eighteen, and she was at her high school graduation. She was set to go to college in Charlottesville, Virginia in the fall and I wasn't sure there was much I could do about that. I had to allow what may come, come. I had to let fear and control go; I had to trust with her skill, strength and cognitive prowess that she not only would survive what was in store, but she would thrive, be happy.

During her high school years, I had shared everything I knew about our collective past with her. She knew about her great grandparents; she knew about my father's work. She knew about my mother, the enigma, who must certainly be dead. She knew how Nathan had found me, marked me, fallen in love with me. She knew about the prophecies and my internal struggles with fate and free will. She knew Grayson and I had a long settled convoluted past; she anticipated Nathan and I would have a future.

I did not share these sentiments.

I wasn't sure when the protective barrier framing us would lift, but I had a feeling I'd find out sooner than later. I had mailed invitations to Grayson's house to distribute to whomever he deemed necessary. I wasn't sure if he would pass it on to Nathan, but regardless—I was not going out of my way to hide from him anymore.

"Remember. If anyone strange approaches you—"

"Yes, mom, latch onto friends, and the enemy loses strength. Got it." She reached across the car, placing her hands on my shoulders with sheer bravado on her face. "Mom! I've got this!"

I exhaled. "Okay. Get out of my car. See you soon." I gave a little push, laughing at her.

"Love you!" she exclaimed, super-excited, practically bouncing out of my car, as if she had springs on her feet. I watched her rush off into a living painting of white and dark grey gowns. She quickly disappeared. I grabbed my phone off of the passenger seat before finding a spot to park. I texted Kassidy to let her know I had arrived, and would meet her at the tea shop that we frequented before returning to the school for the ceremony.

I stepped out of my car as the wind whipped my hair into my face. "Dammit," I muttered, dropping my phone. I slammed the door to my car, trapping my skirt into the door. I looked up at the sun, glaring into it, counting to four. "I've got to calm down!" I yelped to myself, reopening the door, getting my skirt out before closing it again. I reached down and grabbed my phone.

A large, misshapened shadow fell over me once I stood back up, and I heard squeals of delight. "Liz! Layla! Sam!" I was shocked. In the hustle of bustle of everything associated with a graduation, I had forgotten I had even *invited* them to the ceremony. They obviously had never been to our house, or even to our town over the years. The last time we had even seen them had probably already been four or five years prior. I knew they wouldn't believe how much of an adult she truly had become.

I noted that they hadn't brought their own kids, or spouses for that matter. "You guys are alone?" I asked.

"We started this together, girl. We're here for you now."

They enveloped me in their embrace, and tears pressed at my eyelids. "She'll be so happy to see you guys. It's been so long. Too long!"

"I'm headed to a cafe to meet one of my friends before the ceremony—do come with me and we'll catch up. Kassidy will love to finally meet you all." In spite of my quick invite, I was dreadfully nervous. This was the first time that any aspect of my old life was intersecting with my newer life. In eighteen years, I had kept both worlds separate.

Now the collision began.

Of course, everyone got along just fine and I needn't have worried about it. Kassidy and the others shared stories about my past and my current state of things. It felt good to be exposed—there were no secrets in this group. Kassidy had finally become privy to the prophecies, and of course, the others had been there at the start.

Even so, I was still a little spooked and kept glancing around. Liz with her keen eye noticed, but didn't vocalize anything. She just grimly pressed her lips together.

I glanced at my phone. "Come on guys—it's time to grab our seats."

Liz walked next to me and put her arm around me as we walked back onto the sidewalk. "Oh honey, you've done such a great job! Salutatorian! Look at this place you chose to live, too, it's so beautiful here."

"Thank you," I said, squeezing her hand and pulling slightly away. The others walked ahead of us in conversation. There was a brief pause, but I knew it was coming.

"Do you know if…" she started.

"Nathan's coming? Or Grayson? No. I never made it back to my mailboxes to see if anyone was coming."

"But you're no longer in hiding," she stated.

"No… My guess is the veil lifted once I sent everyone the address to the school." I waved up ahead to the school as we approached it. "Unfortunately, I can only assume some idiot is going to approach her, as early as tonight." I sighed. "The good news is, I know she's safe."

"Well, we will help out in any way we can while we're here."

"I'm so *happy* you're here," I said, squeezing my eyes shut as I walked next to her.

"Open your eyes, Miss Violet" she laughed, and I opened my eyes, finding myself just outside of the entrance to the school. Liz took a step back as Kassidy moved in at my side, taking position. Other people were walking in and out of entrance, yet I was still frozen in spot.

Kassidy's son, Marcus, had finished his sophomore year at college and so he was home for the summer. He walked up, dressed in slacks and a white polo. His dark blond hair hung to his shoulders, and his blue eyes shone as he saw his mother. He and Amara were close, although she always refused to tell me if they had ever talked about dating. As far as I knew, they were still just good friends.

"Mom. Violet."

"Hey, honey! Look—some of Violet's friends made it to the

ceremony! Isn't Amara just going to be so excited?" Marcus looked over my friends with a quick hello, and a slight feeling of unease fell over me, which was *incredibly* strange.

I had never had any ill feelings about either of Kassidy's kids. They were both *great* kids, and had played major roles in our lives. Positive roles. They were kind, smart and funny. When Marcus and his sister had both gone off to college, they made sure to visit with Amara whenever they returned for a visit. Nothing about Marcus's demeanor or facial expression changed—he was as friendly as ever as he greeted my friends —but something wasn't right.

Or maybe I was just paranoid.

I ran to the restroom alongside Liz and made mention of Marcus. "Oh, I don't know, Violet. He seemed fine to me. I think you're just—"

"Losing my mind?"

She started to laugh, but suddenly I had to grasp the countertop to keep myself from falling. "Vi?"She reached out to steady me. "What is it?" she whispered to me as other people entered into the bathroom.

A woman walked in at that moment and distracted me so that I wasn't able to answer her. I had only met her once, but I would recognize her anywhere. She was younger than me, with short, wavy brown hair and brown eyes. Her dark skin was beautiful in opposition to the yellow sundress she had on, and a giant smile spread across her face when she saw me.

"Violet!" she exclaimed, and came up to give me a brief hug. I wasn't entirely sure what she knew about me, my past, Nathan, or Amara—all I really knew was that she was now Grayson's wife.

"Hey, Helena! Wow! Thanks for coming—I wasn't sure if any of you were going to make it!" I exclaimed, surprised by her gracious embrace.

"Of course. Grayson loves Amara as if she were his own. I know he wishes he could have been more a part of her life over the years, but you know how things go… I can't believe this is the first time we've even been here!" She spread her hands out, as if using that expression was going to explain life away.

However, I found it interesting. She certainly couldn't have known everything if she was under the impression she was able to visit us at our home all these years. "This is my friend, Liz. I guess I'll see you out there?" I asked, hesitating.

She reached out and placed her hand on my shoulder. "Nathan is here with us."

I felt punched in the gut, which of course was ridiculous. I had *invited* him. "Okay," I said softly, nodding to Liz to go ahead and exit the bathroom.

I looked in the mirror one last time, and put on my armor.

28

It was unmistakeable. It was unbelievable. His backside was the first thing I saw when I left the bathroom. Grayson and Nathan were in a small circle, speaking with Layla, Sam, Kassidy and Marcus. My unease with Marcus was stronger than my sheer terror of seeing Nathan. He seemed as if he was standing slightly outside of the circle… No, that wasn't it. His body language screamed defensive…opposite Grayson and Nathan. Well surely that must be it. He felt threatened by these other men in her life, these important men who were never around, yet somehow held to the highest esteem.

Right?

I first made eye contact with Kassidy. She stepped outside of the group to mouth a 'wow' at me. Liz caught it and stifled a laugh. "Guess she's never been affronted by the two brothers beautiful, eh?"

I glared at her, stumbling a bit, trying to shake off the dizziness that remained from the bathroom. "You okay?" she whispered.

"Yes."

Grayson turned first, his haunted look overcoming his face

for a brief moment before smoothing over to normal. He grabbed me into a hug as greeting and whispered, "I hope you're ready for this." He released me.

I met his eyes one last time before looking at Nathan.

As my eyes met his eyes, those shockingly green eyes with hazel flecks, the rest of the room faded away—except for the energy of Marcus. I could still sense him as he paid close attention to the exchange with Nathan. I was too enthralled with Nathan, though, to give it any attention, and then Marcus faded away, too.

A bright light connected my heart to Nathan's, and the tattoo on my collarbone burned. I saw him swallow—hard—and I probably returned the motion. I have no idea. At that point I was stone, immobile, incapable of moving, only capable of being frozen in time and space save for my roving eyes.

His face was still beautiful, even after all this time. To be fair, I had seen a few pictures of him over the years, but photos do *not* do this man justice. His once amazing chocolate hair was short—and grey hair had consumed far more than just the temples of his fading chocolate head. He had a neat goatee—mostly grey, of course. He wore a light blue polo, with the sleeve length resting at that perfect spot to accentuate his bicep. Apparently he still worked out—and it showed. My eyes traveled down the rest of his body, my heart rate beginning to race. I shrieked to myself, finally realizing what I was doing. The noise of the crowd slammed me back into the present.

His eyes traveled back to my face at the same time, his face illuminating a faint smile.

A voice came over the loud speaker, telling us we needed to get to our seats, and people began to file into various doors to get inside the small theatre. As Amara was salutatorian, we were able to sit in the second row. Marcus went first with

Kassidy behind him; Layla, Sam and Liz were next, with Helena and Grayson behind her. Somehow or another, I found myself behind Nathan as he held the door open for me.

I wasn't sure if I was breathing anymore. How could I handle this? Why did I think it was a good idea to invite him? It was hard enough watching Amara graduate—but to deal with Nathan, too—

I felt his hand on my back as he followed behind me, a tingling left behind when he removed it. He still hadn't said a word to me, nor I to him. But when all of a sudden I felt a huge tug, all the way to the right side of the room, I stood rooted in spot and Nathan slammed into me. Helena was deep in conversation with Liz, so she didn't notice that Grayson was not walking down the aisle behind her. He had turned to face Nathan.

Over my head, they mentally communicated, until Nathan hissed aloud, "I told you, I'm retired, I don't work for them anymore, they are not *with* me." Grayson curtly nodded, and then, ever so slightly, reached for me. I saw Helena's profile up ahead, Nathan's heat from behind me, and started to panic. Grayson shook his head, as if to return to reality, and I started to back up, trying to push Nathan out of the way.

Amara.

Amara is in danger.

"No, she's not," said Nathan in his deep, calming voice. My mind was trying to grapple with hearing Nathan's voice, in real-time rather than my memories, and dealing with the clearly not-invited men across the way.

"Nathan," I croaked, "She's—"

"*Safe,*" he said, looking down at me. He looked slightly green, as if he was struggling with my proximity as much as I was his. His breathing was ragged. "They may talk to her after the ceremony, but they won't try anything. I promise. She's safe here."

I reached one hand up to press against him—I was so dizzy—there was too much going on—I was going to faint— "Violet?" he asked, concern replacing the green shade. His hand covered mine and he dipped his head close to my ear so that only I could hear. "Are you alright?"

"I've just been so… dizzy… today," I said faintly, trying to steady myself. I looked up at him with a slight smile on my face. "I thought it was because of you, but maybe not." Just then, I felt like Marcus's eyes were boring into my back from the second row. I quickly turned to look at him, but he wasn't even looking in our direction.

However Grayson was, and he indicated we should quickly sit before we drew any more attention to ourselves.

He whispered as I sat down, "If this is too much, I'll get him out of here."

I slightly shook my head, indicating everything was fine.

Nathan's leg was touching mine, and I was nervously bobbing my leg up and down. He reached out to steady my leg, and I half-laughed. "Sorry," I said sheepishly.

Kassidy was trying to catch my eye from down the row, but I couldn't give her the attention she required. I was having a hard enough time remembering to breathe at this point, what with being trapped between the Brothers Sexy, Marcus, and the uninvited men.

And then it hit me, truly hit me. And the thought felt like concrete the size of a car pressing on my chest.

My *husband*. I was sitting next to my *husband* who I hadn't seen in almost twenty years. *Oh my God*, I was about to crack. I choked a half-sob out, but luckily, the graduation march started to play and the students began to walk down the aisle. It distracted me from the looming panic attack that was trying to emerge.

It was a small class, less than one hundred kids. The last two to march on by were Amara and her best friend Nicole, because they were the ones who were going to give speeches. Amara looked liked a proud bride, marching to her groom. Nicole looked a little nervous.

My heart pressed at my throat. She turned to face as us she walked by, her mouth tilting upwards into the bravest of smiles. This was the first time in her life she was laying eyes on her father. I could see a happy sparkle in those eyes, and I could feel Nathan's body still in the shock from seeing her. Before she turned away for good, I knew that only I would be able to make out the hint of worry for her mother lurking beneath the sparkle. Even so, she was positively beaming as she turned away. An extra spring to her step had appeared.

I couldn't help myself; I needed Nathan, and I needed him *badly*. I reached for his hand and luckily he did not fight me off as my fingers desperately entangled themselves into his. Grayson was leaning into Helena as Amara walked by, but none of this passed by him.

I felt like only Nathan and I were present to witness the ceremony. It was just for the two of us to celebrate our daughter. As she gave her speech, I couldn't help but muse on the fact that Nathan and I—our love—had somehow manifested into this beautiful soul. I also couldn't help but feel his arm pressing next to mine, not just during her speech, but the entire ceremony. When we stood, his body hummed alongside mine. When we sat, he leaned into my seat.

It was impossible not to be drawn together.

The magnetism of the past was still present, and no matter how angry, or hurt, he was—whatever trials and tribulations he had suffered at my hand—he couldn't separate himself from me. Nor could I, him.

The ceremony ended, and the caps flew into the air. I yelled until my voice bloody well gave out, and Nathan, overcome with emotion, couldn't contain himself. As everyone was cheering, he grabbed me with enthusiasm and lifted me off of the ground. I squealed out loud—out of shock, out of excitement for our daughter.

I saw Helena nudge Grayson to look at us. As I was landing from flying in the air, I saw Grayson's look of relief. *How odd.* Nathan set me down, arms wrapped tightly around me, and the hum of our physical contact was so strong, I was sure everyone around us could see it. I reached up and wrapped my arms around his neck, burying my face into his neck, inhaling him and the moment as best I could.

He didn't speak and I couldn't stop from crying—overwhelmed with more emotions than I knew even existed. His grip on me continued to tighten and I was sobbing, ugly crying, in public, all over this man I hadn't seen in twenty years. He held my shaking body as long as the moment would allow; luckily the chaos was good cover for what had happened.

Nathan magically produced a handkerchief and I pressed it to my face, trying to desperately regain control of my emotions. He briefly touched my face with his palm, wiping the rest of the wetness away, but his eyes were swimming, too. I almost lost it again by making eye contact, but the crowd began to dump themselves into the aisles so everyone could meet the kids out in the common area.

Nathan and I were then separated, and I found myself with Kassidy's arms wrapped around my shoulders as we walked out of the auditorium. "She did it, Vi! She did it!" I squeezed her back in return, and again, I felt an indescribable heat signature from Marcus who was behind me.

We all stood in a half circle, waiting for Amara to join us. Layla and Helena were in deep conversation about food; Liz, Kassidy and Sam were discussing college; and I was standing on my tiptoes, peering around Kassidy trying to find Amara. I wasn't sure where Grayson and Nathan had gone. I had a feeling their abrupt disappearance had to do with the men who were after our girl.

I caught a peep of her dark red hair coming towards us, and I was vibrating with anticipation. She was just about to step up to us, within several feet of us, almost with us, just about there, and then the uninvited men intercepted her. *Dammit.*

She looked startled at first—then flustered—and then devil-may-care. She brushed them off like she was a *pro*, and continued on her path towards us. And then Marcus—*wait, where did he come from*? Somehow Marcus wasn't a part of our group anymore. *Dammit. What was going on with this kid today?*

Amara positively beamed at him as he approached her, blocking her from my view. He reached down and gave her a huge hug, lifting her off of her feet in much the same manner that Nathan had just lifted me. *Well. That's that.* He was definitely in love with her, but I still couldn't tell if she felt the same way about him. She wrapped her arm in with his and continued the rest of the way towards our group.

She half-waved at me, clearly distracted, looking for, probing for, seeking out, what I was assuming, her father. Nathan was nowhere to be seen, nor Grayson.

She stopped first at Kassidy, slipping off of Marcus's arm. She went for hug after hug after hug. She ended up at Grayson who had suddenly appeared out of nowhere, and he gave her a full-body, avuncular hug while whispering something into her ear.

I'd have to remember to ask her what he said.

She turned to me, smiling brightly, and then to my right, Nathan was back. The others were either engaged in conversation again, or pretending to be—I wasn't sure. In sheer fascination, I watched Nathan's skintone drop several shades whiter than normal. His body was subtly shaking as I reached out to grab our daughter.

"You're amazing," I said, whispering in her ear.

She pulled back, all smiles and no tears. She faced Nathan dead on, and said, "Hi, Daddy."

I thought he was going to disintegrate into speckles of dust right there before us all, but somehow he managed to retain composure. He cleared his throat before speaking, however, and his first words spoken to his daughter were, "Hi, baby."

29

We were all in my backyard, celebrating the kids' accomplishments. Neighbors stopped by to say hi, other kids and their parents came as well. I chose not to leave my house, but several kids and their parents were party-hopping—small community and all. Kassidy, Amara and I had decorated the yard with twinkling lights trailing across the yard from the back porch to the beautiful gazebo one of our friends had built. I had secretly painted runes on the inside of the gazebo, only visible under blacklight, only knowledgable to Amara and me.

Or so I thought.

Marcus was inside of the gazebo, still creating odd feelings in me of unease. I wanted to ask Kassidy if everything was alright with him at school, but that would have to wait. Someone had changed the music to death metal and I saw a bunch of boys laughing around the speaker. I walked up to the porch.

"Now, boys, you know us Wood girls do *not* like this type of music." I turned it back to classic rock, and one of the kids snorted something about old fogey music.

I turned and looked back at my mingling life. People drinking, dancing, smiling, laughing. My old friends speaking with new friends. Grayson casually leaning back in a chair, with his arm around his wife. Dogs roaming—not ours, though. Malcolm had passed a couple years prior and I was animal-free at the moment.

And then... And then *Nathan*. I caught sight of him, cautiously heading my way. I found it humorous that he was cautious. After all I had done to him, to us, he was somehow nervous about how I would receive *him*.

He handed me my glass of water that I had left on his table, and I took a sip of it, squinting up at him in the fading light. "Hi, Violet," he softly said.

"Why hello there, Nathan," I smiled in return.

We both looked out at the sea of people.

"You've created quite a life without me," he sadly said.

A lump formed in my throat, and I tugged at the chain around my neck. After I'd sent the invitations, I'd pulled my wedding ring back out. I had placed it back around my neck on a chain and worn it as a necklace.

It had been kept hidden all of these years in case he could use it to track us; but once he knew where we were, there was no need to hide it. It had felt like dead weight at first when I put it back around my neck, but became lighter over the past two weeks. At times I felt tremendous heat from it, and I knew in those moments, Nathan must have been thinking about me.

"That's where you're wrong. You've always been a part of our lives, even if not in the physical body."

A beat passed.

Nathan asked, "Is it hard? Watching this moment? When she's becoming an adult?"

"Of course. But... it's not the hardest thing I've ever had to do."

I turned to him.

"Nathan—I—" He cut me off, but I no longer felt fear for what I had to say.

"Violet, please… You don't have to…"

I looked down, holding my glass. I took a deep breath and faced him, searching for… Well, I wasn't sure what I was looking for. "No… Nate, I do. I can't apologize for something I willingly did. We know why I did it, right or wrong. I *am* sorry, though, for the pain it caused you, caused us. It wasn't something I wanted to do, but I believed it was the only way to protect her. I know you don't agree, because I know you searched for us while you were still working for the government. And while that makes me angrier than you could possibly believe… I also understand."

He nodded in agreement, and opened his mouth, but I lifted a palm to stop him from speaking. "And I know how angry you are with me. And how scared you've been. And I know you've been getting updates from Alexandra and Gray and whomever else, so you almost always knew we were okay, and always knew any major things that happened. I know it's going to take time to fill in the blanks, if you're even willing to give me that… I know I don't really deserve it. But I'd love to learn to be friends again. I know you can't ever trust me, or forgive me, but—"

And this time he didn't let me continue.

"Violet," his voice cracked in a way that made me shut up.

He took my glass and placed it next to his on the little round patio table behind us. He grabbed my hands within his own, and looked at me, a multitude of expressions crossing his brow. "I forgave you the moment I realized you were gone. You're right. I don't trust you, but I believe that's something that may be able to be—slowly—earned. I… I didn't stop loving you just because you were gone, or just because you hurt me. I do want to take the time to fill in the blanks—for both of us. You don't know everything, either. It's not just one-sided. Don't forget that."

"Marcus!" screeched a laughing Amara in the background.

Nathan dropped my hands, and his own hung slightly tightened next to his side. "We do, however, need to talk about that boy."

A smile curled at my mouth. "I know." Marcus's good looks were cast golden by the fading sun. "He almost looks a little like you, don't you think?" A slight growl erupted from underneath Nathan's chest. I tickled his chin, and said, "Now, now. There's room for both of you. Besides—you *both* have to compete with Grayson." I smirked.

Nicole ran up to me, "Cake time, Violet!" And she disappeared in the direction of the gazebo.

"Come on, you can have the duty of cutting the cake, Nate." I paused as my hand unwittingly reached for Nathan's. "Oh. Sorry." I dropped it back at my side.

Nathan reached out and squeezed my hand. "It's okay, Violet. I don't know what the hell I'm doing, either."

He then took over, pulling me to my own gazebo while holding my hand. He gave me a wolfish smile as he bravely walked us over to the cake. We were aware of other people's reactions. Nobody had ever seen me with a man, and not everybody even knew about Nathan to start. It was worth it to see Amara's smiling, teasing face.

"Well, hey, there, guys. Cake time?"

She raised her eyebrows suggestively. I rolled my eyes in response, and Nathan looked uncomfortable, which made both of us laugh. I leaned into her ear, and said, "Take it easy. Your father just admitted he doesn't know what he's doing any more than I do—easy goes it—for all of us, okay?"

"Yes, mommy," she batted her eyes innocently.

Nathan took the cake knife, and began to cut it while I served the delicious slices to our guests. Amara was laughing with Nicole, eating cake, and dancing under the now shining moonlight.

Afterwards, the kids went to a local community center where they would stay for the rest of the night. It was an anti-drinking Grad Fest, trying to keep the kids sequestered by doing safe activities rather than getting smashed. The kids all thought it was lame, but they attended it anyway. They were to be kicked out around eight the following morning, and from there they'd grab breakfast and then pile up at Nicole's house for a rest-of-the-day hangout.

Amara was supposed to be home at dinner time.

Everyone cleared out of my yard, leaving behind twinkling lights and trash. Grayson, Helena and Nathan helped me pick up trash and put recycling away. The night grew quiet, and we all walked out to my front wraparound porch. It was certainly surreal, having these three people at my house as if it was normal.

Helena gave me a hug as we started to descend the stairs. "That was a wonderful party, Violet. Thank you again for inviting us." I walked her to her car, and then stepped back as she got into it. Nathan and Grayson were a few steps behind us, deep in conversation about something. Grayson smacked Nathan on the back, and then came up to me as Nathan leaned across the car window to tell Helena good night.

Grayson ran his hands through his hair before speaking. I crossed my arms, slightly chilled by the night. "I'd like to talk to you and Nate alone tomorrow—we need to talk about the men who were here, and Amara's future."

I furrowed my brows a bit. "Look, just because the veil of protection is lifted, it doesn't mean you guys can just come into our lives and tell us what to—"

"Calm down, Violet. That's not what we're doing. I'm just saying now we can have *all* information at our disposal at *all* times. Okay?"

He defensively placed his hands. "Okay," I gave the ground a little kick.

"And Violet, please be good to my brother. He's been through a lot."

I narrowed my eyes. "Seriously? You are no angel, Grayson."

"I'm not talking about us," he said soberly. "You and I both know that ended a long time ago. I'm taking about the two of *you*," he positioned me towards Nathan, who had moved closer to my house now that he had said good night to the two of them. He seemed unsure, as if he didn't know whether or not he should leave. "He doesn't know where he belongs. You've got to remind him that it's with you. I don't think I've ever seen him look so displaced. And that's saying a lot, Vi, and you know it."

"So you're giving me your blessing again?" I half-laughed into the darkness.

"Something like that. See you tomorrow." He gave me a hug, and slid into his car and drove off.

Nathan approached me and waved goodbye at the end of my driveway. "Well," he said awkwardly, "I guess I should be going."

I looked at my phone, it was a little after nine thirty. "Where are you staying? Where is your car?" I noticed for the first time that the only car remaining was mine. I looked around. "Uhhh?"

"I'm within walking distance. I'm staying at the villas across the street."

I let it sink in, and then asked, "Did you know I lived here?"

30

"No. Just a lucky coincidence."

"I don't believe in coincidences."

"Alright, then I had a hunch that this was the closest place to your house."

"Ah." I paused. "Where's everyone else staying?"

"Up the road a ways."

I was about to ask him to come inside, but a car pulled into my driveway.

It was a tiny, red car that reminded me of Nathan's old smart car from twenty years ago. "That's Dawn's," I laughed, noticing Nathan's expression. "Wonder why she's back here?"

We walked towards the car and she got out, rushing to her father. "Hey, kiddo, what's up?" he asked, looking over her head to me with concern.

"I just wanted to make sure you were real." She pulled back from him. "You're staying with Mom tonight, right?" She looked anxiously from him to me. "I don't want her to be alone."

"What!" I exclaimed, looking at my daughter in confusion.

"You're kidding, right?"

"No, mom. I know how exhausted you must be, and I get that some of that exhaustion is just from seeing Dad again— sorry, Dad—but who better to take care of you, than him?"

Nathan cleared his throat.

Man. Co-parenting was already becoming a pain in my ass.

"It's safer if you're not alone." She pointed her toes out, and placed her hands on her hips.

"Safer?" I snorted. "In *this* town? I'm not really worried about it."

"But those men—"

"Amara," I cut her off, "We can talk about that stuff tomorrow. Tonight is about your accomplishments, and accomplishments *only*. All other things can wait."

"Can it, Dad?"

Wow. What a traitor. She was literally looking *past* me to get validation from her *father*.

He stepped closer behind me, and while I wanted to push him away out of frustration, I mentally counted to five and chose to just take strength from him instead. Even so, I was fuming quite a bit on the inside.

"I'll stay tonight if that's what your mom wants. But I'm only half a mile away, at that villa place—"

"Mom?" She pleaded with her eyes.

I didn't understand. I felt like there was something she wasn't telling me.

"Is everything alright?" I asked, taking a step closer to her.

"Just get Dad's car and come back here, okay?"

I pressed my lips together.

"I'll drive y'all there."

I looked at Nathan, shrugging my shoulders. "We have an extra bed, or the couch, or a hammock out back. Let's go get your car," I agreed, not knowing why.

After Amara left us outside of his car, I shivered again.

"You don't *really* have to stay at my house, Nathan. I'm not sure what's going on with Dawn, but—"

"Why are you calling her Dawn now?" He interrupted me.

"I'm not sure. I just do sometimes."

He looked away at the fading taillights of her car. "C'mon, I'll drive you home."

Back at my house, we sat inside his car. "Got rid of the smart car?"

"Long time ago," he chuckled. "Interesting her car reminds me of that old thing."

"I know. I about died when that was the car she wanted." I looked out his window, somberly. "I've missed you, Nathan."

The only sound was our breathing. I glanced at him, but he was looking out the windshield gripping the steering wheel. "This is all so...surreal. When Grayson told me you'd sent invitations... I was just... I haven't seen pictures of Amara since her freshman or sophomore year. She's changed so much."

"Pictures?" I asked, him turning to me.

"We've kind of been writing to one another." He looked sheepish.

I perked up. "Oh, *really*?"

"Through Alexandra, don't worry. But I hadn't gotten any new pictures in a long time, and hardly any letters. I think she just got so busy with school. The last time I saw her in person was in Sylt—"

"So you *have* seen her before? In person?" Silence.

He swallowed. "Trust, Vi. For both of us. There's a lot you don't know."

"Nathan."

"Another time... you were in Florida," he started.

"You saw...us?"

He seemed distant, staring ahead again. "Yeah... You had a sundress on the first time I saw you. You were so tan... Your hair was shorter than it is now." He glanced at me. "You were walking on a boardwalk like you owned the place. Men kept turning their heads as you walked by, but you paid them no attention."

"Where were you?" I swallowed thickly. I remembered that trip. It must have been when Kassidy had dragged me to Destin, Florida for a whole summer. It was the longest amount of time I had stayed away from home. Malcolm had come along with us. I remembered being on edge the whole time, and Kassidy constantly telling me we were safe. The kids had had a blast, and there was that one night I had gone off by myself.

I went to a local shopping area to wander in and out of stores. I eventually crossed the street to the boardwalk leading to the beach. I remembered the flavor of my mango smoothie as I carried it off of the boardwalk onto the sand, staring out at the sea. I remembered how small and lonely I felt that night. I also remembered feeling spooked, but I could never pinpoint where it was coming from.

"I followed you from the mall to the beach. You seemed so lost, yet so beautiful. So strong. Once I saw you, I knew Amara was close by, and so I stayed until you guys left town."

"How did you hide from me?"

"The same way you hid from me."

"How many times did you see us?"

"Almost daily once I figured out where you were staying."

"Did you approach Amara?"

"Yes."

My breath caught. "Oh my God. She never told me."

"She didn't know who I was. She may not even remember the encounter."

"Oh, she'll remember. If you tell her it was you, I'm sure she'll remember."

"That boy was with you guys, Marcus. I remember him."

"Yes. That's Kassidy's son. I am not sure how Amara feels about him, but I suspect he's in love with her."

"He's dangerous."

"He's a good kid, Nate, he's not dangerous—"

"He has a tattoo of an arrow on his shoulder."

"Yeah, he just got that a few weeks ago."

"Did you ever hear that I made a prophecy?"

I hadn't forgotten about his prophecy by any means, but I also hadn't given any attention to when Marcus had gotten that tattoo. A chill swept across my body, a chill of dread. "You think Marcus is *The Arrow*?"

"I don't know. I just know something was uncomfortable with him."

I caught a whiff of something unfamiliar, and asked Nathan to roll down the window. *Smoke.* I smelled smoke. So did he. "What the hell?" I asked, opening up the door.

31

I ran into my backyard, tall flames starting to erupt into the sky. "My gazebo!" I shouted as Nathan grabbed his phone to call 911. I frantically raced to my water hose, pathetically spraying it at the gazebo. Nathan pulled me back after he hung up the phone.

"There's nothing you can do!" he shouted into the fire as it burned.

Firefighters showed up, and we stood off to the side as they put the fire out. The police chief, an old friend of mine, showed up and said he suspected arson. I went inside my house to grab a sweater to fight off the chill left behind from the smoldering cinders to find he was warily eyeing Nathan. Firefighters were beginning to clear out."You sure you have no idea who did this?"

"No, Joe, I really don't. And stop giving Nathan the stink eye. He had nothing to do with this. He used to work for the government himself. He's one of the good guys."

"Oh yeah," challenged Joe. "Doing what?"

It was eleven o'clock now. I was beyond tired. My beautiful little gazebo had been torched—and I suspected I knew who the mastermind was. I also suspected this is why Amara had wanted her father to stay with me. She must have caught wind that Marcus was going to do something stupid.

But why?

"Joe—stop. Nathan is my freaking husband for Christ's sake." *Husband.* It felt weird to say; stranger to hear.

"Husband? Yeah? So what? Where was he with Amara's first steps? When she first rode her bike?"

"Whoaaaaaa, Joe, calm down," I laughed in spite of everything. "It's been a long day for everyone, and you know how stupid kids get with these big events. We may never find out who did this, and chances are, this won't be the last call tonight."

Joe grumbled, but stuck his hand out to shake Nathan's hand. "Nathan, nice to meet you." He turned to me. "Violet—go get some sleep. You're right. We can deal with all of this later."

Everyone left but Nathan, and he and I flopped down on my couch, strung out from the day's events. A long, not exactly comfortable, not exactly awkward silence stretched out. "I'm so sorry, Nate. This is a small town. Joe's been around since she was a baby," I sighed, leaning my head onto his shoulder. "I know I don't deserve this shoulder to lean on right now, but it's here, and it's you, so I'm taking it."

"I'll allow it," he said, quietly laughing. A few more moments passed before he continued, "Here's the thing, though. I'm in your life for less than a day and your house almost burns down. Because a kid is jealous of me and Grayson? Or because this kid is…?"

"Not now. Please. Let's just stare at the TV and ignore life for the rest of the night. Please. Please. Please." I took my head off of his shoulder, begging him.

"I've got a better idea. Why don't I run to the store, get us some drinks, and you can take a hot shower while I'm gone?"

"Perfect," I said, standing up. "But I still *have* some whiskey here, and while a shower sounds amazing... No offense... But I'm a little weirded out with you being in my house while I'm otherwise detained."

"Welllll," he drawled, standing up next to me. "I could always shower *with* you."

My eyebrows danced in my hair. "Wow. That was a totally Grayson thing to say."

He plopped back down on the couch, and groaned. "I'm sorry. I'm probably still in shock from today's events, and haven't slept this past week in anticipation. No excuses... These are just reasons."

"How about this? I'll shower, and then *you* can shower, and then we just go to sleep?"

"And meditate at four?" He tiredly smiled, the deep lines of his face showing his age.

"Ha. Those former militant mediations are an evening endeavor."

"I was joking. I meditate at night now, too. Before bed. As I fall asleep."

"So was I. I haven't meditated in years."

We gazed at each other, caught in the past, frozen in the present. He murmured my name, then placed his face into his hands. I looked down on him feeling empty. "What did I do?"

He looked up at me, locking in on my eyes. "I've missed you, too." He looked pained as he said it, and I stepped away.

"I'll be back in about twenty," I quietly said.

I felt like a new person after my shower, and grabbed some oversized shorts out of my room before handing them and some towels to my guest. After *his* shower, he and I found ourselves propped against one another on the couch again, eyes mutually closing to an old black and white TV show on the screen.

I woke up to his snores, and he jerked himself awake.

"Sorry," he mumbled.

"Come on, Nate. This is ridiculous." It must have been four in the morning. I pulled him up, and walked him to my bed, my sacred spot no man had ever touched.

"Yeah, okay," he mumbled some more.

He sleepily got into bed with me, and, shockingly enough, I instantaneously passed out upon my head hitting the pillow. I expected he had done the same.

The sun was brutal when it tried to peek through my blinds the next day. I groaned, forgetting there was a grown man in bed with me, so it was quite a shock to turn on my side, stretch my arms out and touch another person. I caught my scream just in time, though, and did not wake him up.

He was facing away from me, and I could see his tattoos peeking out from his undershirt. I kept myself from tracing the runes. *So in life, is death.* That used to mean so much to us. I pressed my hand to my own runic script over my chest—*eternal love.*

I felt connected to Amara whenever I traced it.

Nathan grunted in his sleep, and turned onto his back, muttering something under his breath. I held mine, wondering if he was waking up, but luckily for me, he did not. I could continue my study of him. He had a new tattoo on his ring finger—an interesting design—but I did not recognize what it meant. On his other forearm was a picture of a sunrise on it, with the initials 'A.D.' embedded into it. Well. It didn't take a psychic to figure out what that meant.

I leaned forward to inspect it more closely, but quickly I was caught. His voice was gravelly as he spoke. "I got that soon after I caught word she had been born. If you look closely... You'll see the dawn has Violet in it." He rubbed his face and then sat up next to me. "What time is it?"

I pointed to the clock on his side of the bed. "Almost eleven. I can't believe we slept this late." I paused. "What's with the ring tattoo?"

"I wanted everyone to know I was taken," he said seriously.

I bit my lip, hesitant to meet his eyes. I could tell my hair was crazy from sleeping on it wet. Nathan of course, looked fine. "We need to get up. We've got to meet everyone at noon and I need to beat my hair into submission."

He chuckled. "You look fine, Violet."

"Must be nice to wake up a Roman God every day, but I'm mere human, remember?" I stood up, groaning as my feet hit the floor. I opened the blinds to look outside. "Beautiful day out there." I turned back around to Nathan, who had lied back down to apparently stare at my ceiling. "Say... How long are you staying?"

"I don't have to be anywhere for the next week."

My heart skipped a beat in spite of the grogginess. "You're more than welcome to stay with us. I know it might be weird, but... I do have an extra bed, or the couch, or..."

"Or the hammock." He smiled. "What about in here, with you?" He patted the bed, motioning for me to sit down.

"Oh, Nathan," I sat down, holding his hand. "I don't want to give Amara the wrong idea."

"Yeah?" He asked, taking my other hand, tracing the veins on it after he had sat back up. "I think maybe you're afraid of getting the wrong idea yourself." He said quietly.

"Nathan. We can't *be* together." I laughed at him, removing my hand, standing up and walking into my closet.

"Why not?" I heard him ask from behind me.

I pulled a dress out of the closet, and put one hand on my hip. "Come on, Nate. Don't be ridiculous." He was now standing next to the bed, looking down at his boxers with confusion.

"Where the hell did those shorts go?"

I laughed. "They must be stuck in the sheets." I threw my

dress down on the bed and started looking underneath the covers.

"Why can't we be together?" He asked from somewhere in the sheets. "We're married, remember?"

I blew hair off of my face in frustration. "*Nathan*," I said, as if he were a child. "That's the most impractical thing I've ever heard you say." He met me underneath the covers, looking impish, and I narrowed my eyes. I covered him with the comforter and pulled the shorts out from underneath another section of the bed, proclaiming, "Found them!"

At that moment, we both heard a noise from the doorway. He peeked his head out from underneath the covers, and I was holding a pair of shorts, dangling them above Nathan's head like a prize. My cheeks flamed red like the firetruck from the previous night.

"Oh my *God*," said Amara. "If *this* isn't the weirdest damn thing I've ever seen in my life." As our faces continued to burn in the late morning sunlight, Amara's smile deepened, making us even more embarrassed. "Also, Mom? Why the hell is our gazebo charred out back?"

I pushed Nathan back onto my bed, throwing the shorts at him. "To answer your question, *this* is why," I said, growling at him. "And take your pants!" I turned to our daughter. "Amara, what are you doing here? I thought we weren't seeing you until tonight." I stood up, pushing Nathan down yet again as he struggled to stand next to me now that he had his shorts on.

"Well, mom, I live here," she said, and that's when I noticed two of her friends were with her.

"Hi, Miss Wood. Nice bedmate," said one of the girls, slyly.

"Nice to meet you, Mr. Murphy!" called the other one, leaning around her friend, giggling.

"Glad to see you two getting along so well," Amara's dimple grinned at me. *Damn dimple.* Same as her dad's.

"Look, you guys, this man merely *slept* in my bed. *Nothing* happened. I promise. I wouldn't do that. Besides," I started.

"Besides," he continued finally allowed ground next to me. "This *man,* and this woman, were both exhausted last night, especially after we found that the gazebo had been torched." He had gained some traction and was no longer embarrassed. "Know anything about that?" he pointedly asked the girls.

Amara could dish it back out no problem. "No way, Pop." She batted her eyes innocently.

He narrowed his.

I decided to take back control. "Out you guys. Am—do you need anything?"

"Nope—just wanted to change shirts and say hi to my *parents.* I got mud all over the one from last night. We're on our way back to Nic's until dinner tonight."

"Mud?"

"Long story. About as long as how Dad ended up in your bed."

"So see you tonight?" I asked, pushing her out of the doorway.

"Kisses!" she said, blowing kisses at us as she ran down the stairs and out the door. I followed the sound of their laughter, walking to my balcony and looking over my cactus covered lawn as I waved goodbye to her. She made the crazy motion with her fingers at her temple before shutting the doors. They drove off, and left me to my thoughts.

"Jesus."

I turned around, thinking I was speaking to Nathan but apparently he hadn't followed me onto the balcony. "Nate?" I asked, unsure. How had he disappeared so quickly? I peeked my head out my doorway, but he wasn't in the hallway, so I decided to just go ahead and get dressed. I walked into my bathroom wearing only underwear, carrying the dress I was about to slip on.

And there he was.

Brushing his teeth.

Oh. My. God.

He spit, and then wiped off his face with a hand towel. I quickly covered my bare chest with the dress, and he smiled a debonair smile, taking no shame in looking at me from head to toe. For the second time in about thirty minutes, my cheeks flamed firetruck red.

"Stop it," I muttered. I tried to rationalize that the *old fart* in my bathroom was just that—some old fart I barely knew. Not my husband. Who was very clearly attracted to me, as I was to him. His smirk died a bit as he tentatively approached me. I almost fainted as he wrapped his arms around me, holding my essentially naked body up to his chest. The dress slipped to the floor. The vibrations that almost always seemed to happen when we touched started up like an old skin I had long shed. I trembled; he trembled. Our egos eventually dozed and we meshed into one, solid essence. There were no lines of demarcation. One heart.

My phone buzzed in the bedroom, breaking us out of the trance. I pulled away, picked up my dress and slid it over my head. I turned to brush my own teeth, and through the mirror, I watched him watch me. It was my turn to spit and wipe my face. He had moved to lean in the doorway as I groomed; I went about brushing my hair, and putting earrings into my ears. Once I was finished, I met his gaze in the mirror before turning around and walking out. He reached to grab me—held my arm, not allowing me to pass— but as I didn't turn towards him, he let me go.

The mood had changed between us, but luckily he didn't force me to talk about it. However, he did hold my hand all the way to the car, inside of the car, on the way to the restaurant, and only let go after we sat down. I went along with it without thinking, but it was obvious everyone else had plenty to think about it.

Brunch ended, and just like that, all the girls had gone, taking Helena with them. She had to get back to work, but Grayson was able to be left behind. He planned to take a flight out when he was ready to leave. Grayson wanted to spend some more time with his brother, or so he said, and Helena thought it was a great idea.

32

This is how I found myself in my house, cooking dinner, with both brothers hanging out in my kitchen as we waited for Amara to return. Nathan was sitting at the table drinking a beer. Grayson, however, was going through my cabinets, openly snooping.

He pulled out several coffee mugs, and put them on display for Nathan to look at. "You know, you really can tell a lot about a person by going through their coffee mug collection."

One said 'Fresh Out of Fucks' with pink hearts all over it; another said 'Hot Mess, But I'm Blessed'. Yet another was shaped like a pumpkin. "Oh, stop," I said, taking the coffee mugs and putting them back into the cabinet, glaring at them. "Amara got the first two for me, so there."

I cleared my throat, turning my attention back to the onion on the chopping block. "So how is Alexandra? I know Dawn is super sad she isn't here." They weren't forthcoming with a response, so I paused mid-chop to look back at them. "Guys?"

"She's not doing well. That's why I'm leaving for Sylt next

week. You're more than welcome to join me." Nathan looked over to Grayson. "We're pretty sure she's transitioning soon."

"Oh, no!" I exclaimed, tears instantly pressing at my eyelids. Alexandra had been such a stabilizing influence in my life after I had left Nathan. I couldn't imagine a world without her comfort and guidance.

"She's in her nineties now, you know? She's in a care facility and… I just think it's her time."

"I'll look at my schedule and see if we can go."

"I'll pay for it. You don't need to worry about—"

"It's fine, Nathan. I can pay for it."

"But—"

Grayson looked slightly amused at this banter. "You two are like an old married couple. Oh, wait…"

I threw a piece of celery at him. "Shut it."

"Are you going, Gray?" I asked quietly, turning back to the big pot of soup I was making.

"I saw her about a month ago and made my peace then."

"You know how much she loves you."

Chop chop chop went the celery. I dumped the smaller pieces into the pot and then added some spices. I glanced back at him.

"I know," he finally responded, standing next to my bay window. He began to sort through the various plants and jars that I had resting there.

"I need to go through her affairs, make sure everyone gets whatever is in her will. I know she has things for Amara," sighed Nathan in between sips of his beverage.

"I'm really sorry to hear this, you two. Alexandra is like a mother to me." I resumed dicing.

"What the hell is all of this?" Grayson was holding up small baby jars with handmade labels on them.

I choked on a laugh as he opened one up and took a whiff. "It's a salt scrub I use with my clients. Please don't eat it." I looked over at Nathan and we both grinned at one another.

There was a knock on the door just then, and both men became extremely alert. I wiped off my hands on a towel and told them to calm down, that it was probably just Dawn with her hands too full to open the door. But I was wrong. It was Joe, proudly wearing his badge. "Violet. May I come in?"

"Sure, Chief. What's going on?"

He seemed all business and no pleasure. Nathan and Grayson joined me in the foyer, and Joe couldn't help himself. "Not this guy again."

"Joe," I warned. I pointed to the other brother. "This is Grayson, my brother-in-law." Grayson reached out and shook his hand. "And of course, you met Nathan last night." Nathan's hand was rejected and I half-laughed as Nathan played it off by putting his hands in his pockets.

"I just wanted to let you know, it was definitely arson. I know you had a big party last night—"

"Yeah, and you ate some of the cake." I tried to make light of the situation.

"So there's no way to know if what we found was evidence or just something left behind *from* the party. But we found something that we believe belongs to one of Kassidy's. That Marcus kid."

By my lack of response, Joe simply nodded. "That's what I thought. Would you like to press charges?"

"No," I quickly said.

Naturally, at the same time Grayson and Nathan both said, "Yes."

I pressed my lips together and glared at them, taking Joe by the arm and walking him back towards the front door. "This is a family matter, Joe. Everything will be fine."

"Violet, you need to keep him away from our girl if he's really the one who started it."

"Thank you for coming by, Joe. I will let you know if I need your assistance."

He abruptly took my hand in his, and peered into my face. "I trust you, Violet, but you've got to take this seriously—"

"And I do. I promise. If I need you, I know I have you, and I am deeply grateful for it."

After he left, I cursed my way back to the kitchen. I could tell the brothers were having a frantic conversation behind my back. Some of it was out-loud, some of it must have been telepathic, but I wasn't trying to figure out what they were thinking anyway. I was simply wondering how to approach Amara.

The soup simmered on the stove; I began slicing bread for us to eat with it. I could hear the door open and could feel the essence of joy and light come barreling in through it. And there she was, looking tired, but happy to see her uncle and father. "Yay!" she exclaimed, jumping into Grayson's arms. "I'm so happy you're still here!" She turned towards Nathan, giving him a quick, friendly squeeze. "Are you staying the night with Dad?" I could tell Nathan was taking it all in in wonderment. She was so open, so fresh, so willing to accept them. Accept him.

"I'm not sure. Is there enough room for all of us, Violet?"

"Yes," I said, cautiously slicing cheese, only half-paying attention to them. "You guys can share the pull-out bed."

"What? Daddy can't stay in *your* bed again?"

"No," I growled at her.

Amara started to laugh, plopping a grape she had taken from the fridge into her mouth. I smacked her hand. "Don't ruin dinner."

"What did I miss?" asked Grayson, looking intrigued, looking from me to Nathan to Amara. Nate shook his head in response, and Amara giggled some more.

"Dad had a hard time finding his shorts this morning, that's all."

"Hey, Am? Will you please go make the bed for them?"

"Of course." She pirouetted out of the kitchen into the living room, and I could hear her making the bed.

"Look guys—let's just handle this tomorrow. Please? I don't want to bombard her with any of this stuff yet. We're all tired and could use a good, happy meal, and then decent sleep. Tomorrow we will tackle—everything—okay?"

Grayson narrowed his eyes, but Nathan said amicably, "Of course. Let me help you set the table."Grayson's eyes continued to narrow as Nathan and I played house. We ignored him.

Dinner was a success, and he Grayson helped me clean up while the other two went into the living room looking for either a game to play, or a movie to watch. I expected Grayson to make unwanted judgments, or unwanted comments, but rather than being wicked, he simply helped me.

We played a game of Clue, put a movie on and ate popcorn. We all promptly fell asleep in various states of discomfort. Amara and Nathan were on the pull-out bed; Grayson was asleep in a recliner, and I was on the floor resting against it. Eventually we all woke up and decided to go to our various ways. Amara made sure her uncle and father were tucked in, and I put my arm around her as we told them good night.

She went into her room, closing the door. I took a quick shower and turned my nightlight on, reading for a little while before dozing off again. I heard someone use the restroom out in the hallway, and listened for the feet to pad back down the hallway. The person didn't, and I hesitated turning my nightlight off.

"Nathan?" I asked quietly.

Sure enough, he stepped in my room. "Hey," he said lightly, coming closer to my bed. "You're still up?"

"I've been dozing off and on ever since we left you guys alone. Sorry that bed's so crummy. Is Grayson stealing all the covers?" I teased.

"Yeah, right," he said, hands in his pajama pockets. "I wanted to thank you again for dinner tonight. I really appreciate it. It's been forever since someone's cooked a meal for me."

"Well, it wasn't just for *you*," I teased further, stifling a yawn. "And it was only soup." I closed my book, looking past him. I didn't want him to leave, so I said, "Good night, Nathan."

He didn't want to leave, so he stood rooted in spot, even after returning my good night. He laughed a bit, and said, "I don't know what I'm supposed to do."

I stifled another yawn, and opened up the covers. "Just get in here. We'll deal with repercussions from those two tomorrow."

He smiled a crooked smile and slid in next to me. I turned to face my balcony doors, and felt his body press against mine for the second night in a row. I felt him hesitate at the proximity, but with a slight release of tension from his body, he wrapped his arms around me. I instantly tensed up, but the longer he held me, the stronger his resolve became, and the more relaxed I became. His breathing soon changed into a slight snore, and it lulled me to a restful state.

It was probably the best sleep of my life.

***

"Well, well, well," I heard a judgy voice say from outside my door.

"Look who ended up cuddling with your mother anyway, leaving me all alone last night. So tragic," another voice drily chimed in.

Amara snorted with laughter, lighting up the whole house with her light.

I rolled over and looked at the clock. *Almost ten!* How had we all slept so late again? "Who turned on the light?" I asked, rolling back onto my stomach and covering my head with my pillow.

Nathan was still lightly snoring, so I jabbed him with me foot. "Whoa—what?" he asked, confused as he felt around on the bed for… I wasn't sure what for, actually. It appeared he was still dreaming.

"We've been caught," I said, lifting the pillow off of my head and pointing to the door. He first looked at me, rubbing his eyes and totally confused, then looked behind him, realization setting in.

"Ohhhhh," he said, turning back to me, sheepishly smiling. "What time is it?" he asked.

"Nine forty-five, daddy. Now get up! Gray and I have been cooking for you two slacka—"

"Amara!"

"Sorry, mom. Come on!" she exclaimed, leaving the room.

"She's become quite a character," said Grayson, casually leaning up against the doorframe. "Did you two enjoy yourselves last night?"

"Shut your face," I yawned. "Nothing happened except sleep."

He raised an eyebrow, "Really? I find that hard to believe. But, it's none of my business, so…"

Nathan groaned, trying to sit up. "Why do I feel like a train ran me over multiple times?"

"Because we are no longer young, that's why."

Grayson smirked. "I hope I'm never as old as you, two," then followed after Amara. "Breakfast is ready, get up."

I threw my pillow at the doorway. "I'm up, I'm up. Let's go eat and then solve all the world's problems." I headed into my bathroom to brush my teeth and slip on a robe. Before closing the door, I looked at the man in my bed; hair astray, crumpled sheets all over him, one foot hanging off of the bed. I rolled my eyes, and he grinned.

After breakfast, we continued sitting at the table. I didn't want the lighthearted, fun, family feeling to go away, but I knew it must turn serious. I was playing with my fork, looking down at the markings on the table. "Wow, for adults, you aren't very forthcoming," Amara finally said. She stood up, collecting plates and putting them in the sink. She looked back us, admonishing us as we all guiltily stared back at her.

"Well, honey, I know how nice it's been for all of us to finally be together. I just didn't want to ruin it by talking about… things."

"But, Amara's right. We need to talk. And now that we're all together again, there's no place like the present." I shot a sharp look at Grayson as he said it, and he put his hands up. "No judgment, Vi. You know I think you did the right thing."

The room grew still. Amara was chewing on her lip, Nathan put his head in his hands, and I started to sweat in a panic. I couldn't do this. I couldn't talk about this. Maybe never. It was just too raw, too painful. "Well, judgment or not…We will never know, will we?" Nathan grimily looked across the kitchen to his daughter who forlornly shook her head in return.

"No. We won't."

33

"And look," she said, closing the gap between the four of us. It was time for reckoning. We had all played a part in her separation from them—none of us truly challenged my decision—we all had just let it happen. She could theoretically blame any one of us individually, or as a group. "I have mixed feelings about the whole thing. I understand why it happened. But I didn't get to grow up around my *family*. And while my life has been great, Mom, I just..." She placed her hands on the table.

"I know. I know." I mumbled, not having any idea what else to say.

"I was lucky enough to spend some time with you, Gray, and obviously Grandma, and some of Mom's friends, but the only relationship I had with my *father* was through pictures and letters Grandma made me promise not to tell you about, Mom."

"So this is why I didn't know. She asked you not to tell me?" Nathan and I hadn't talked about any of this yet, and knowing Alexandra had plotted against me didn't sit so well. Nathan saw the angry look on my face and reached out for my hands.

"We still have a lot to talk about Violet. Just the two of us." I nodded, trying to retain my cool.

Amara ignored my question, and stepped back from the table, "I don't know if I'm angrier at Mom, or the stupid government for thinking they could control me. Or whoever else is after us." We sat in silence like reprimanded children. She was really worked up now. "Furthermore—"

Nathan stepped in. "Amara. I love you, more than you'll ever be able to comprehend. But please don't take your anger out on your mom, or *only* on her. You weren't there when she got pregnant—it was a different time. We were actively being hunted, your mother in particular. Frankly, things are as calm as they are and *have* been be*cause* of her sacrifices. While I obviously wish it had never happened this way," he said, reaching across the table to grasp my hand again, "I do not hold a grudge for what she did. I simply can't. I love her too much." He said softly.

Amara was speechless and dumbfounded that Nathan had more or less taken my side. I was worried that it was just going to hurt her even more, maybe make her feel *more* rejected by Nathan because he *hadn't* hunt her down to find her.

Tears escaped. He turned to face her. "But the real issue is, this peaceful treaty that we unknowingly have, well, it seems to be coming to an end. I feel a change in the atmosphere, and I think the tides are beginning to turn. Darkness just seems to be...growing."

Amara sat down with us. I could tell she wasn't done with arguing about her childhood, but she was willing to let it pass for now. "Why, they already *have* turned," interrupted Grayson. "How much do you know, Amara? How much have you told her, Violet? I'd love to sit here and hash out our feelings and sort through this familial mess, and trust me,

Amara—if anyone knows what it's like to be isolated from one of your parents, it's *me*. You'll never not wonder if things could have been different, but you cannot let it control you. It doesn't matter. It happened the way it happened; you are who you are. So I get it," he reached across the table and squeezed her hand. "But we can't talk about this now. We have to talk about our visions, this *Arrow* and the last known prophecy."

"There's been another," I said quickly and quietly.

"What?" they all exclaimed, looking at me.

"But first—Am, please tell them who you are. This is your Moana moment." I gave a small smile.

"Nice, Mom." She stood up, walking to the fridge to refill her water. "Who I am? Or do you mean, *what* I am?" Her voice got pensive. "I am probably the last light bearer, at least in our family. I am a clairvoyant, and clairaudient. I have always had telepathic skills, I have visions and maybe even make prophecies." She glanced at me in question. "I am *The Bullet*, and have the weight of the world's balance on my shoulders. My mother is *The Weapon*. And it's Not. Fucking. Fair." I hung down my head. "I know *The Arrow* has some uncanny ability to turn me Dark."

"Does *The Arrow* know who he is?" asked Grayson.

Silence.

"Do you love him?" I asked into the quiet. Amara slid her butt onto the counter next to the sink.

"I don't know. No. Maybe. But it doesn't matter. There is literally no path forward with him. So… there's that."

"He burnt down your mother's gazebo," Nathan said showing his opinion on the matter.

"I know."

"How did this happen?"

"Some goons at college marked him. They knew he was friends with me, Mom. How would they have even known that?" She asked, looking at me from behind dark eyelashes and scared green eyes. "That's why he got that stupid tattoo. He started telling me about prophecies and destinies and I never let on that I knew anything. He always tells me I am too naive, and accuses me of keeping secrets from him."

"Does Kassidy know?" I paused, mortified she had been aware of all of this and hadn't told me.

"No."

"*You* know Kassidy knows things about us. I never told her all of it, but..."

"What are the names of these 'goons'?" Grayson interjected.

"Oh, let me think... One of them was a Jr... like a Jason Jr or something."

"Jason!" exclaimed Grayson. "Oh my God, he *did* have a son!" He looked over at Nathan with anger in his eyes.

Nathan had been relatively quiet, listening to this interaction. Horrified, he muttered, "The same damn players. God dammit."

"So me being separated didn't help at all!"

"No, Amara, I don't think that's really true—"

"But how would they have found out about Amara if nobody else did?"

"Probably just from this Marcus kid. Maybe he talked about her to them, and when they found out where he was from, they put two and two together."

"They're so young. This is just awful to pull them into this." I closed my eyes, tapping my fingers.

"I was young, too, when I got pulled in," said Nathan, looking over at Grayson. "Warriors tend to be on the younger side, Violet."

I opened my eyes. "You're right. I was one of the older ones." I stood up, starting to wash dishes because I couldn't sit at that table for one more second not doing anything.

Shaking, I naturally dropped a plate on the floor and it shattered into several pieces. "Dammit," I cursed.

Nathan came up behind me, picking up the pieces of the broken plate. He placed them in the trash for me, and then forced me to stop with the dishes.. "Violet. She's going to be okay." He gripped me by the shoulders, staring earnestly into my face. "She's got all of us to protect her."

"Bah. I don't need protecting! Mom, there's *nothing* to be afraid of because I refuse to partake in any of this nonsense! I'm just going to go to college like a normal kid." Amara came up next to me, and gave me a hug.

"Ha. She sounds just like you, Violet." Grayson said wryly.

I pressed my eyelids together and exhaled. They were all hovering around me, afraid I was going to snap. I did. "Dawn, I need you to go to your room. I need to talk to the two of them in private."

"What! I'm an adult, Mom, and this is about *me*. Whatever you say, you need to say it in front of me!" She demanded, shocked I was playing the parent card.

She wasn't used to this. She and I had almost always had a democracy, but what she didn't realize was the democracy existed because things had always gone *my* way. This time, she wanted things *her* way and it wasn't in accord with what I, as her mother, knew to be best.

"Once we decide what to do, I will of course include you. But I need to talk about this with your father—"

She couldn't help herself, because, as she had just pointed out, she was still just a kid. "You're kidding me. He's been here for what, two days? And you're just going to let him control my life?"

"Amara, that's not fair. *Nobody* is ruling your life, I just need to pow wow with them about how to keep you safe."

She began to step away in frustration, and sounded slightly hysterical. I felt the two men flank my sides, and I knew that that particular power play was not helping. "I thought you'd been doing that for the past eighteen years, Mom, with*out* them. Now you need their help?"

"This is different. The protection we had is no longer with us. You're going away to college—"

"Whatever," she said, stomping her feet and running to her bedroom, slamming the door and blaring music.

The three of us stood by the sink, sort of in shock at how south that conversation had quickly gone. "Teenagers." Nathan said, trying to lighten the mood. I was pinching my nose, trying to remain calm.

"She's not normally like this."

"It's okay."

"No, it's not. We need to intervene, Nate. We need to find Jason's spawn and—"

"No, we don't. We need to talk to Marcus's mom and—"

"*No.* You're both wrong. I'm going to find Marcus right now and find out what the hell is going on!" I slammed my hands on the table. "Ouch," I said pathetically.

"What's the new prophecy?" asked Nathan, escorting me back to a proper chair. He sat down opposite me, and Grayson was pacing in the background.

"Amara said it a couple of weeks ago. We were watching TV, I had begun to doze off and all of a sudden she was in this daze, speaking in a monotone voice I had never heard before. At first it sounded like gibberish, but then it became very clearly English." I spread my hands out on the table. "It scared the shit out of me."

"Do you remember it?" Nathan asked, gritting his teeth.

"Yes. She kept repeating it over and over again. I couldn't forget it even if I wanted to forget it." I took a deep breath. "*Once The Path of The Bullet is clear, it is The End—The Long Peace, a New Child—or a New God.*"

Grayson stopped pacing. "What the fu—"

"Is this just about us? Aren't there others? Can we find them, and stop all of this, once and for all? Eradicate Darkness? No more little pockets of people fighting against those who wish to control Nature—just the entire planet working together? Is it possible?" I was hysterically grasping.

"I'm sorry—did you not hear what you just said.? A *New God*? That sounds like total annihilation! A reset," Grayson sputtered.

I kept going. "What of the runes? What about our ancestors? It literally can't just be us."

"Why not?" Grayson bitterly switched gears. "You don't want to feel the incredible burden of all of this bullshit? Does it make it easier for you, to think others are just as important as we are?"

"Grayson, that's not fair. I'm simply using *logic*—"

"I'm assuming you are correct, Violet. If you look through history, you can see various peoples, from all over the world, doing the same thing. There are prophecies, there are miracles, there are battles. It didn't start with us, and it looks like it won't end with us," Nathan intoned.

"The Long Peace. She did not say *Forever* Peace." I sighed. "But we play a part."

He sighed. "Yes."

"We are destined to play these parts."

"Well—we could argue that—"

"Is free will bullshit? Or is free will your destiny when you make the right, or best choices?"

"I'd love to debate this crap with you guys—and your seeming lack of care about this *New God* is astounding—but we have a more pressing issue. Marcus, remember him, he who burnt down your gazebo? Is threatening your daughter?" Grayson beat his hands on the table to get our attention. "Wake up!"

"Okay. Okay. You're right. But we're doing it Violet's way

—"

"I'm rusty, Nathan. I have barely used any of my skills since I've been here. Only the rare occasion I've been forced to use them. I wouldn't know the first thing how to protect myself, what chants to use, *anything*."

Grayson lifted his shirt. "Great. Then it's my way"

"Grayson," Nathan hissed angrily in his direction.

"You forget, brother, I'm not exactly like you. I've always believed in an eye for an eye. *That* is what creates balance."

"Your gun is a power shift. And Marcus is just a *kid*."

"*Kids* murder all the time. That's naive—"

"Guys, hush," I said, closing my eyes, seeking out Marcus's heat signature. I realized I didn't need to *do* anything to tap into my dormant skillset. I simply had to *be*.

34

Trying to tune into my inner wisdom, I ignored the banter between the brothers. I immediately connected with my third eye, and slowed my breathing down. I felt a hum from deep within me, and I realized it was some old mantra that I used to chant to open myself up to receive. Almost immediately my eyes burst open.

"He's at the beach. And Amara has sneaked out to see him. God dammit," I swore, jumping out of my seat and racing to her room to check on her. Her music was still blaring, but the doors to her balcony were wide open. I never had had any reason to worry about her just walking out of her bedroom before and leaving, sneaking out of the house.

I looked east toward the beach to see if I could detect anything, and all I could see was the sudden darkening clouds off of the ocean. I heard the sound of feet on the stairs, and jumped as thunder boomed in the distance. I looked below me and saw Nathan and Grayson on the street. "Stop it, you two," I called out.

They looked up at me. "Vi?" called Nathan, unsure.

"Let's get up on the catwalk. I don't think it's safe to go

down there at the moment."

"But what about—?"

"Trust me."

Grayson started using all sorts of expletives, looking like he wanted to throttle Nathan and me, but Nathan still climbed back up the stairs and met me on the landing. Together we went up the other flight of stairs to get a better view of the beach, Grayson slowly climbing behind us. "Just there," I said, pointing off in the distance to the small group of people gathering around, what I assumed, was my daughter.

"That storm is moving in rapidly. They're going to get soaked."

"Maybe."

There was a fire pit on the beach, and even though it was daylight, *Darkness* was closing in. It was almost like the sun had been blown out, it happened so quickly. I could feel it gathering on the beach and spreading outwards like tentacles exploring its surroundings. Strangely, nobody else was around—it was quiet. No beachgoers, no neighbors.

It was very strange.

"She's going to stop it, Nathan. Look. Feel." I was not sure where this calm inside of me had come from, but I was grateful. Nathan looked ready to jump off my balcony and try to fly over to the beach to grab Amara. Grayson was furious, but I placed my hand on his shoulder to calm him. Somehow I instinctively knew she was handling it on her own. She was fighting them off, much in the same manner I used to fight off Scouts.

There were differences, though. I had been a *lot* older, and had had training. I had been told that this was my purpose, and there was a certain method to attain results. I was sure she'd explored runes a little bit, tarot, maybe chanting, meditating, etc, but this was all her inner power working in her favor.

I was in awe. I closed my eyes, and felt Nathan *and* Grayson step back from me.

Maybe it was some sort of weird relationship built between mother and daughter, but I damn well felt a connection to her all the way down to the beach. I could feel her pulling from me, and I willingly gave. And so together, we zapped the hell out of those boys down there. They didn't know what hit them, equally untrained, young and foolish.

Thunder clapped like it was coming from within my heart, and when I opened my eyes again it was pouring down rain. The young men who had gathered around the fire pit, arguing with my daughter, were now sprawled out on the wet sand, save for one person standing *next* to Amara. I assumed it was Marcus; but I couldn't be sure. I couldn't make out faces or anything. They were too far away.

It looked like they were still arguing in spite of what had happened, but Amara began to pull away, heading in our direction. Marcus tried to pull her back, gesturing to the beach, to the lightning above him, to everything. "She's coming back," I yelled into the screaming thunderstorm.

I ran all the way down the stairs to meet her in the driveway, getting soaked. Nathan and Grayson flanked me as we stood rooted in spot as she and Marcus approached us. Before I had run downstairs, I made sure that the boys on the sand were okay; they seemed to be stirring and getting up. I knew they'd be safe from the storm.

"What the hell were you thinking?" I yelled into the wind as she got closer to us. "You could have been hurt!"

She pushed Marcus in front of her, towards the brothers and me, yelling back, "Marcus has a lot to tell you!"

At first he looked angry, but as the lightning zapped into the electrical lines across the street, he looked positively spooked. Timidly, he asked, "Can we at least go inside?"

I stepped in front of Nathan and Grayson, who were like unmoving pillars, stern faces, strong offensive stances. I nodded at them, indicating it was okay, and they moved aside as I grabbed Amara and Marcus, walking them to my front door while I ran inside and got towels. The brothers were furious; Amara looked stubborn and Marcus now looked defeated.

I whispered to Amara, "Can you tone the storm down?" She looked nonplussed, then half-nodded her head and the thunder immediately died down.

Again. I was in total awe. What the hell *was* that?

We dripped in my foyer until we were dry enough to come into the kitchen. Marcus' surliness was met with fury from Grayson, angry curiosity from me, shock from Nathan, and finality with Amara. When this new generation of Veritas Truth seekers who had found Marcus, and subsequently my daughter, drove slowly down the street to leave, Amara had flipped them the finger until the last car was gone. Marcus hung his head low.

"Real mature, Dawn," I murmured.

We spent a couple of hours in my kitchen interrogating Marcus, getting as much information as we could. Amara chimed in when she felt like it, and she was obviously very hurt by what had happened. There had been tears, silence, pleading and anger over the past few hours. Marcus was very sullen in most moments.

Grayson had tried intimidating him, to some success at first, until Marcus realized I was running the show and would not allow anyone to hurt him. This in turn infuriated Nathan, who, generally speaking, was more like me, but apparently when it came to his daughter, could be like Grayson.

I think the power of Nathan's love scared the shit out of Marcus.

This is when he finally gave us answers to what we asked —but most certainly, not everything.

I couldn't believe Amara had kept so much from me, and that Marcus had been so easily turned when he was away at college. At this point, though, everything seemed inconsequential as Marcus implied he wasn't going to hang around those boys anymore once he got back to school. I wondered if this would be the case, but I also knew Amara wasn't attending the school he was at, so hopefully Marcus would leave her alone.

But. The enemy knew where my daughter was, and what school she would be heading off to in the fall. This was not lost on any of us. It had begun.

It wasn't until early evening that I sent Marcus home to his mother. Kassidy had called me, looking for him, and I told her that I would send him on his way shortly.

As fate would have it, Nathan turned out to be living in Charlottesville, so we agreed, it only made sense for me to pack up and move there as well. Amara didn't even seem reluctant about it—which surprised me a bit. She had always been independent. I didn't really think she'd want us to be up there hovering around her. But maybe she assumed we'd be busy with our own lives and wouldn't interfere in her life.

Unless it came to all of this *hocus pocus* crap.

Which is what we were now calling it.

After dinner, I had a teenager who couldn't believe all the shit we'd told her, but I could also see lots of things clicking in her mind. She realized she'd been living with half-understanding of things over the years. I could sense a lot of anger towards me, and I knew she and I would have to hash that out, but for now, things were okay. Kassidy had texted, saying Marcus was home and that she hoped he hadn't gotten into any fights with Amara—apparently he wasn't acting normal.

Imagine that.

We pulled the bed out again for the brothers, and I was about to pass out on the way to my bedroom. It had been an exhausting few days. "Playing this game again, are you, Violet?" asked Grayson. Nathan was in the bathroom, and Amara was already in her bedroom—door to the balcony locked.

"What do you mean?" I asked, walking over to him on the bed, joining him.

"You're making Nathan start out here again with me?

"Oh, I don't care. I'm going to bed. I just figured after the insane day we've all had, he'd want his space."

He had returned from the restroom, and I half-turned to him while standing back up. He gave me a quick kiss on the cheek, and told me good night. I smirked at Grayson before returning to my room, falling asleep almost instantly.

***

Amara went to her friend's house early the next day after saying goodbye to Grayson, who Nathan and I drove to a train station before sharing our own goodbyes. Back at my house, it was quiet with just the two of us there. Amara had pulled out a beautifully carved box, not much larger than a tissue container, and left it for us to peruse.

"What's this?" I asked, picking it up. It had runes carved into it, painted in that glowing, magical blue paint that the runes were often transcribed. There was a tiny lock on it, and I saw that she had placed the key next to box on the table. I unlocked it, and hissed as soon as I saw what was inside.

I had a pretty good feeling Nathan knew what I was going to find.

"Are these all the letters you've sent her?"

Nathan looked uncomfortable, tracing the runes on the box. "My mom handcrafted a matching box for me, and told me to keep the things she sent to me inside of it. She also said if we were to align the boxes…" He trailed off, fingering the intricacies and craftsmanship of it, closing it back again and locking it. He lifted up the latch, inspecting it.

"What are you looking for?" I asked. The desire to look at those letters was burning a hole in my stomach. I sat down at my table as he inspected it.

"There should be a notch here… Yes… It looks like it will click into my box. Hmmm," he said, turning it upside down. "I'm not sure what's supposed to happen when you click it in with mine, but I guess we will find out, eh?" He placed it back on the table, unlocking it, but keeping his hand over it. "The thing is…" he paused. "Actually, I don't care if you read them. That's fine." He kept his hand on the box for a beat, and then sat down next to me, clasping his hands.

My fingers were clumsy as I began to pull out photos, some faded, some that looked no older than a couple of years. "I can't believe Alexandra thought to do this for her," I murmured. There was an old picture from when Nathan and I had just started dating. I had never seen it before; we were laughing, holding forks at an outside pizza joint we used to go to. "Wow," I said, holding it up. "We were so young.."

Nathan took it from me, and laughed as he saw it. "I can't believe she sent her all of these. Yes, we were young."

He pulled out one of the letters, and opened it up. "Ah… I remember when I wrote this." He laughed to himself, and handed it to me after skimming it.

"You know what?" I slid my chair next to his, and covered his hand with m own. "I don't think I'm going to read these. It's between you two."

"Mom sent pictures to me, too, you know. Both of you," he looked sad. "Every few years I'd get an updated version of you." He said softly.

I swallowed hard, trying not to think of what we had lost by my actions.

"Look, Nathan—"
"Violet, I think you should move in with me."
Silence.

Part III: The Road Home | Epilogue

35

The three of us somehow made it to Sylt in one piece. Amara and I hadn't seen her grandmother since Amara's second year of high school where we met up in Washington D.C. for a long weekend visit.

Inside the care facility where Alexandra was actively passing away, we decided Nathan and I would go in first. Amara was happy with this since she was so jet lagged and tired. She plopped into a chair with a blanket and almost instantly fell asleep. I gave her a kiss on the top of her head and walked with Nathan to where his mother would die. Alexandra looked peaceful, wrapped in blankets, and eyes closed.

Nathan sat on the side of the bed and grabbed her hand while I kneeled at her side. "We've made it, Mom," Nathan said softly. "Violet and Amara are both with me. We're together again. It worked..." He hesitated. "I forgive you your part. I know you always did what you thought was best for all of us."

I broke. Of course. I was like a damn water faucet these days. I quietly sobbed into Alexandra's hands, and for the briefest of moments, I felt life within those fingertips. It was enough to turn my dam off, and I looked up. "She just made movement with her hand, Nate," I gulped.

Her eyes began to flutter open, and I gasped. Her green eyes remained somewhat unfocused, and were looking off into the distance at something we couldn't see. "Mom?" asked Nathan, unsure of himself. She took a deep, rattling breath in, and made eye contact with first me, then Nathan.

Her scratchy voice managed to eke out, "Amara?"

"Asleep in the waiting room. We're all together, Mom."

"Grayson?"

"Said goodbye last month," he said quietly.

"But all.. All together? Forever?"

"Yes, Mom. Violet and Amara are home again."

"Violet," she croaked. Exhausted, her eyes closed again.

"I'm here, Alexandra." I squeezed her hand. She turned to look at me.

"My boys..."

"I know. I'll try to keep them safe and happy as long as I can, until I send them back to you." Her lips curved into something that resembled a smile. She closed her eyes again, and I could feel the warmth of tears on my face.

"Tell Grayson... So sorry..."

"He knows, Mom. He knows how much you love him."

"Good."

She took in a raking breath. "Amara's safety..."

"I'm here, Grandma." Amara stood in the doorway, alert and breathtaking.

Alexandra lifted up her entire upper half of her body to get a good look at her. "Amara," she breathed, raising her lips in that sort-of-smile again. Nathan moved and let Amara sit next to her and hold her hand, Alexandra resting back down.

"Thank you for all of your guidance, and for keeping Daddy and me connected. It was everything. And please, as we discussed… contact me if you need me after your transition. I will be able to connect with you."

I looked sharply at Nathan, and he just met my eyes with a shrug of his shoulders.

Alexandra closed her eyes once more, saying something under her breath. It appeared she was chanting something, but I wasn't close enough to hear her, nor was Nathan. I wasn't sure if Amara would recognize any of the chants, but a smile came across her lips, and she whispered, "Thank you, Grandma. We are safe, always under your care." She leaned into Alexandra and wrapped her arms around her frail shoulders.

I had stood up next to Nathan, holding him around the waist as we watched Alexandra take her last breath underneath Amara's embrace. As the breath escaped her lips, I swear I saw her spirit leave with it, a small glittery essence floating from up above her head, lingering briefly before dissipating.

Nathan turned into me, loudly sobbing into my shoulder. I held him as best as I could, considering how small I was compared to him, and Amara stood up and quietly said, "I'll go let the nurse know." She paused next to Nathan, placing her hand on his back.

"Daddy… She's free now." She slipped out of the room, and he looked up, looking after her as she stepped out.

He turned to look back at me, eyes red, face blotchy as he tried to regain composure. "I'm sorry."

I took his face in my hands, and said, "Don't be. I love you." I whispered, searching his eyes, willing him to give me some of his sadness and grief. He half-smiled.

"So you'll move in with me then?"

I just wrapped my arms around him again, and held him as he sighed away some of his distress. The magic of a hug never ceased to amaze me.

***

We were in the hotel room, and Nathan was talking to Grayson on the telephone out on the balcony. Amara was lying in bed with me, hopelessly flipping through German channels. "Ugh. Why didn't I ever take the time to learn German?" I patted her on the leg, laughing.

"You still can, you know."

"What's the point? This is probably the last time we'll ever come here." She looked at me deep in thought, but it saddened me when she said that.

"So. Anything you want to tell me about Dad?"

I raised an eyebrow and responded, "Anything you want to tell me about Grandma and her secrets you keep?"

She faced the television again. "No, I don't, but I do want you to tell me what's going on with you and Dad." She found a children's station on the TV, and I had a major flashback to when she had been little watching Cookie Monster in German.

I sighed. I wasn't ready to have this conversation with her, considering I hadn't really had it with Nathan himself. He was still my husband, yes.. But we'd be a part so long—I just didn't know if it was a good idea. It was apparent we still had feelings for one another, but so much had happened in between space and time and… I was used to being alone. I enjoyed it.

"Moooooom!" she yelped, trying to get my attention. Apparently I had lost myself in my thoughts.

"Honey, I don't know. I really don't. I just…" I looked at him sitting on the balcony, staring off into the fading light. We were all still jet-lagged, but he looked particularly terrible. He had apparently gotten off the phone with Grayson while we were sitting there talking.

"Don't be stubborn, Mom. Just take the plunge. You guys still love one another—it's *beyond* obvious. You were destined to be together, it's written in the runes, it's been in prophecies!" She jiggled me with her toe. "Go be happy, for once. You deserve it."

"I thought you didn't believe in that stuff." She gave me a wicked smile.

"I'm gonna go to the little store downstairs and grab a beer, because I am old enough to drink here! You go talk to Dad. He's *really* sad, Mom."

I glanced outside again, and his hands were on his head. I stood up as Amara walked to the door. "Don't be gone long, it's a foreign country and as you pointed out, you *don't* know the language."

"Bah. They all speak English downstairs." She stuck her tongue out at me.

I walked over to the balcony, opening the door. "Want some company?" I asked, still standing halfway inside.

He looked up at me, his green eyes dull from being exhausted. "I spoke with the crematorium. They're hoping it can be done before we leave the country." I stepped outside and placed a hand on his back, slightly hesitating.

"You need to lie down and rest, Nathan. You look terrible," I said quietly.

"I know. I think I need a shot of whiskey though to relax enough to fall asleep."

"Let me call Am and tell her to bring some upstairs. She just went downstairs to grab herself a beer." I rolled my eyes.

"Do you think it's safe enough?"

"Yeah. I don't feel any sort of hostilities. Do you?"

"No, it's not that. I just meant because she's so young."

"Oh. I'm not worried. She's fully capable of holding her own against unwanted advances. She's smart, too. She's just grabbing *a* beer for the experience. She doesn't like alcohol."

He stood up, and I opened my arms up to him again, letting him rest his entire bodyweight against me. Luckily, I was leaning up against the balcony door. "Come on inside, Nate, lie down." I whispered.

"Okay."

I dimmed the lights and was able to get him to lie down in the bed, closing the curtains most of the way. I texted Amara to ask for a whiskey, and told her to be quiet when she reentered the room. We actually had adjoining rooms, although I wasn't sure what the sleeping arrangements were supposed to be. When she came back into the room, she handed me the whiskey and nodded she was going to go next door. I heard the TV turn on and saw the lights flickering.

I had Nathan sit up and take the two shots, and then he lied back down, on top of the covers. I slid next to him, holding him as best I could. He sniffled from time to time, but he finally fell asleep.

The next morning we all woke up uncomfortable, raw, but hungry as hell. We took showers and got dressed, ready to head out for breakfast. Amara, of course, was the least affected by the jet lag so she was the most alert and awake. Nathan still retained some of his dullness from the previous day, and I was personally just sad about everything.

And unsure.

Unsure about what the future held. It was nice, playing the part of a cute little family, but I also felt very awkward, and at times it didn't seem genuine. Or perhaps I was worrying too much about nothing. Trying to stay out of the drama, I chose to watch Nathan and Amara interact. Once I was able to remove myself from the whole situation, it turned out to be amazing watching the two of them talk. Wit and intelligence were matched. Empathy and understanding, a simple knowing.

Finally, at one point, Nathan realized I was being quiet. He reached for my hand and squeezed it, asking if I was okay when Amara had gotten up to use the restroom. I smiled wistfully. "I've just been enjoying watching the two of you interact. It's sweet."

"Ah," he said. "She's a character. When you were in the shower earlier, she asked what my intentions with you were." He choked back a laugh, sipping on his coffee, peering at me from the top of the mug.

"Oh, did she? That little rotten egg," I said, rolling my eyes. I took a sip of my own coffee, and then innocently asked, "And what did you say?"

A smile spread across his beautiful, exhausted face, and his green eyes lit up, the first time I had seen since his mother had passed. "I told her I wanted you to move in with me."

"And?"

"And she thought it was a great idea."

"Really?" I asked, surprised.

"Why is that so shocking?"

"I know we talked about this last week but I'm still blown away she even wants me *in* Charlottesville, let alone *living with you!*"

"I can only relay what she said. She said she wanted you to do it, and that she liked the idea of us being close by."

At that moment, the waiter dropped off our check, and our daughter returned to the table. Her eyes widened and she asked, "What? Is there toilet paper on my shoe?" She looked down at her flip flops.

"You want me to move in with your father?"

The same grin that had been spread across her father's face found its way across her face. "Yes, I do. I think it's a fantastic idea for my parents, who love one another, to actually make things work out after all this time. They should live together, and be married together. Like the way *real* married parents do it," she playfully said.

I groaned, and looked at Nathan who was now trying to have an emotionless expression wipe across his face. But, I could tell he was anxious for me to agree to the terms. "And you are okay with us living in Charlottesville? Maybe even a walk away from campus?" This I did not know. I wasn't sure how far Nathan lived from the campus of where she was going to attend.

She continued to smile, and I finally gave in to her joyful spirit and now *my* face began to show the glimmer of a smile, awkwardly so. "Yes."

I looked back to Nathan, whose face now showed hopefulness. "You want us to try and be a normal...family."

"Yes."

"Nathan?"

His face collapsed into an eat-shitting grin, just like my daughter's. "More than anything. I think it's worth a shot. I don't think it will be easy by any means—I think we'll need some outside help—but, Violet..." He trailed off.

I took in a huge, ragged breath. "Okay. I will move in with you. I mean... What could go right?"

Amara jumped up and hugged me. "Mommy and Daddy, sitting in a tree," she sang, being silly. She grabbed the ticket and went to pay for the meal. "Dad—this is where you kiss Mom," she instructed before turning away.

Nathan leaned across the table, and did just that.

The Brothers in youth must be separated to keep The Order or one will perish; The Weapon will bestow upon a brother The Bullet. All will be in peril during these times. Pairing brings forth Peace, or War. Sacrifice leads to Safety. The Bullet must dislodge correctly, or else All shall perish. If The Bullet is dislodged upon her Own Accord, Great Peace shall be bestowed at Her Behest. Or, Darkness will permeate Light, and the Conclusive War is fought. The Bullet and The Arrow meet. Until after time passes, a one-time defeat. But shall they join, Thurisaz. Once The Path of The Bullet is clear, it is The End—The Long Peace, a New Child—or a New God.

What could go right?

When Violet Took Flight

What the Bleep?

In *When Violet Got Bored*, questions about some of the mumbo jumbo our dear Violet mentioned in her story were tackled. Let's do that again! *When Violet Took Flight* has far fewer mentions of techniques, talismans and things, but here is a short list to get you started before accessing good old fashioned books, or Google, on your own.

- **Hibiki** translates to 'echo' in Japanese. This echo can be felt as a sensation one may feel or 'tap into' during a Reiki session. As with anything else, any judgment about this sensation is naturally through the lens of the human feeling it. The *International House of Reiki* can share more here: https://tinyurl.com/2avb9d5d

- Wait a second, you mentioned **Reiki** again! Yes, I am a Reiki practitioner/teacher, but yes, I also love science. I do not think these two things are at odds with one another. In short, Reiki is a hands-on or hands-off practice, stemming from Japan, that helps clients relax. Feel free to go down all the rabbit holes. There are a million.

- **Chakras**—what? Yes, we are moving onto India now. Chakra means 'wheel', and references energy points in/around the body. Did you know that your heart chakra gives off the largest magnetic field of any other organ in the body? You can dig into rabbit holes with this one, too.

- **Runes**—The plan is for the third book to delve into some of the mysticism of this overall story. If not, maybe a *Guide to Violet's World* will happen in the future! While the runes mentioned are simply from the *Elder Futhark*, this family's connections to runes supposedly goes back to Odin himself. Therefore, the symbols are even more special, written or un-written.
- **What could go right?** This bind rune symbolizes 'good luck'!
- **The cover?** This bind means 'protection'.
- There's a reason why my stressed-out characters are **always taking deep breaths**. Harvard has decided to chime in on it, too with the article entitled "Breath control helps quell errant stress response". Uhhh, yeah! Check it out here: https://tinyurl.com/yc2c7a8h
- Everyone has access to breath—even if you're struggling to breathe, if you find yourself coughing, air is working its magic—but if you **have an access to a hug**, even better. *Psychology Today* says: Hugging reduces inflammation and blood pressure. Hugging can also help fight against the common cold. Hugging promotes the release of oxytocin and increases feelings of bonding with others. *So go get you one if you can!* https://tinyurl.com/26s7me2z
- General mythology—The obsession started at least as early as 8th grade. :)

Also, you've probably noticed Violet and company visit *Sylt* quite a bit. While Sylt is a real island which looks teeming with life, no, I have never been there. I wrote this so long ago, I can only surmise I was looking for a location further north than Germany that was *still* Germany to utilize in my tale. After researching websites and perusing social media accounts, in spite of some German heritage, I can't understand a lick of the language. Thanks to my Grandma, I only know German cuss words. The island looks *amazing* though, and while everything that occurs there in my story is from my brain and its limitations, I sure would love to visit one day and have a real experience there. *Have you been?*

Violet's Empowerment Scrub

- 1/2 cup Dead Sea salt (a brand like Minera)
- 1/4 cup Jojoba oil (or melted coconut oil, olive oil, etc)
- 1-5 drops essential oils (like Rocky Mountain Solar Plexus Chakra Oil Blend)

Optional

- A few drops of Vitamin E
- 1 tsp dried herbs

To Use/Tips:

- Using 1-2 tbsps, methodically spread evenly across your feet, upper arms, etc. *Rinse off!*
- Do not use daily or if you are allergic/intolerant to any of the ingredients.
- If you have sensitive skin, be extremely careful. Test small areas.
- Shelf life will vary depending on how you store it.
- Rule of thumb—if it stinks, toss it out.

About the Author

allison keli is a writer, bodyworker and educator. She blogs about health, parenting and spirituality topics. Her books include the children's fantasy/science mash-up *Phenix & Fox: Shooting Stars*, the paranormal historical fiction series *The Hauntings of DoG Street*, and the magical realism series *The Light Thrower*.

You'll often find her annoying her neighbors by feeding squirrels, rescuing snails and talking to plants. She currently resides in the eastern U.S. with her husband, almost-middle-schooler son, kitties Dragon and Pilot, and the resident hamster of the household, Luka.

Website

Newsletter

Instagram

Meta / Facebook

Leave a Review

Rocky Mountain Oils Discount

Wrapping up in 2025...

Join life through *Amara's* eyes in *The Last Light Thrower*. The novella is set for a full title reveal and release date in 2025. Shocking twists and turns help the third installment race the series to its ultimate end. Some things will be lost forever, yet some things will never change.

The ultimate battles between destiny and free will, Darkness and Light, prophecies and self-fulfillment take center stage as Amara is forced to avenge... Well, you'll have to wait and read the book to find out what she's avenging. It's a doozy!

www.ingramcontent.com/pod-product-compliance
Lightning Source LLC
Chambersburg PA
CBHW021802130726
47987CB00008B/2978